The Irish Secret

Ronna Brooks

authorHOUSE®

AuthorHouse™
1663 Liberty Drive
Bloomington, IN 47403
www.authorhouse.com
Phone: 1 (800) 839-8640

Published by AuthorHouse   04/25/2015

ISBN: 978-1-5049-0941-9 (sc)
ISBN: 978-1-5049-0942-6 (e)

Dedication

This book is dedicated to
Ron and Jeanie Brooks
Thanks for always believing in me
Love you

Prologue

There it was, the biggest ship she had ever seen. Having a love for adventure since she was a child, this is the first adventure on her own. Being raised in foster care, Beatrice was always getting into mischief. Building a fort out on the creek behind the house and getting the other children in the house to sneak out in the middle of the night. Pretending they were Knights and Queens just like the latest book she had read. Reading was Beatrice's favorite way to pass the time. "Haven't I told you enough times to leave the others out of your mischief? You're grounded, now go to your room." That is where Beatrice spent most of her time. Reading and dreaming about visiting the far off places that she has only read about in books. Now she was here. Ready to take on her greatest adventure yet. Thanks to a rich Great Uncle Charles passing away. One that she never even met.

Chapter One

"COME ON EVERYONE, INTO THE kitchen. It's time to sing to Beatrice". Said Kristy, Beatrice's foster mother. "Mom, I told you I didn't want anything big. Especially not a cake and singing". Said Beatrice. Beatrice loved her foster Mother. Being one of the lucky ones to be placed with the same family since her entrance into 'the system'. She started calling Kristy Mom when she was three and it just stuck. Now she was 21 and not so ready to start out there in the 'real world'.

"Hey Kirsty, there is someone at the door and they are asking for Beatrice". Said Billy. One of the four other foster children.

There he was, a tall man in his forty's. Wearing his blue uniform with his glasses pushed up onto his forehead. "Yes, can I help you?" Asked Kristy. "I have a package for one Beatrice Maloney" he said.

"I'm Beatrice, who's it from?" Replied Beatrice.

"Well, you will need to sign here and then open it to find out who it is from." He replied smiling handing her a pen and a small orange piece of paper.

"Thank you" Beatrice said as she took the strange large envelope.

"Well open it. I can't stand the suspense." Said Kristy.

With shaking fingers and a heart beating like the Little Drummer Boy was in her chest, Beatrice opened the large envelope. Inside was a smaller white envelope containing a letter from a lawyer in Ireland and a check for $300,000.

"What's it say, what's it say, what's it say?" chanted Kristy jumping up and down and clapping her hands.

"It says that I had a Great Uncle Charles in Ireland. He died and since my Mother is unable to be reached, they tracked me down and the money goes to me." Said Beatrice.

Holly cow, she had never seen that much money with her name on it. Beatrice was always under the impression that she didn't have any family left since she was put into foster care at the age of two. The letter seemed authentic and so did the check. "I will have to check this all out in the morning." Beatrice said out loud. Not really talking to anyone special.

"Well, I am here to help you honey. Are you alright? You're looking a little pale?' Kristy asked while putting her arm around Beatrice's shoulders.

"Yes, I am fine. Let's go have some cake. I need it right now." Replied Beatrice.

Waking up in the middle of the night soaked with sweat and a fast beating heart was not a new concept for Beatrice. She had night mares since she was a child. She can remember waking up with Kristy shaking her and calling her name from the age of five up to twelve years of age. Every doctor Beatrice saw said the same thing. "There is nothing physically or mentally wrong with Beatrice. Some children have night terrors and she will grow out of it as she gets older." Eventually they slowed down and then stopped when she was twelve. So why tonight she thought while standing in front of the open refrigerator. Finally settling on grape juice with a glass of ice, she turned, screamed, jumped and dropped the glass of juice on the kitchen floor when she bumped into Billy. "What the hell." Shouted Beatrice. "Why are you sneaking up on people like that, I could have had a heart attack and you could have a dead person on the kitchen floor instead of my glass of juice"

"Sorry, I didn't mean to scare you. I just heard the noises coming from your room and then I heard you get up. You haven't done that in a long time. What's wrong? I thought you might want to talk like we used to when we were kids." Said Billy.

"Oh, I'm sorry I woke you up. I guess it's that letter and the money that has me going through it again. I just don't know. This seems so unbelievable you know? Me with family and money. Can you believe it?" Said Beatrice.

"If anyone deserves it it's you Bea. You're the one that has been here the longest and you are the big sister I never thought I would have. I don't think that I could have made it in this situation without you". Said Billy. Having been in three other foster homes before this one. Billy was headed down a bad path. Rebelling, cutting school, bad grades and getting into fights. Finally landing into Kristy's house and Beatrice. Billy seven and Beatrice eleven, she took him under her wing and showed him that together they could take over the world. One book at a time. Beatrice would read to Billy every night and Billy would bring her a cookie after her night terrors. Together they bonded like two children that were blood related and born into a family of their own.

"I just don't know what to think of all of this. What to do. Or how to process this information. I mean, I had family all of this time and didn't know it. Now they are gone and I have no one to answer any of my questions. I guess I will have to sleep on it and investigate more in the morning. Thanks for the talk Billy". Said Beatrice.

"No problem Bea, that's what brothers do". Replied Billy. He hugged Beatrice tight as they headed back up stairs.

Heading for the bus, Beatrice bumping into a little old lady with her basket full of groceries as Beatrice rounded the corner to the bus stop the following morning sent the ladies groceries into the street and brought her out of her deep thought. Did she really have family out there somewhere? Was this Uncle Charles for real? What about the money? What would she do with the money? School, travel or maybe buy a car? "Oh, excuse me ma'am" said Beatrice. "I was in my own little world and I didn't see you there. Are you alright? Let me get these things for you."

"Yes, I'm fine dear. Thank you for helping me and you should be more careful." Replied the lady.

As if on cue, a man appeared and helped Beatrice pick up the ladies items and place them back into her basket. Beatrice couldn't help but notice his strawberry blonde hair as he was

bent over picking up cans from the street. His hair was long enough to reach his shirt collar and ears but not long enough to cover them. Beatrice, frozen to her spot, went slacked jawed and her mouth completely dried up at the site of the man when he stood up. Standing at 6'1" he wore blue jeans, a green flannel shirt over a white tee shirt, with brown boots and had the bluest eyes Beatrice had ever seen. The temperature outside was only 66 degrees when Beatrice left the house that morning. But for reasons Beatrice could not explain, she was sweating bullets standing in front of this man. He smiled a perfectly white smile at Beatrice and then moved to the back of the line for the bus.

Boarding the bus, Beatrice sat towards the front. She tried to keep her mind on all of the questions she was going to ask the lawyer, but her mind and her eyes kept straying to the strange man at the back of the bus. A couple of times, she caught him looking at her. By the third stop, the bus was crowded and Beatrice had to move over to let a woman sit down and when she looked again, the man was gone. That was funny, she never even saw him get off of the bus. Continuing her ride to the lawyer's office, Beatrice wore a smile on her lips and private thoughts about him in her head.

"Look Mr. Evans, I hear what you are saying and I don't believe that you are wrong, but really, this is all on the up and up" Beatrice said with her green eyes as big a saucers. "Where was this family member all these years?"

"Per Kristy, I did some checking for you. Yes, you had a Great Uncle Charles. From what I can find out, your family linage was small. We know that your Mother died when you were two years old in that car accident. Apparently, she had an Uncle Charles that lived in Ireland. His estates' lawyers say that he never knew that you existed. You were only found out when they attempted to locate your Mother. She, apparently, was his last living relative. The money is yours and the check is good. Congratulations Miss Maloney and my condolences." Explained Mr. Evans.

"Holy cow" Beatrice sighed. "Thank you for your time. May I take a business card for future reference?"

"Of course" Replied Mr. Evans reaching out to shake hands. "Keep my card and let me know if you have any trouble at the bank with your check"

"Thank you I will, have a nice day." Beatrice said exiting the office with her head down staring at the check in her hands. Glancing up just as a bike rider came down the sidewalk. He veered right to miss hitting Beatrice, hit the parking meter instead and landed on the hood of the car parked there. Sprawled there on his back in a sprawled eagle formation, a crowd gathered along with the police. Beatrice was sent on her way and the bike rider was given a ticket for riding his bike on the sidewalk.

While waiting for the bus to take her back up town, Beatrice watched all of the cars go by. Thinking that now she had the means to buy a car. But what kind should I get? What color would go with my green eyes? "Great here comes the bus." Beatrice said out loud. More to herself than to anyone special. Just as the bus was pulling up to the curb, Beatrice glanced out at the passing cars and there he was. The blonde, blue eyed man from earlier. In the passenger side of a black SUV. He glanced at Beatrice as it drove by. "Now this is getting creepy" said Beatrice out loud.

As Beatrice entered the house, she smelled food. "Stuffed cabbage, that's my favorite. How did you know that I would need something to make me feel better?" Asked Beatrice.

"I just know it's your favorite. Didn't things go well with the lawyer?" Asked Kristy

"He said that the money and the letter are real and that I am the last living relative for this Uncle Charles person. I can't believe that I had family and did not know it. Not that I am not happy for being here all these years. I guess I just got lucky. You have been great. You are the Mother I know. I love you." Beatrice said

"Oh honey, you know that I love you too. I am so glad that you got to stay here with me. What are you going to do now? Are you going to continue with school?" Asked Kristy

"I just don't know what to do. I think that I am going to sleep on it. Will you go to the bank with me tomorrow? I just don't feel comfortable on the bus with this money." Beatrice asked.

"Absolutely, we can go after I get everyone else off to school." Replied Kristy

After her fill of the stuffed cabbage, Beatrice headed up stairs to her room. Thinking of what she was going to do with the money. School just wasn't for her. At least not right now. Beatrice wanted to travel. See the parts of the world that she read about all her life. Falling into her nightly routine, turning down her bed, brushing her teeth and dotting her favorite pair of boxers and t-shirt. Beatrice laid on her back with her arm over her eyes, she drifted off to sleep with thoughts of the blonde, blue eyed stranger.

Beatrice stood there starring up into the bluest eyes she has ever seen. Both of her hands on his chest feeling the heat seeping through his white t-shirt. One of his hands was cupping her face while the other was on the small of her back bringing her closer to him. As he pulled her closer, she smoothed her hands slowly up his chest to his neck. Forcing her to stand on her tip toes. Placing her hands around his neck, he leaned in until their lips were barely touching. Very lightly he kissed her lips, then again on her jaw bone then he kissed her neck. Shivers ran down Beatrice's body so violently, it felt like someone was shaking her whole body.

"Wake up Bea, wake up." Urged Billy with his hands on Beatrice's shoulders gently shaking her. "You're having a dream."

"Wait, what, Billy? What are you doing here?" Asked Beatrice slightly disoriented.

"There were some strange noised coming from your room when I walked by. I tried knocking, but the moaning noises just got louder. Are you alright?" Replied Billy

Beatrice could feel the heat in her cheeks. Thankful that the room was only lit by the hallway light. She was sure the color in her cheeks would give her away. "Yes, I'm fine thanks Billy. I was just dreaming." Said Beatrice

"That must have been some dream from all the noises you were making" said Billy smiling shyly and looking down at his feet. He has always felt like a brother to Beatrice, but lately he has been feeling shy and awkward. Not really sure where these feelings were coming from, Billy stood up and went to the door to leave.

"Then what did you wake me up for" Beatrice said smiling noticing the look on Billy's face and the way he seemed to be backing out of the room. "I'm fine, really it wasn't a night mare. Go back to bed and I will see you in the morning" Beatrice smiled but noticed the awkwardness that was beginning to form between them.

Choosing to put those thoughts out of her head for the moment, Beatrice laid back down and tried to go back to sleep. A glance at the alarm clock said it was 3:32 am. "How am I supposed to sleep now? And what was I doing dreaming about him?" Beatrice said out loud to herself. Closing her eyes, she drifted off to sleep thinking about the money and what she planned to do with it. She really wanted to travel but to where? What would Kristy think about her leaving for destinations far away?

"Now that I have some money, would you like to go out to lunch?" Beatrice asked Kristy as they were leaving the bank. Not quite sure as to how to break the news to Kristy of her up and coming plans to travel to New York. She had always wanted to go there. Growing up in the Central Valley of California, Stockton to be exact. It was nice and all but not as exciting as Beatrice thought things could be. She wanted lights, big city, people and adventure. She thought what better place to get all of that than New York.

"Thanks for lunch, but you didn't have to do this" said Kristy.

"I wanted to. How do you like your salad?" Asked Beatrice.

"It's wonderful thank you, you've hardly touched your sandwich and fries. What's wrong?" Asked Kristy

"Can I ask you something?" Asked Beatrice

"Sure, you can talk to me about anything. You should know that by now." Replied Kristy. Just then her eyes got as big as giant serving platters. "You're pregnant!" Exclaimed Kristy. Loud enough for the two people at the next table to stop eating and stare at them.

At that comment, Beatrice had soda coming from her nose and mouth all over the table and her lap. Her sandwich bread soaking up the liquid and her French fries swimming in it. Laughing, she grabbed her napkin to help clean up. The waitress came over with a towel and asked if everything was alright. After the waitress left, Beatrice leaned in and whispered "Holy cow, I can't believe you just said that. I'm still a virgin for Heaven sake! I only dated one boy in high school. Don't you remember John? He took me to that dance. After that it was like I adopted a puppy. He followed me everywhere and once you found him on the porch at 6 am when you went to get the paper."

Laughing as hard as Beatrice, Kristy nodded her head in response. Dabbing her napkin at her mouth as well. "I remember, at one point I thought I was going to have to adopt him or start feeding him on a regular basis! I'm sorry for interrupting you, go ahead and ask me your question honey."

"Well, one question is why was I allowed to stay with you for all these years? I mean I have seen kids come and go, but I got to stay. Aside from Billy, I have been with you the longest. And the other is, why have you continued to let me stay with you past my eighteenth birthday. It's not that I am not great full, I'm just trying to figure things out." Explained Beatrice

Kristy knew that these questions would come at some point. She just wasn't prepared for them now. How could she sit there and lie to Beatrice. She loved Beatrice like she was her own and didn't want Beatrice to hate her if she knew the truth. Of course, Kristy was bound and unable to tell Beatrice the truth. She knew it was coming though, she has heard word that Joe was in town. A bitter sweet smile came across Kristy's face at the thought of the little blonde two year old girl that come to her house on that February night. She remembered it like it was yesterday. This poor blonde baby of two years old was brought to her house in the middle of the night. Kristy was told that her name was Beatrice. Beatrice was dressed in a lavender colored dress with white tights, white socks and little white shoes. She was clutching her teddy bear and blanket with tears streaming down her little cheeks. Now sits a twenty one year old woman asking questions that Kristy was not at liberty to answer, not now anyway.

"Well" Kristy began "Since there were no other family members that could be found at that time and the fact that you were not a trouble maker, I guess that is why they just left you with me. After you turned eighteen, I just loved you like you were my own and wanted to give you the best start I could in life. I wanted to see you succeed in school and life." Kristy said shrugging her shoulders. She hoped that Beatrice would believe the explanation she just gave and not call her on it. The less Beatrice knew about the truth the better.

"I can understand that. I mean the first memory I have is of you. Remember that rocking chair that was in my room? We spent hours upon hours in that chair with you reading to me. I think that is where I got my passion for reading. Thank you for that by the way. Reading has gotten me through some difficult times as a child." Beatrice said.

Beatrice's jaw fell to the floor and she just began starring past Kristy to the window behind her. "There he is" Beatrice whispered

"There's who?" asked Kristy as she turned in her chair to look behind her. She looked right into the eyes of Joe. He smiled and then walked away.

Chapter Two

"Who is that guy Bea? Do you know him?" Kristy said looking at Beatrice to gauge her response.

"No I have never met him, but I can swear he is following me." Replied Beatrice

"What makes you say that?" Asked Kristy

"On my way to the lawyer's office, I ran into a lady and knocked her basket into the street and he showed up out of nowhere and helped me help the lady with her stuff and then I swear I saw him in a passing car when I was getting on the bus to come home." And then, Beatrice paused, turned beat red and then said "There was last night"

"What, wait, what do you mean last night?" Kristy replied her voice just a little louder than she planned it to be.

"I had a dream about him. He was kissing me and then Billy came in and woke me up. He said that I was making noises in my sleep and thought I was having a night mare." Beatrice shrugged her shoulders in response.

"Oh so you have never talked to him then?" Asked Kristy

"No but he keeps showing up where ever I go. It's getting creepy. Maybe we should go. I am not feeling comfortable with this guy hanging around." Said Beatrice picking up her purse and paying the check.

"Right behind you." Replied Kristy looking around as she got up from the table. She had never seen Joe before, but she was told that he was in town. She was assuming that was him by the description she was given. Having him around was not a good thing. It means that they have found her. Signing up to be a foster parent was a good cover, so Kristy thought. That way she could keep Rose's daughter without anyone calling suspicion to her. Joining Beatrice at the counter, they walked out together. Beatrice's head down as usual, Kristy with her head up and scanning the parking lot for Joe.

The next few hours Kristy spent on the phone trying to figure out what to do next. She spent the last nineteen years taking care of Beatrice. Trying to give her a life that she deserved to have. Not one running from the Cassidy family. She finally got through to Aengus. "Yes, Aengus, I understand. Like I said, he was standing outside the restaurant where we were having lunch. Beatrice said that she has seen him around town a few times this week." Explained Kristy.

"Okay, I'm going to see how much they actually know. Apparently they know enough to have found her. Sit tight and I will get back to you soon." Explained Aengus.

Splashing water on her face trying to get her composure back, Kristy was trying to figure out how she was going to keep Beatrice from reading that something was wrong. Leaving her room, she ran into Beatrice coming out of her room with her purse in hand and sunglasses on her face. "Going somewhere?" Asked Kristy

"Oh hi, yeah my friend Amanda called and asked why I wasn't in class today. She said that she wanted to talk to me and to meet her at the library. Is it okay if I go? Do you need me for anything?" Replied Beatrice.

"No, I'm good you go and have fun. You have your phone on you right? Please call me if you need anything. Would you like to take the car? I don't need it for the rest of the day." Said Kristy. She wanted to make sure Beatrice was as safe as possible without alerting her and standing at the bus stop made Kristy nervous.

"Sure, I would love to take the car. Are you sure you won't need it? I won't be but a couple of hours. Said Beatrice

"That's fine. Go and have fun. Be careful." Said Kristy as she headed down stairs to check on the other kids and help them with their homework.

Beatrice just loved it when she got to take the car. Now more than ever because she had the money to buy one. She had been thinking about that for a couple of days now. One thing that she knew for sure was that she didn't want a mini van like the one she was driving now. She giggled to herself. What she really wanted was a sports car. Navigating to the library on auto pilot with the radio blasting, Beatrice almost missed him. The blonde stranger in the black SUV that just passed her. Turning her head to see, she almost ran into a light pole, swerving and jumping the curb, Beatrice corrected herself and kept going. Shaken and scared, Beatrice ignored the horns honking, checking the rear view mirror to make sure no one got hurt she kept going to the library.

Amanda was at the library where she said she would be. Her brown hair sporting a pony tail, her upper body a black leather jacket over a white sweater and her mouth a pencil. Almost every time Beatrice saw Amanda, she had something in her mouth. A pencil, her keys, gum, paper clip or her finger. Beatrice approached the table, pulled out a chair and sat down. "Hey girlfriend, what's up?" Asked Beatrice

"Not much, where were you today? I missed having you in class to help pass the time. You sick or something?" Asked Amanda

"No, not sick I just had some things to take care of today. Did I miss anything good?" Ask Beatrice

"Ha, no, just a three hour lecture on immigration." Said Amanda laughing

Looking at all of the pamphlet's spread out on the table, Beatrice picked one up and asked Amanda she was doing with all of these.

"This, my friend is what I wanted to talk to you about. You know how we are always talking about traveling? Well, I talked to this guy today and he said the best way to travel and get paid for it is to apply to work on a cruise ship. I got the number and wanted to talk to you and see if you wanted to do this with me. My parents are going to kill me if I do this, but I don't want school right now. I just want to have some fun. You in or not?" Said Amanda.

"Oh wow, what timing. Of course I'm in. Who do we call? Where do we go? Can we go now? Kristy let me take the car so we have transportation." Beatrice exclaimed.

"Cool, let's roll." Amanda said as she jumped up and grabbed her things. "I will call this place on the way."

The girls exited the library arm in arm laughing all the way to the car. A job on a cruise ship was just what Beatrice needed right now. A way to travel and make money while she was at it. Not that she needed the money anymore, but what an opportunity. Beatrice was going to take advantage of this no matter what anyone said. Telling Kristy was the only thing that gave Beatrice butter flies in her stomach and a frown on her face.

"Hey, why the long face? I thought that you were excited about this. We are going to the office to sign up for this right?' Asked Amanda.

"Yes of course that's where we're going. I was just thinking about telling Kristy. I don't think that she is going to be all that happy with my choice. But...." Beatrice let the rest of her thought trail off. She was having her own inner fight.

"I know what she has done for you and what she means to you but you have to live your life. Not the one that someone wants you to live. We need to go out there and make our own choices. Our own mistakes and our own adventure. And what better way to do that than with a friend. Your best friend." Amanda said with her arm out the window, hair blowing in the wind and a smile on her face.

As the girls got out of the car, Beatrice had this feeling that made her turn and glance around the parking lot and the other businesses. A jewelry store, a music store, and a coffee shop lined the rest of the business building housing the cruise line office. Across the parking lot was a thrift store with two cars parked in front.

"Hey are you coming? We don't want to waste any time come on." Shouted Amanda standing in the doorway to the office.

"Yes I'm coming. Keep your shorts on will you?" Replied Beatrice. She sighed, turned towards the office door where Amanda was waiting and hit the lock button for the car.

Standing inside the thrift store looking out the window, Joe watched Beatrice and Amanda enter the cruise line's office. Follow, observe and report was his mission. He didn't know that his subject would look like that. As he watched, he noticed Beatrice looking around the parking lot. Looking for him, he was sure. All he could do was stare at her with her long blonde hair blowing in the wind. That day at the bus stop, he got a look into her green eyes. Eyes that have haunted him every night since that day. Today what caught his eye was her legs and the way she filled out the jeans she was wearing. "She can't be more that 5'3" and beautiful." Said Joe out loud to himself.

When Beatrice and Amanda left the office, Beatrice did another scan of the parking lot and surrounding stores. Amanda watched Beatrice looking around while she waited for her to unlock the car. Amanda thought her behavior was odd even for Beatrice, but she just watched and didn't say anything. They had all of their papers signed and ready to go. The only thing they needed to do was tell their parents. Beatrice and Amanda chatted all the home about what they were going to pack. What they would take and how much fun they were going to have. By the time Beatrice got home, she was shaking she was so nervous about telling Kristy. Beatrice pulled into the drive way and sat there trying to figure out just how to break the news. Kristy might understand and take the news pretty good, but Billy. She hopped that he would not revert back to his old ways after she left.

Walking into the house, Beatrice noticed how quiet it was. It was never this quiet. "Hello, is anyone here?" Beatrice called out as she put her purse down on the entry table and hung up the keys on the hook by the door. Her papers, she kept with her in the big manila envelope given to her at the meeting.

"Here in the kitchen." Called Kristy.

Beatrice tool a deep breath and headed through the living room in route to the kitchen. "Hi, what's going on? Where is everyone? It's never this quiet around here." Said Beatrice standing in the entry to the kitchen.

"Billy is spending the night at Jeff's, Jackie and Suzy are doing the weekend trial with their mother and that leaves you and me. Are you hungry, I made lasagna and salad? What's that you have? Explained Kristy

"I'm glad that it's just you and me. I wanted to talk to you about something." Said Beatrice

"Ok, shall we talk over dinner? Asked Kristy. "It's all ready. Help me get everything to the table."

"Sure, let me get the salad." Beatrice started her explanation of her meeting with Amanda and their decision. "I met up with Amanda at the library. She said that I didn't miss anything good at school today." Beatrice took her usual seat at the table. Beads of sweat started to form on her upper lip and her heart rate picked up. "She had a great opportunity to talk to me about."

"Oh really and what might that be?" Kristy asked as she spooned lasagna on a plate and handed it to Beatrice.

"She had information about getting a job on a cruise ship." Beatrice said with her head down serving herself some salad. Beatrice was not sure how she was going to eat this food. Her stomach is in knots.

"And what does that have to do with you?" Asked Kristy

"I kind of went with her today and applied." Beatrice said as she shrugged her shoulders. "We were approved and hired. We leave a week from tomorrow."

Lasagna fell out of Kristy's mouth and landed on the table when her jaw dropped. "You're kidding me?" Kristy stuttered picking up her napkin bringing it up to her mouth. "What made you do this? Is this for real? I just can't believe you just said that. Start talking and do it now." Kristy said with her lips pursed together,

Beatrice put down her knife and fork next to her plate. She picked up her napkin, dabbed her mouth and laid it gently in her lap. Taking a deep breath, she looked Kristy in the eyes and started "After I got that money, I was thinking about putting school on hold for maybe a year. Do some traveling. Then Amanda had this information fall into her lap and I thought it would be a great way to see parts of the world and make money at the same time. I thought that I could put the money my Uncle left me in the bank to earn interest and just travel for a while." Beatrice did a big exhale. It seemed she was holding her breath for the whole explanation.

Sitting back in her chair, putting her hands in her lap, Kristy stared at her hands for a bit before she spoke. "I see." She said as she raised her eyes to meet Beatrice's

"Please don't be mad at me." Beatrice said in a whisper

"I'm not made at you honey. Just surprised is all" Kristy said sitting forward taking a bite of her salad. "Isn't Amanda older than you?" She asked

"She is twenty five and I am twenty one. It's not that big of a difference" Said Beatrice

"Like you said Bea, you are twenty one and can do as you please. I am just shocked at all of this" Replied Kristy "Can you give me any more details?"

"Sure, we signed up to be maids. We will be making up the rooms on a daily basis. We will get time at each port we go to and a weekly pay check. All meals are free and he said that he would make sure that we are roomed together." Beatrice said smiling her best smile

"Well, if that is what you want to do than I am going to support you honey" Kristy said with her heart in her throat. She didn't want to lose Beatrice, but she needed to let her spread her wings and fly. Kristy also thought this cruise thing would keep her out of the danger of the

14

Cassidy Family. Later that night she would call Aengus and inform him of Beatrice's plans.

"Will you help me get the bank account started and go shopping with me to get the things I will need? Oh and maybe give me some pointers on how to tell Billy?" Asked Beatrice

"Sure, spending as much time with you as possible before you go off and travel the world, how could I resist?" Kristy replied smiling "Now eat before it gets cold"

The next week just flew by. Faster than Beatrice thought it would. Kristy went with her to the bank and got that part situated. At Kristy's resistance, Beatrice deposited $50,000 in Kristy's account. Beatrice wanted to know that she would be all right. After all that she did for her Beatrice wanted to re-pay her. Beatrice would always remember the shopping trips and the long nights packing and talking with Kristy. The conversation Beatrice had with Billy almost broke her heart. They parted with the promise to keep in touch via the phone and e-mailing. Beatrice was satisfied that he would be good without her being close.

The night before Beatrice's departure, Kristy let the rest of the children stay up late and make cookies, play games and have just a fun time together. The following morning, Kristy let the others skip school so they all could go to the bus station together. A lot of tearful hugs and goodbye's called for a whole pack of tissues. Beatrice and Amanda boarded their bus to Long Beach after they heard the final boarding call. They wanted to spend as much time as possible with their families. Finally the bus was pulling out of the parking lot. Beatrice was sitting next to Amanda hanging out the window waving her arm off.

Kristy said a small prayer that Beatrice would be all right. A long conversation with Aengus the night before made Kristy feel a little bit better. It was decided that Kristy would not say anything about Joe and the *Cassidy* family. They figured that they would have a hard time following Beatrice if she was in the middle of the ocean or at some foreign port.

Chapter Three

With luggage in tow, three suitcases and one over the shoulder bag that contained everything she owned, Beatrice headed up to the building on the right with Amanda in tow. Looking for the door marked 'Employees'. At the age of 21 Beatrice just knew for sure that she would be the youngest employee on board *The King.*

"Come on will you" Yelled Beatrice. She was moving faster than Amanda was. Amanda had brought four suitcases and a big leather zipper bag that weighed just as much as she did.

"Hey, can you help me here? I guess you were right, I should have not brought so much with me. But I just could not leave my wardrobe behind" Said Amanda struggling to catch her breath.

Beatrice could not help but stop and laugh at Amanda. Beatrice sat down her own luggage and walked back to Amanda. Both girls started to laugh as Beatrice helped take one of Amanda's smaller suite cases. Both girls struggled to get Beatrice's luggage. Amanda put the strap to her big leather bag over her head to use her body to help and took the other two large suit cases, one handle in each hand. Beatrice balanced her small bag on one suit case and attached the other two together and off they went in search for the entrance.

"Look, there it is over there next to the big windows" Said Amanda

"Okay, I see it. Just a little bit further." Replied Beatrice. As she approached the windows, she stopped and leaned up against the window to wait for Amanda to catch up.

"Man, I'm out of breath. Who knew that I should have really participated at the gym instead of looking for hot guys" Said Amanda as she put her bag down in front of Beatrice's feet. "And speaking of hot guys, look at that one. Those are the most amazing eyes I have ever seen and he's looking right at you, look" Amanda exclaimed pointing at the window

"What the hell" Whispered Beatrice as she looked in the window. She was face to face with Joe. He smiled, turned and walked in the opposite direction. Beatrice turned to run inside the building and tripped over Amanda's large leather bag. Down she went on her face, hands hitting the ground along with her dignity.

"Shit Beatrice are you all right?" Screamed Amanda bending over to help Beatrice up off the ground. "And who was that guy anyway? Do you know him?" Amanda went on with her questions not giving Beatrice a chance to answer them.

Beatrice stood up and brusher herself off. Starting with her pants then her hands. "I don't know him but, and you're not going to believe this, I think that he is following me" Beatrice explained. "Come on, I will explain later, we are going to be late"

"Only if you promise to tell me everything later." Replied Amanda

"I will, I promise. Let's get in there before we are late and we miss the boat." Said Beatrice.

Beatrice held the door open for Amanda and all her luggage to enter the building first. Pushing and pulling her own luggage, Beatrice followed Amanda to the counter. Both girls produced their paperwork along with their passports. They were giving their room number, tags to put on their luggage, directions to boarding the ship and their instructions there after.

Beatrice tried to concentrate on putting the tags on her luggage, but she kept picking her head up scanning the room. Looking for the blue eyed stranger. Why was he here? Why was he following her? What did he want? Just who is he? While thinking about all of these questions, Beatrice didn't hear Amanda calling her name.

"Bea, hey Beatrice can you hear me?" Asked Amanda waving her hands in front of Beatrice's face.

"Yes, sorry, I was just looking around" Said Beatrice

"Yea, looking for him no doubt." Answered Amanda laughing "Come one let's go, we have to check in by three and it is already two o'clock. I want to look around some before we start working" Amanda said as she took Beatrice's hand pulling her along.

Begrudgingly Beatrice moved as Amanda pulled her hand. Going where Amanda led her with her head and her eyes turning in every direction looking for the stranger. Beatrice was determined to find him and question him.

Stepping out into the crisp, clean, ocean scented air, Beatrice stopped walking and took a deep breath with her eyes closed. She just couldn't believe what she was about to do. She never traveled further than about 100 miles away from home. And when she did she had Kristy with her. Now here she was, about to board a cruise ship, spread her wings and fly. A smile appeared on her lips, a quiver through her body and joy in her heart. Beatrice took off running to catch up with Amanda who was already half way up the ramp to the ship.

The first thing that the girls did was find their room. "Holly crap" Said Beatrice "This room is the size of my closet at home. Look I can pee and brush my teeth at the same time in this bathroom."

"Yea but it's ours for the next year Bea" Said Amanda with a big grin on her face. "We won't be spending much time here anyways. When we're not working, we are going to be out on the ship getting into mischief. I'm not hip on the bunk beds thing. Which one do you want top or Bottom?"

"I guess you're right. It doesn't matter to me I can take either. We don't have to decide right now do we? Let's go check in and find out what we are supposed to be doing." Replied Beatrice

Their instructions were to meet in Ball Room One. When they stepped out of the elevator on the main floor, both girls stopped dead in their tracks at the splendor in front of them. Beatrice's head titled up at the large chandelier suspended above. Gold with red ribbons hanging down. There were windows above the chandelier spilling in sun light. The sun light sparkled off of the gold plated walls. Walls that came down from what looked liked four more flights up thought Beatrice. Bringing her head down out of the clouds, she noticed the carpet was swirled with red, green and gold. In the middle of the room sat a circular shaped bar with stools going around it. Without looking, Beatrice reached out and touched Amanda's arm. More checking to see if she was still there than wanting anything from her.

"I know, right" Whispered Amanda still looking around herself.

"This is just beautiful" Replied Beatrice

"Hello ladies, can I help you" Asked a man dressed in a suit the color of charcoal with a red tie. His name tag said Carl.

"Oh yes" Replied Amanda "We are supposed to be going to Ball Room One. Can you direct us? This is our first time aboard."

"Absolutely" Said Carl "You will need to go down that hall way there. Ball Room One is at the end. And if you need anything let me know. My name is Carl, I am one of the ships director's."

"Thank you Carl" Beatrice responded. Taking Amanda's arm, Beatrice led her in the direction that Carl indicated.

Beatrice couldn't remember feeling anything like it, the soft carpet on the walls. Blood red with purple swirls all through it. As she walked she ran her hand along the walls. Amanda ran her hand along the rail attached to the wall. "Oh Bea, I don't think I feel so good" Said Amanda as she grabbed her stomach with the other hand bending slightly.

Beatrice stopped walking and looked at Amanda "Are you serious? We're still docked" Beatrice whispered "Didn't you know whether you get sea sick or not" Asked Beatrice

"No, I have never been on a boat or ship or anything like it before. I didn't even think about this." Replied Amanda

"Shit, come on let's get to the Ball Room and we can get you a seat and some water. Maybe that will help" Said Beatrice as she took Amanda's arm assisting her the rest of the way.

The Ball Room was large by Beatrice's standards. She helped Amanda find a seat near the front of the stage. And then went to find her some water. She spotted Carl standing off to the side of the room reading some papers.

"Excuse me, Carl?" Beatrice said while she waited for him to finish with his papers.

He looked up and smiled "Yes, what can I do for you" He asked

"My friend is not feeling very good, I was wondering where I can get her some water" Asked Beatrice

"And your name is?" asked Carl with a big smile on his face

"Oh sorry, my name is Beatrice and my friend is Amanda" Replied Beatrice

"Where is your friend?" He asked

"She is sitting over there a couple of rows in from the stage" Replied Beatrice as she pointed in the direction of where Amanda was sitting.

"You can get her some water over there at the refreshment bar and I will have a nurse come check on her, try not to move from that area so the nurse can find you" Carl said as he stepped away.

Beatrice picked up two water bottles, one for herself and one for Amanda and made her way back to Amanda. "How are you feeling?" Asked Beatrice as she took a seat next to Amanda opening one of the waters and handing it to her.

"A little better now that I am sitting down. Man this water tastes great." Amanda said as she started to drain the bottle of water.

"I wouldn't do that if I were you" A masculine voice said from the isle next to Amanda

Both girls slowly looked to their left and then up at the man standing there. He was standing next to Carl. "Hello ladies" Carl started "this is Jeff, he is one of the ships nurses we have on board with us. He is going to take a look at Amanda and see if he can help. If you ladies need anything else just locate me. I will be in the back of the room for this meeting" And just like that Carl was gone.

"So, which one of you ladies is Amanda?" Asked Jeff as he kneeled down in the aisle.

"This is Amanda" Said Beatrice pointing to Amanda "and I am Beatrice" she said pointing to herself.

"I was told that you are not feeling too good" Jeff said to Amanda "Just what is going on with you?"

"After the ride up in the elevator, my head started to spin and then my stomach started to churn and I feel like throwing up" Explained Amanda

"Unfortunately, this is common for some people. I have some Dramamine for you. Take one now and then one every time you feel this way. Try not to take more than six in twenty four hours. Be careful they may make you sleepy. And sip the water, too much at one time can make it come back up. If you know what I mean?" Jeff said as he felt Amanda's forehead, touched her arm and then stood up.

"Thank you" both girls said at the same time staring up at Jeff.

"You're welcome" Jeff said smiling as he walked away

"Man, they sure have some hot guys working her" said Amanda

"You think every guy is 'hot'" Said Beatrice laughing.

Beatrice and Amanda spent the next few minutes looking around and pointing out people that caught their eye. Amanda spent that time pointing out all of the 'hot' guys she wanted to get to know.

A very smart looking woman stepped on stage and started checking the equipment. She was wearing a light brown pencil skirt with a white button down shirt. Her brown hair was pulled into a bun and the nape of her neck and high heeled shoes that matched the skirt. "Hello everyone and thank you for being here" She began "My name in Heather Smith and I am the head coordinator. I am here to welcome you all and to get you all started on your career with Premier Cruise Lines. After my short speech, everyone will need to get your itineraries from one of the back tables" Heather said as she pointed to the back of the room. "The tables are alphabetized, just find the table that will match your last name. In there, you will find everything you need for the next week. We depart port in eight days. During that time everyone will get a picture taken for your badge and name tag. Your floors that you will be in charge of and the dates, times and places of your various meetings. Once you have your picture taken, it will take about twenty four hours until we have them all ready for pick up. Until then you are not allowed to leave the ship. If you leave the ship without your badge, you will not be allowed back on. That badge is your pass for exiting and entering the ship. It is now approximately 3:30, your next meeting will be dinner which starts at 5:30. Between now and then, please pick up your itineraries, get your picture taken for your badges and feel free to mingle or check out the ship and I will see you all in the dining hall by 5:30. Thank you all and welcome"

"How do you feel now?" Beatrice asked Amanda

"Better thank you. That pill really works." Replied Amanda

"Great, shall we get in line for our itinerary?" Beatrice said standing up looking around the room. "My line is over there and yours is over there" Beatrice said pointing in the proper direction.

"Okay, after we get our stuff let's meet up over there by the door, yes?" Amanda Said

"Sure that sounds great" Beatrice said as she turned and headed over to the sign marked L-O.

Standing in line, Beatrice took this time to look around. Standing behind her were two women who were talking to each other. One was from the state of Washington and the other was from Georgia. They were talking about how they needed to get away from their lives and try something new. The one from Washington had fire red hair cut short and looked to be in her thirties. The other one from Georgia had brown hair shoulder length and looked to be in her forties. Standing in front of Beatrice was a man that kept turning around and looking at her. He was about the same height as Beatrice and was balding at the top of his head.

"Hi" the man said to Beatrice

"Hi" Beatrice replied

"I'm George Matson, what's your name?" George asked

"Beatrice, Beatrice Maloney" Replied Beatrice giving a small smile

"I'm from Oregon. My wife left me for her personal trainer and I lost my house and thought I would try this for a while" George said "How about you?"

"The same" said Beatrice pointing to the front of the line "you're next"

George's face turned beet red and he turned to step up for his turn. Relieved, Beatrice scanned the room for Amanda. She spotted her chatting with the guy behind her in line. He was tall, tan and blonde. Amanda is so lucky, where ever she goes she meets hot guys that will talk to her. All I get are the bald and forty type. Beatrice thought to herself.

Beatrice found Amanda waiting at their meeting spot. "Hey, what shall we do now? It is only 4:15 and we do not have to meet up again until 5:30 for dinner." Beatrice asked Amanda

"Let's go to our room and see if our luggage has made it. I would like to change and maybe we could do some unpacking." Replied Amanda

"Sounds good to me. Who was that guy you were talking to" Asked Beatrice

"Some guy from Los Angeles. He tried out to be one of the male dancers in one of the shows that they have on board but he got cut and he decided that this was the next best way to get on board. His name is Jimmy. He' kind of full of himself." Replied Amanda as they waked back to their room.

Chapter Four

'Yes, our luggage is here" Exclaimed Amanda diving right in and unzipping her suitcases.

"I don't know where we are going to put everything in this cracker box." Said Beatrice

"Oh quit being so negative will you? This is going to be great." Said Amanda smiling as she started to put her things away.

Beatrice wasn't thinking this was so great at the moment. She was starting to miss Kristy and the other children in the house. Standing in the middle of their room looking around Beatrice spotted one long dresser with six drawers, one closet that had a full length mirror, Two bunk beds and a bathroom. The only window in the room was a port hole. Looking out Beatrice saw the water came right below the window. The entire room had been painted white. The bed spreads were a cream color and the carpet matched the walls in the hall, blood red with purple and green swirls in it. Taking a deep breath, Beatrice joined Amanda and started un-packing her things. Each one took three drawers and half the closet.

By 5:00 they were done with the task of un-packing. Each had changed into black jeans, black boots and a sweater. Amanda's was red and Beatrice's was purple. "Hey, at least our itineraries are the same" Said Amanda "That way we get to be together for those. So smile or they will think you don't want to be here"

"I'm good" Said Beatrice with a small smile. All though she did not feel good. She had never been away from home before. Home, what home, thought Beatrice. No family, no home, all I have is a necklace that my mother had on her when she died. A small gold heart and a small gold key on a gold chain.

"Hello, Bea?" Said Amanda waving her hand in front of Beatrice's face. "Did you hear me? What's with the stare into to the beyond?"

"Oh, sorry Amanda. I was just thinking about things" Beatrice said. With itineraries in hand, Beatrice and Amanda strolled off together to the dining room.

The dining room was in full swing when Beatrice and Amanda arrived. Music playing in the back ground and groups of people everywhere. There was a bar along the wall to the left and dining tables set up to the right. The sign by the door read:

WELCOME

OPEN BAR 5:30 – 6:00

DINNER STARTS AT 6:00

"Wow, would you look at this" Beatrice said walking in and looking around. Twinkle lights hung all over the room, intermingled with the fake trees. The tables were set in cream and gold colors. Every table had a number on a stand in the middle of the table.

"Yeah" said Amanda looking around with her mouth open. "Let's get a drink"

"Sure" Said Beatrice

Amanda handed Beatrice a beer. She gladly took it taking a long pull. The music stopped and a voice came on over a loud speaker "Hello everyone and welcome to our kick off dinner. Everyone should have brought your itineraries with you. At the top right hand corner of the first page is a number. That number tells you what table you are sitting at. It is 5:45 so if everyone could please start finding your tables, the wait staff will be around to start taking your dinner orders. Thank you and enjoy" Then the voice was gone and the music started up again.

"I have number three, what number do you have?" Beatrice asked Amanda

"Hey, I have number three too." Exclaimed Amanda "This just keeps getting better and better" Amanda said grabbing Beatrice's hand pulling her in the direction of the table numbering three.

At the arrival of table number three, Beatrice noticed a woman with black hair sitting there alone looking lonely and lost. "Is this seat taken?" Beatrice asked the woman.

"No" the woman said with a small smile.

Beatrice sat down next to her. "Hi, my name is Beatrice and this is Amanda" Beatrice said pointing to Amanda

"Hi, my name is Felicia" the woman replied.

"Are you here alone?" Asked Amanda

"Yes" Felicia said

"Where are you from?" Beatrice Asked Felicia

"New Mexico" Replied Felicia

"I've never been there" Said Amanda "What's it like?"

"Hot" replied Felicia

A sudden burst of laughter between the three women made all the others at the table stop what they were doing and look at them. This brought more laughter from the women.

"It feels good to laugh. I haven't done that it quite some time" Said Felicia

"Are you okay?" Beatrice asked Felicia

"Yes, it's just been a tough couple of years for me. My husband died in a robbery at a grocery store. I had to move in with my in laws in Santa Barbara. They took me in, but I could tell they didn't want me there. I heard about this opportunity and took it. I didn't even tell them I was leaving. I just got up and left one morning early and came here." Said Felicia

"It sounds like we could all become friends" Said Amanda raising her third beer up in a cheers motion.

This sent the three women in another round of laughter. After four beers, a four course meal consisting of soup, salad, lobster and chocolate cake for desert, Beatrice and Amanda walked Felicia to her room before heading to theirs. "I think that we all could be friends" said Amanda for the second time. Beatrice knew that Amanda had one to many beers and would be feeling it in the morning, Beatrice pulled out her key for the room, unlocked the door, opened it and came to a dead stop. Amanda ran into the back of Beatrice. "What the hell" Exclaimed Amanda. When Beatrice didn't move, Amanda looked over her shoulder into the room.

The whole room had been tossed. All of the clothes were out of the dresser drawers and thrown all over the room. Both beds were askew and had their suitcases unzipped on top of them.

"What the hell happened in here?" Beatrice said

"I don't know but I'm going to find out." Amanda said as she reached for the room's phone. She hit the zero and got a lady from a switch board. Amanda told her what happened and the lady said she would have security there shortly and not to touch anything. Beatrice and Amanda waited out in the hall for security.

After their arrival, a series of questions ensued. Both Amanda and Beatrice told the security how they left the room when they went to dinner and yes they locked the door. "Hello Ladies, I hear we had some sort of a break in." Said Carl as he walked up to Beatrice and Amanda sitting on the floor in the hall outside the room. Amanda had her legs brought up to her chest with her head resting on her knees. Beatrice was crossed legged with her hands in her lap her head down. Beatrice brought her head up to look at Carl, noticing he still had on his suit without his tie. His shirt had the top two buttons un-done, hands in his pockets. Carl smiled at Beatrice and stepped into the room. After a long thirty minutes later, Will, one of the security came out of the room.

"From what we can tell there is nothing missing that should be there. We swept for prints and will test them to see if any of the one's we took don't match yours or any of the staff. Go through your things to see if anything is missing. I will have my assistant return in the morning to get a list if there is one. I will have one of my men patrol this area the rest of the night. Here is my card with my direct extension if you need anything else tonight." Will said as he handed Beatrice one of his cards

Beatrice stood up off of the floor and took his card. "Thank you for everything" Beatrice said. She turned to help Amanda up off of the floor and lead her into the room. "Look at this place, who would do this?" Beatrice said out loud

"I don't know but I am too tired to put this all away right now. I think I had too much beer" Amanda said as she flopped down on the bed putting one arm over her eyes.

Beatrice spent the next three hours putting all of their things back in the dresser drawers and in the closet. She spent time arranging their things in the bathroom and laid all of Amanda's jewelry out on the dresser for her to check when she woke up in the morning. As far as she could tell nothing was missing. Beatrice secured their luggage and placed them, locked and labeled, outside the door as directed for pick up to storage. How Amanda could sleep through all of the noise she was making thought Beatrice. Finally at 3:30 am, Beatrice climbed up to the top bunk and laid down. Taking her mother's necklace in her hand, she thought she was glad she never ever took it off. It might have come up missing. The next thing Beatrice knew, she was being shaken awake.

"Rise and shine" Amanda said as she shook Beatrice's foot that was hanging off the edge of the top bunk. "Our first meeting is at 9:00 and I want to get some Breakfast first"

"What time is it?" Asked Beatrice as she sat up rubbing her eyes.

"It's 6:45. I just got out of the shower and it's your turn so hop to it would you" Amanda said smiling. "I'm sorry about last night. I guess those pills I took really make you tired, especially if you drink. Did you put all our stuff away?"

"Yeah, I stayed up until three or so this morning. I left your jewelry out so you could check to see if anything was missing." Beatrice said on her way into the bathroom.

"Thanks, it's all here. I think I am going to put this in the safe in the closet. Is there anything you want me to put in there?" Asked Amanda

"No I'm good thanks. Give me a minute and we can head out, I'm hungry too for some reason. Must be the sea air." Replied Beatrice

Breakfast was being served on the upper deck. Tables and chairs had been set up around the swimming pool. Along one side of the deck was a long table with various fruits, breads and pastries. At one end of the table was a bar for ordering omelets and at the other end was another bar serving waffles.

"I could get used to eating like this every day" Said Beatrice digging into her waffles. Which were piled high with strawberry's and whipped cream.

"Yeah me too, but then we wouldn't be able to fit into our uniforms that we are being fitted for today at 2:00." Replied Amanda as she poured syrup all over her waffles.

"What's first on the agenda for today?" Asked Beatrice

"It says we are going on a tour of the ship from 9-12, then we have our fitting for our uniforms at 12:30. After that lunch is being served from 1-2:30 back here on the upper deck. Then we have safety training at 3:00. That one we have to meet back in the ball room." Explained Amanda

"Hey look there's Felicia. Hey Felicia over here" yelled Beatrice waving her hand in the air so Felicia could see her.

"Good morning, how are you guys today?" Felicia asked Beatrice and Amanda as she sat down with her plate of fruit and an omelet. "What is your schedule like for today?"

"I was just giving Beatrice the run down, let me see yours and I will check it against ours to see if we are going to be together at all today" Amanda said taking Felicia's schedule. "Hey look at this we are the same" Exclaimed Amanda

"Oh that sounds just great, I wasn't looking forward to being alone today" Felicia said as she leaned back in her chair letting out a deep breath.

"Hello Ladies and Gentlemen" a loud female voice said. "We would like to welcome you to our first day of training. We will have three days of training and then we will be getting ready to welcome our guests. We set sail in seven days. Up here next to me are seven guides. I have comprised seven lists of people. When you hear your name called please join your guide to get under way. Thank you"

The first day of training was a lot of walking. Learning where every room, cleaning station and emergency areas were located. Beatrice's group walked every inch of the ship. Passing the gift shop, the weight room, the casino, and various types of bars, the kitchen, the laundry room and a tour of the engine room. By the time Beatrice, Amanda and Felicia reached the ball room all three of them were exhausted. Finally sitting down in a chair with a bottled water each.

"Hello Everyone" Carl's voice came over the loud speaker. "Now that everyone has had the tour and fitted for their uniforms, how does everyone feel?" This comment got a few groans and some cat calls from the group. Carl laughed and then said "Well this is your last event of the day. When I blow this whistle, everyone needs to go to their rooms and retrieve your life jackets. Putting them on securely, as you were shown early today. Then you will all need to meet at your designated life boat. You will need to do this without using the elevator. Oh, and this is a timed event. Once this test is completed, you will have the rest of the evening to yourselves. And remember, if you leave the ship, take your badge with you as you will not be able to get back on without it" He then blew that whistle.

Everyone in the room started running in every different direction. Like a group of mice going for the same piece of cheese. Beatrice, Amanda and Felicia waited a minute to let the majority of people get out and then they started on their journey to their rooms. It took twenty five minutes to the end of the test. Several people got lost. After the all clear was called out everyone started walking back to their rooms.

"Hey after we get changed do you girls want to go out for dinner tonight off of the ship? It will be my treat." Beatrice asked the other two.

"Yeah, that sounds great" Exclaimed Amanda

"Sure, if you don't mind me tagging along" Said Felicia with her head down looking at the floor as she walked along side Beatrice.

"Of course not. We are like the three musketeers" said Amanda

"Okay then, let's get changed and meet by the exit at 5:00. Sound good" Beatrice said

"Great I will meet you guys there" Felicia said with a smile on her face and a sudden bounce to her step.

At the end of the hallway they were walking in, Amanda and Beatrice turned right and Felicia turned left to get ready for a night on the town.

Chapter Five

THEY DECIDED TO GO TO Johnny Rocket's for dinner. Amanda arranged for a taxi to pick them up from the ship and take them into town. The air was crisp and cool. Beatrice choose to go with jeans and a green hoodie. Felicia went with jeans and sweater. Amanda choose a short red swirling skirt, a silver sequined blouse and silver strappy sandals. Walking alongside each other down the street, the girls were chatting, laughing and having a good time. Felicia was filling them in on her husband's family and the things they would have her do when Beatrice stopped dead in her tracks.

Amanda stopped walking and turned to look at Beatrice. "What's wrong" Amanda asked Beatrice. Who was standing in the middle of the sidewalk with her mouth open and eyes as big as the moon just starred across the street.

Beatrice stood stock still, mouth open starring right at Joe. He stood across the street leaning against a light pole with his hands in his pockets. He was starring right back at Beatrice. They stood like that for what seemed an eternity to Beatrice. Until a van passed up the street between them. When the van passed all the way, he was gone. Amanda and Felicia stood there starring at Beatrice who had her eyes wide open, not blinking and her mouth open. Amanda started waving her hand in front of Beatrice's face saying "Hello, anyone in there? Earth to Beatrice"

Beatrice started blinking and closed her mouth. "Sorry, I... um.. I thought I saw someone I know" Explained Beatrice

"That must have been some someone by the way you were starring with your mouth open like that" Commented Amanda "If you're through starring, the restaurant is just up the street"

As they continued to walk, Beatrice caught herself reaching up and touching the necklace she wore. The one that was her mother's. She always wore it though never on the outside of her clothes. She kept it inside her shirts. The key and the heart nestled between her size C cupped breasts. The girls took a booth towards the back of the restaurant. Beatrice and Amanda on one side while Felicia took the other. After the hostess gave them their menus and departed, Amanda spoke up first "Are you going to tell us what that was all about or what?"

"Let's order first and then I will tell you." Replied Beatrice

When the waiter appeared, Beatrice ordered the Smokehouse single, French fries and a chocolate shake. Amanda had the same and Felicia ordered the Houston with a strawberry shake.

"Now spill it" Amanda ordered Beatrice

Beatrice took in a nice long breath before she started with her explanation. Using those couple of seconds to try and decide just how much of the story she was going to tell. "Well, about two weeks ago, I was waiting for the bus to take me down town. While I was walking I was not watching where I was going, as usual. Anyways I bumped into this lady and knocked her basket into the street. Out of nowhere this guy shows up and helps me help this lady with her things. Then he gets on the bus with everyone and sits to the back, but he keeps looking at me. Then I look up and he is gone. I never even saw him get off of the bus. Ever since then, I keep seeing him everywhere I go. He was standing across the street earlier when we were walking, that is why I stopped. After a van drove by he was gone." Beatrice said shrugging her shoulders. She decided it was best not to mention the money part of it.

"And you have never talked to him?" Asked Amanda

"No, not once. He has just smiled at me. But I did have a dream about him once." Beatrice said as her cheeks turned red.

That got a laugh out of the others as there food arrived. They relaxed, started eating and chatting about the things they wanted to do at some of the ports they were expected to stop at. They learned more about Felicia and her husband before he died. She was born and raised in New Mexico. Las Curses to be exact. That was where she met her husband. They got married after only two months. They didn't tell any of his family. "That is why they don't like me" Felicia said. "He was a store manager at the time. Working nights to help with money. A man came in with a gun to rob the store and my husband tried to stop him. The man killed my husband." Felicia stopped talking, put her hands in her lap and her head down.

"I'm so sorry Felicia" Beatrice was the first to break the silence at the table. "But look, you have us now isn't that right Amanda?" Beatrice said looking at Amanda who had tears in her eyes.

"Of course Felicia, the three musketeers" Said Amanda wiping the tears from her eyes. "Now that I am completely stuffed, do you guys want to walk around a little bit before we head back? I have the number of the taxi service in my purse. All I have to do is tell them our location and they will pick us up and take us up back."

"Sure that sounds good, okay with you Felicia?" Ask Beatrice

"Yes, I could go for a walk." Felicia said as she started to get up from the booth. "I need the ladies room first"

"I will go pay the check and meet you by the entrance." Beatrice said taking her purse and heading for the counter.

Out in the open air, the girls stood under the awning and looked around. 'Man it is cold out tonight" Said Amanda

"That's what you get for dressing like a hooker" Beatrice said as she gave Amanda an elbow to the side. Felicia just laughed. Beatrice looked to her right trying to see which way to go and then to her left. "Holly shit, that's him" Beatrice exclaimed.

"Who, that guy" Amanda said as Beatrice took off running down the street. Felicia and Amanda started running after Beatrice.

Beatrice could see him up ahead, about five feet in front of her. She was gaining on him when she bumped into a man coming out of a store. They both fell down to the ground causing a commotion. Enough of one to make Joe turn around. He spotted Beatrice on the ground rolling off of a man. His first instinct was to go and help her. But he just stood there and watched. When Beatrice looked up she saw him standing there starring at her. Beatrice apologized to the man and stood up. When she looked again, he was still starring. Amanda and Felicia caught up to Beatrice at this point. Joe turned around and walked around the corner. When Beatrice, Felicia and Amanda reached the corner themselves, they saw him drive away in a black SUV.

"You should call the police" Said Felicia

"I don't know. I just wish I knew who he is and what he wants" Said Beatrice

"All I know is after all that I need a drink. There is a bar across the street let's go" Said Amanda as she started crossing the street.

Beatrice and Felicia followed suit and crossed the street. They all took seats at the bar. Amanda ordered a beer, Beatrice ordered a strawberry margarita and Felicia ordered a tequila sunrise. Amanda and Felicia started a conversation with the bar tender while Beatrice was lost in her own thoughts. Why was he following her? Who was this guy? What did he want? All of this started after she received that money. The first chance Beatrice got, she was going to call Kristy and see if she was all right.

As Joe drove to his destination, all he could think of was Beatrice. His initial mission was to observe and report. Now his mission had changed to retrieve the necklace. He had no idea why or what it was for only that he needed to get it. "She must have it on her" he thought. "That is the only place it could be since I didn't find it in her room on the ship" Once Joe reached his destination, he sat in the SUV and thought about Beatrice. He wanted to go and help her when she ran into that man. Every time he saw her he got this unfamiliar tug on his heart. Her blonde hair, green eyes and her legs just did something to him. He dreaded getting out of the SUV. He knew that once he did, he was in trouble for coming up empty after the search and now he slipped and she saw him. Actually chased him down the street. Maybe he would just leave that part out of his report.

"Yes, Aengus, I understand" Said Joe "like I said, the item did not turn up as a result of a search of the room. My thoughts are that it is kept on her person"

"And do you have a plan to get close enough to rectify this situation?" Aengus asked Joe

"Yes Sir I do" Replied Joe

"Fine, just keep in mind that the time is running out. If we are to get into that box, it needs to happen within the next thirty days. It is in your hands. Report back in one week. Don't disappoint me." Aengus said as he hung up.

Joe poured himself two fingers of whiskey before he sat down to contemplate his plan. The plan was simple in his mind. Get close to Beatrice and retrieve the necklace. The only problem is that she has seen him and her mannerisms suggests a feisty personality. Joe kicked off his shoes, drained his glass of the ember liquid and put his head back against the chair he sat in. As his eyes closed, his thoughts were of Beatrice. Her long blonde hair, her green eyes and her lips on his.

After a couple rounds of drinks the girls were standing outside the bar waiting for their taxi. Amanda and Felicia were talking and laughing about Amanda trying to pick up the bar tender. Beatrice still thinking about him.

"Hey Bea, you have been awfully quiet tonight. I'm worried about you." Said Amanda

"Yeah I'm okay" Replied Beatrice. "Just thinking about things"

"You sure you don't want to call the police" Asked Felicia

"No not yet." Said Beatrice

As the taxi pulled up Beatrice thought she was not sure of anything. More than anything she wanted to go back to Kristy's. Out here on her own like this she felt scared, unsure and a bit lonely. She missed Kristy. After all, she was the only mother Beatrice had ever known. One thing was for sure, as soon as she could get away she was calling Kristy.

Beatrice and Amanda walked Felicia to her room so she wasn't alone. Felicia was a late hire so she got a room to herself. "See you tomorrow and thanks for dinner and drinks. I had a great time tonight. Maybe we could do that again." Felicia said as she unlocked her door.

"Yeah for sure" Replied Amanda

"Yeah, see you tomorrow" Said Beatrice

As Beatrice and Amanda walked to their room. Beatrice asked Amanda "Do you mind if I take a few minutes, I want to call and check on Kristy?"

"Sure no problem. I think I'm going to go pass out" Amanda said laughing. She stopped and gave Beatrice a big tight hug then left down the hall towards their room.

Beatrice took the stairs to the upper deck and stepped outside. It was cold enough to pull the hood up on her hoodie. The sky was clear with the stars twinkling above. She walked over to the edge and looked down. On that side she could see the water. It looked like black glass. Pulling out her phone she checked the time 9:30. What the heck, she thought and dialed anyway.

"Hello?" A soft voice said in a whisper

"Kristy?" Beatrice asked "Did I wake you?"

"Bea, no, I received an infant yesterday and I was just putting him down. How are you honey? It's so good to hear your voice. Tell me everything. Are you all right? What's going on? Have you made any friends yet?" It made Beatrice smile to hear Kristy go on and on with her question's. Just hearing her voice made Beatrice relax just a little bit.

"Yes, I'm fine. It's been hectic around here learning everything. Amanda and I made a friend. Her name is Felicia and she seems nice. I was calling to check on you. Make sure that you and the kids are getting along. You know the usual." Said Beatrice

"Oh yes, we're all doing great. I think that Billy might have a girlfriend." Kristy said laughing. "But you know him, he keeps things locked up inside."

"You remember that guy we talked about before I left? The one I told I had a dream about?" Asked Beatrice

Kristy paused a little bit then said "I think so, why?"

"You haven't seen him around lately have you? Asked Beatrice

Kristy got a sick feeling in the pit of her stomach, "Not that I have noticed, why do you ask?"

"I don't know, I just thought that I saw him tonight. The girls and I went off of the ship to have dinner and I swear I saw him twice tonight. The second time I tried to chase him down the street but I lost him when I ran into a man coming out of a store." Explained Beatrice

"Oh my, were either of you hurt?" Kristy asked

"No, it's just starting to freak me out you know." Beatrice said

"Well, the next time you think you see him, stop and jot down a description of him and call the police." Said Kristy

Beatrice didn't have to see him again to describe him. She had his face committed to memory. "Okay I will. You take care and tell Billy and the others I said hi. I will call you in a couple of days. Love you" Said Beatrice

"I love you too honey and call me every day please. I would like to know how you are doing and if you see that guy again. Ok sweetheart?" Asked Kristy

"Sure and good night." Beatrice said before she hung up. Beatrice stood outside breathing in the cool air before heading inside to her room. Beatrice felt a little bit better after hearing Kristy's voice. She jogged down four flights of stairs, holding onto the hand rail for guidance. Once at the bottom of the stair case, she took a right then her first left and four doors down was her room. She let herself in as quiet as she could.

Amanda was already asleep, so Beatrice went into the bathroom then slipped into her jammies and crawled up the ladder to her own bed. She fell asleep dreaming about those blue eyes and that hair. How she wanted to run her fingers through that strawberry blonde hair.

It was dark outside as she ran. Through trees and bushes, sweating and trying to catch her breath. All she could think about was if she didn't keep running they would catch up to her. She didn't know what they wanted. It was getting harder and harder to see. Slowing down and reaching for an object to guide her, Beatrice touched a tree trunk, then a large rock. She heard water off in the distance. Slowly making her way out of what she thought was a forest, she spotted the moon. Creeping closer to the sound of the water, Beatrice stopped and looked down. She was standing on the edge of a cliff. Very faintly, she saw and heard the waves crashing on the shore. Footsteps were getting closer, she looked for a place to hide. As she turned around to move a bright light shined in her eyes and a hand grabbed her arm. Beatrice started to scream....

Chapter Six

"Bea wake up, wake up. For crying out loud what the hell was that about?" Asked Amanda as she shook Beatrice's leg.

"What? What happened?" Asked Beatrice rubbing her eyes.

"You were making a bunch of noise and then you started to scream. Scared the hell out of me." Explained Amanda

Amanda started backing down the ladder that lead to Beatrice's bunk when Beatrice started climbing down herself. Amanda retrieved a bottle of water from their small refrigerator in their room and handed it to Beatrice. Beatrice sat down on Amanda's bed and drank the majority of the bottle.

"Why are you all wet?" Amanda asked Beatrice

"Sweat" Replied Beatrice "It happens when I have s night mare"

"Will you please tell me what the hell is going on" Amanda said. "First there is this strange guy you insist on chasing down the street and now you are screaming in your sleep and having night mares"

"Okay, but if I tell you, you have to swear not to say anything. I'm not sure about a lot of it myself" Beatrice began.

"Yes, of course. You know me Bea, I won't say anything. We have been friends since grade school." Amanda said crossing her heart and putting her hand up.

"As you know, I was put in foster care when I was two due to my mother's death. Well, on my birthday, I received a registered letter in the mail. It said that I had a Great Uncle Charles and he died and left me money. They tracked me down since my mother was unable to be reached. The money totaled $300,000. Since then, I have seen this guy everywhere. I don't know what he wants or why he is stalking me. Kristy has not said she knows anything about it. I mean how could she, she is just my foster mother. But I asked her why she was able to keep me all of these years. I mean I have seen children come and go in her house but I was always allowed to stay." Beatrice stopped to drink more water.

"And what did she say?" Asked Amanda

"She told me that I was not a problem child and since I didn't have any family, she was able to keep me" Replied Beatrice

"Well, that sounds reasonable." Amanda Said

"What time is it anyway?" Asked Beatrice

"It's 4:43 in the morning. Now tell me about your night mare." Said Amanda

"All I can remember is that I was running through a forest at night and someone was chasing me. I reached the edge, which was a cliff, someone shined a light in my eyes and then grabbed my arm" Beatrice said shrugging her shoulders as she finished off the bottle of water.

"Wow Bea that was some dream. Do you think it was that guy grabbing you in your dream? No wonder you wanted to tackle this guy on the street. Look, if we see this guy again, please let's call the police." Amanda pleaded with Beatrice

"Okay, if we see him again" Beatrice said

"Now, it's just about 5:30 and the clock is set to go off at 6, so what do you say we get dressed for the day and head out for some air before breakfast?" Amanda said as she put both her hands on Beatrice's shoulders giving them a small shake.

"Okay, that sounds pretty good. Me first" Beatrice said as she gave Amanda a push and slid into the bathroom laughing.

Beatrice and Amanda strolled around the lido deck together after getting showered and dressed. Laughing and talking with several different people they met along the way. One man offered to accompany them the rest of their walk, but Amanda respectfully declined. The sky was blue, the wind was minimal and the temperature was 59 degrees. Stopping along the railing both Beatrice and Amanda starred out at the water. Small waves passed under the ship and a large pelican perched on a pole near the dock.

"Hey you guys, aren't you going to come have breakfast?" Felicia said as she joined them at the railing. "What are you looking at?"

"Oh nothing. We were just taking a walk and stopped here to look out over the water" Replied Beatrice

"Now that you mention it, I am kind of hungry" Said Amanda as she headed for the breakfast bar.

Beatrice rolled her eyes so far back she almost fell over "You're always hungry. If I could eat like you and stay skinny like you, I would be in Heaven"

*   *   *

Training day two went similar to day one. Today, they grouped everyone according to their positions. Beatrice, Amanda and Felicia stuck together throughout the day. Learning the rooms they were assigned too, where all of the equipment was located.

"I had no idea there was an art to making a bed" Said Amanda during lunch with Beatrice and Felicia.

"Having a hard time with that one? I had a tough time not running over the cord with the vacuum. I sucked it up once and shorted the darn thing out. They had to bring me another vacuum." Said Beatrice

Amanda and Felicia both looked at each other and busted out laughing. Beatrice said "it's not funny" and then busted out laughing with them. She laughed hard and tipped her head back and knocked a woman walking by and spilled her orange juice on the floor. Everyone stopped laughing as Beatrice jumped up to assist the woman.

"I am so sorry. I didn't mean to knock into you." Beatrice told the woman.

"It's okay, I really didn't need another glass." The woman said as she wiped orange juice off of her shirt with the napkin Amanda handed her. "Whatever you all were laughing at must have been something, my name is Star. I'm one of the dancers."

"Hi, I'm Beatrice and this is Amanda and Felicia." Beatrice said as she pointed at them respectively.

"It's nice to meet you ladies. I hope you will come see one of the shows" Star said as she walked away.

Beatrice, Amanda and Felicia looked at each other and began laughing all over again. As soon as they put their dishes away and headed back to do more rooms, Carl appeared out of nowhere and blew his whistle. Starting the timer for safety test number two. This test only took twenty two minutes. The goal was to get everyone accounted for in proper gear in under eighteen minutes. The rest of the day went smooth for Beatrice, Amanda and Felicia. They were making up the rooms from one end of the ship to the other. After seven hours of making beds, cleaning toilets, dusting, vacuuming and putting in all the essential odds and ends of complimentary items, exhaustion set in.

"I am so tired I can hardly move" Said Amanda

"Me too" Said Felicia

"I'm going to the room to lay down before dinner" Beatrice said as she headed down the hall towards their room. Hanging onto the railing for support.

"Hey, wait for us" Amanda shouted as her and Felicia started walking to catch up to Beatrice

* * *

"You were so right, having dinner on the ship tonight was a great idea" Said Amanda

"Oh yeah and why is that?" Asked Beatrice

"So I can drink and eat as much as I want. I don't have to worry about driving or how I'm getting home." Amanda said has she drained her second margarita.

"I think that we should go off of the ship tomorrow night for dinner." Said Felicia "Thursday night is our party and then the guests come on board Friday night and we set sail then too. It will be my treat this time."

"Sounds great" Amanda said

"Yes, and I promise not to go off chasing strange men down the street." Beatrice said laughing.

"That was the most excitement I've had in a long time" Said Felicia

"I am so exhausted, I can hardly lift my fork to eat" Beatrice said as she put the fork down after she had finished her chocolate cake. "I think I am going to go to bed now. Tomorrow had better not be as busy and hard as today"

"We promise nothing around here" Carl said as he strode up to the table. "May I sit down?"

"Of course" Said Beatrice

"How have you all been getting along so far this week? Hasn't been too much for any of you?" Asked Carl

Beatrice noticed that he had on another suit. This one was deep blue with a white crisp shirt and a red stripped tie. The blue color of the suit seemed to bring out the color of his brown eyes. This thought brought Beatrice a thought of blues eyes dancing as they looked at her. She wished she could just stare into those ocean color eyes, touch the face that contained them.......

"Good Lord Beatrice, did you fall asleep at the table?" Asked Amanda

"Huh? What?" Beatrice responded as she came out of her revere.

Everyone at the table began to laugh including Carl. "I was just asking the ladies here if they would like to join me for dinner tomorrow night. I know a wonderful little restaurant in town that serves a mean pizza. Maybe some beer as well. Would you like to join us?" Asked Carl

Beatrice looked at Amanda and Felicia. They both had smiles on their faces and were shaking their heads in a 'yes' motion. "Of course, that would be wonderful" Beatrice replied

"Great, I will meet all of you by the exit about five? Does that sound good?" Asked Carl

"Sure, we will meet you there. What should I wear?" Asked Amanda

Carl smiled as he bent his head down. When he picked it up Beatrice could see his cheeks had turned slightly red. "Anything that makes you comfortable." Carl said looking straight at Amanda

"Thanks again" Said Beatrice and Felicia at the same time

"Good night ladies" Carl said as he patted the back of the chair he was sitting in and he walked away.

Beatrice noticed how quiet Amanda was in their walk back to their rooms. Amanda had a small smile on her face as she walked. Felicia and Beatrice looked at each other and smiled as well. "Did the cat get your tongue or what? You are being extremely quiet Amanda. What's up?" Beatrice asked

"I don't know, I was just thinking about Carl. Don't you think he is handsome? And his deep voice. How old do you think he is? I wonder why he asked us out for dinner tomorrow night." Amanda said

Amanda had not noticed that Beatrice and Felicia had stopped walking. She suddenly looked around and she was standing alone in the hall. She turned around to see Beatrice and Felicia starring at her with their mouths open. "What?" Asked Amanda has she shrugged her shoulders.

"I don't know Amanda, I have never seen you like this over a guy that is older than you. You have always slobbered over the young ones." Said Beatrice as her and Felicia walked to catch up the Amanda.

"He is handsome, especially in those suits that he wears" Felicia said as she blushed and put her head down.

This brought on yet another laughing session with all of them. They laughed all the way to Felicia's room. All of the people they passed in the hall looked at them like they were all crazy. A young man that passed them turned around and started following them down the hall. He asked "What's so funny and how can I get in on this?"

Amanda stopped walking, turned around and looked at the man. She smiled and sashayed over to him. Once she reached him, she put her finger at the top of his chest just below his atoms apple and started trailing her finger down his chest. He was wearing a plain black t-shirt that fit his muscular form well. He had brown eyes and short brown hair. "What's your name honey?" Amanda asked

"Ben, Ben Wilson" he replied in a voice that was barely a whisper.

Amanda let her finger trail down his chest to his waistline and then back up to his chest. All the while she never took her eyes off of his. She licked her lips, placed her hand flat in the middle of his chest and gave him a small push. Just enough to make his upper body tilt back slightly and said "Sorry Ben" and she turned and strutted back to Beatrice and Felicia who had their hands over their mouth's trying not to burst out laughing, again.

Once Amanda reached the others Beatrice said "now that's the Amanda I know" locking arms with Amanda and Felicia "let's get some sleep. Tomorrow is going to come sooner than we think."

Ben stood dumb founded to his spot and watched the girls walk down the hall arm and arm and turn left. His friend who stood back and watched Ben get tore up by Amanda, walked over and put his hand on Ben's shoulder "Dude what the hell just happened" He said to Ben trying and failing to hide his laughter.

"I don't know but did you get the license plate of that truck that just ran me over" Ben said as he shook his head and turned to walk off.

Beatrice and Amanda walked Felicia to her room and then headed off to their room. Once there, they went into their nightly routine. Taking turns in the bathroom, arranging the beds and the task of setting the clock.

"So, Amanda how about Carl tonight, huh? How are you feeling about this, I've never seen you like this over a guy" Beatrice commented

"I don't know, there is just something about him. He reached over and touched my hand tonight at the table. It sent chills up my spine. That has never happened to me before. I can still feel the heat from his palm." Amanda said as she pulled her hands up to her chest.

"Tomorrow night should be interesting then. If at any time you want me and Felicia to take a walk just let me know." Beatrice said as she climbed up onto her bunk

Amanda shut off the lights and laid down on her bunk, closed her eyes and drifted off to sleep with thoughts of Carl. In his suit and stripped tie and beautiful white smile. The sparkle in his brown eyes when he was talking to her tonight at the table. Beatrice on her bunk with her eyes closed and one thing on her mind, Joe..........

Chapter Seven

THE NEXT DAY WENT BY faster than Beatrice thought it would. She got the art of making the beds down, taking only four minutes for the bunks and six minutes for the larger beds. The goal was to get a whole room done in under thirty minutes, and not ruin another vacuum cord. With the completion of her final room, she found herself staring out the port hole that doubled for a window. The ocean lapped up against the ship in rhythm waves. Beatrice's right hand found her necklace, reaching in she took the heart and the key between her fingers rubbing them gently. Her mind drifting off to what it would be like to be out in the middle of the ocean. The waves, the sky and the sea life she might encounter. She pictured herself out on deck with the wind blowing her hair around her face. She closed her eyes and titled her head back ever so slightly.

"Penny for your thoughts" a masculine voice said from behind Beatrice

Jumping and screaming, Beatrice turned around to see a very tall man with a buzz type haircut, wearing a uniform looking at her smiling. Beatrice noticed right away the dark color of his bronze tan and electric ocean blue eyes. Holly crap it's him, Beatrice thought to herself. "You scared me" Beatrice said in a voice higher than she expected it to be.

"Sorry, I didn't mean to scare you. I'm just going through the rooms checking the plumbing. You know, to make sure they all work properly." The man said as he put his tool box down outside the bathroom door.

Beatrice tucked her necklace back inside her shirt as smoothly as possible and made a motion to leave "Sorry, I will get out of your way" she said

"No hurry. Where are you off too?" he asked effectively blocking the door.

"Oh you know, more work elsewhere" Beatrice replied. Her first instinct was to run and find Amanda, but there was something about his eyes and his voice that made her stand in one spot and stare at him.

"Beatrice, that's an interesting name" he said as he looked at her name tag.

"Yes, thank you. I don't see a name tag for you, what is your name?" Beatrice asked. Suddenly she was curious.

"My name is Joe" he said as he looked at Beatrice. Being this close to her was intoxicating. Her blonde hair tied up in a bun high up on her head with soft curls that have come loose framing her face. Her face, so beautiful, housing those vibrant green eyes.

Beatrice suddenly realized she was staring at him. She cleared her throat and broke away from the staring contest that was happening. When she lifted her head back up, she noticed he was still starring at her. "Haven't I seen you before?" Beatrice asked

"Um, I don't think so" Joe said "Oh wait, do you mean the other night in town? Where you the woman that ran into some guy on the street?" Joe was trying to stay calm and sound convincing although he knew he wasn't.

Beatrice steadied her nerves, relaxed her stance and leaned her hip against the desk that was by the door. "Yes, that was me. I was trying to catch up to you." Beatrice said. She thought it was now or never. She had been wanting to see him again so she could question him and now he was standing in front of her.

"Catch up to me? Why would you want to do that?" Joe asked

"Because I've seen you a lot lately. Back in my home town, and now here. I could swear it was you. But you have changed your appearance haven't you?" Beatrice asked

"Um, I think you have me confused with someone else" Joe said. He could feel the sweat forming on his fore head.

"No, I don't think so. You are the one that has been following me around. Back home, the bus stop and the restaurant and then here at the office and then the other night. You have shaved your hair and got a tan, but I swear it's you. Now why have you been following me? What do you want from me? Do I need to get security over here?" Beatrice asked. Her voice getting louder after every question.

Joe put his hands up in a defensive motion and said "I'm sorry to have ruffled your beautiful feathers ma'am, but I think you have me confused with someone else. I think I should get back to my work. Sorry to have bothered you." And Joe stepped out of the door way and into the bathroom, leaving the doorway open for Beatrice to exit.

As soon as Joe entered to bathroom, Beatrice bolted out the door in search for Amanda. Beatrice ran down the hall looking in every room along the way. Finally at the last room in the hall, she found Amanda. "Him, come it's him. I talked to him. I know it's him. Hurry before we lose him" Beatrice said pulling on Amanda's arm. "Follow me, hurry"

Amanda had no idea what Beatrice was talking about, but she followed her anyway. "Where are we going? What the hell are you talking about?" Amanda asked Beatrice as she pulled her down the hall.

Beatrice pulled Amanda into the room where she left Joe and turned towards the bathroom and he was gone. "He was here, I swear he was here. I talked to him." Beatrice said

Amanda put her hands on Beatrice's shoulders "Will you please calm down and tell me what the hell you are talking about?" Amanda asked

"The guy, you know the one I told you about that has been following me. The one I chased down the street the other night?' Beatrice asked

"Yes" Amanda said

"He was here. Right where you are standing. I was finishing up in here and he appeared in the doorway. He said that he was here to check the plumbing on the ship. He shaved his head and got a tan, but I swear it was him. I could never forget those blue eyes." Beatrice said as she sat down in a chair.

"Are you sure?" Amanda Asked

"Oh Amanda, I'm not sure of anything anymore. What should I do now?" Beatrice whispered

"For one thing, I am not leaving you alone until we figure this out. Come on let me help you gather things up in here. Is this the last room you have to do?" Amanda said

Beatrice could not speak, all she could do was shake her head yes. Beatrice stood up to help Amanda gather all of the supplies in the room, the vacuum, the cleaning basket and all of the other odds and ends.

Clearing out of that room, Amanda led Beatrice down the hall to the room she was last cleaning. Beatrice just stood in the door way watching Amanda gather all of her cleaning supplies in what seemed like lightning speed. Beatrice felt like she was watching a movie on fast forward while she was half asleep. She vaguely heard Amanda's voice although she didn't comprehend anything she was saying. Was she losing her mind, going crazy, that's it Beatrice thought she was going crazy.

"Beatrice" Amanda shouted "snap out of it and grab your cart. We need to meet Carl and Felicia in one hour so get moving. We are going to tell Carl some of this story and see what he thinks."

Once all of the cleaning carts were stored properly, Amanda led Beatrice to their room and shoved her in the bathroom. "Take a quick shower and I will pick out some clothes for you to wear"

Beatrice went through her routine of taking a shower with the exception of washing her hair. She just left it up in the bun it was in. Stepping out of the bathroom, wrapped in only a towel, Beatrice sat down on 'Amanda's bed. When Amanda stepped out of the bathroom, she found Beatrice sitting on the edge of the bed starring at the wall with tears running down her cheeks. Immediately sitting down next to Beatrice, Amanda put her arms around her and pulled her close. Beatrice put her head on Amanda's shoulder and let the tears come. They sat like that for a while, Amanda stroking Beatrice's back in an attempt to calm her.

"It's going to be okay Bea, I promise we are going to figure this whole thing out." Amanda told Beatrice in a soft soothing voice. "Let's get dressed and get out of here for a while. Get some food and maybe a drink? Come on, get dressed hm?"

All Beatrice could do was shake her head yes as she stood up and reached for her clothes. Putting on the jeans and sweater Amanda laid out for her was taxing all of Beatrice's energy. All she wanted to do was crawl into bed and pull the covers up over her head. Standing in front of the mirror brushing her hair out, Beatrice had to fight back the tears that were threatening to start again. A series of knocks at the door brought Beatrice out of the fog she was in, Reaching over, she opened the door to find Felicia standing there smiling wearing a pick knee length dress with a white sweater over her shoulders.

"Hi, are you guys ready to go?" Asked Felicia "Wow, you look great" she said to Amanda as she entered the room.

"Thanks, you like?" Amanda said turning in a circle for Felicia to see her on all sides.

Taking a look at Beatrice, Felicia asked "What's wrong with her"

"She was cleaning her last room when a man came in to check the plumbing, Beatrice thought it was that same guy that she says is following her. I don't know what to do to help her. I thought about talking to Carl tonight to see if there were people checking the plumbing on the ship today. Ever since then she has been in this funk." Amanda Explained.

"I don't know if Carl will hear anything you have to say with you wearing that outfit." Felicia said laughing.

Amanda had choose a pair of white skinny jeans with a lavender silk blouse that was cut extremely low in front. It showed off her rather impressive D-cup cleavage. "Really? You think?" Amanda said smiling

"For sure girl, I think he likes you," Felicia said

"Alright, I will grab Beatrice, you shut and lock the door." Amanda told Felicia

"Got it." Felicia said as she shut and locked the door.

Beatrice let Amanda and Felicia lead her down the hall to the elevator and up two flights and then to the exit. That is where Carl was waiting. He wasn't wearing his usual suit this time. He had on a pair of jeans with a white button down long sleeve collared shirt cowboy style with pair of black cowboy boots. He smiled when he saw Amanda and the others walking his way. "Hello ladies, are we all ready to go. It will be nice to get away for a while won't it?" He asked.

"It sure will." Amanda said smiling

Carl looked at Beatrice and frowned. "Is there something wrong?" He asked Beatrice

Beatrice, who had not said a word since retrieving Amanda, just shook her head no and gave a small semblance of a smile.

"I think she is just tired." Amanda chimed in. "shall we be going?"

They all walked to the plank entrance and showed their badges. Amanda walked next to Carl talking all the way and Felicia walked next to Beatrice. Once on solid ground, Carl led them to a limousine he had waiting.

"Wow isn't this something" Felicia said "I've never been in one of these before. Don't you think Beatrice?"

All Beatrice could do was shake her head yes. She was sure that if she opened her mouth to speak the tears would start all over again. And so the evening went. Amanda, Carl and Felicia talked with each other. Beatrice just followed along in her own thoughts. Every now and again she nodded her head either yes or no, depending on the question that was asked. At dinner Amanda ordered Beatrice a beer, but Beatrice just shook her head no and managed to spit out "water please" without crying. After dinner, they all went for a walk window shopping. Amanda had her hand in the crook of Carl's arm walking a few steps ahead of Beatrice and Felicia.

"I think they are cute together don't you?" Felicia asked Beatrice

Beatrice looked at Carl and Amanda then to Felicia and smiled as she shook her head yes. In her own thoughts, Beatrice thought she was losing her mind. All through dinner and the walk, Beatrice kept her eyes open for him. This man who called himself 'Joe'. By the time they returned back at the ship, Beatrice was sure that she had indeed lost her mind. There was no sign of him all night.

"Hey Felicia" Amanda called "can you please make sure Beatrice gets to our room safe? Carl just asked me to go for a walk with him."

"Sure, no problem" Felicia responded smiling and taking Beatrice's arm.

"Are you going to be okay if I go with him Bea" Amanda asked

Beatrice gave Amanda a small smile and her arm a little squeeze as she shook her head yes. She stood and watched Amanda walk over to Carl. As Beatrice and Felicia walked back to the room, Beatrice thought how lucky Amanda was. Beatrice never had a serious boyfriend. There was never anyone she was interested in enough to call a boyfriend. Of course Amanda was four years older and had more experience.

"If I leave you are you going to be okay? You have not said one word all night. I'm worried about you. Amanda wouldn't tell me what happened. Talk to me please." Felicia said to Beatrice as they stood outside Beatrice's room.

"I'll be okay. Thanks for walking with me. I will see you tomorrow." Beatrice said as she stepped into her room.

"Well, if you need anything you will call me, yes?" Asked Felicia

"Yes, of course" Beatrice said as she closed the door. Now that she was alone, she put on her pajamas and crawled up to her bunk, curled up with her pillow and closed her eyes.

Chapter Eight

"You have done enough damage." Angus yelled into the phone "I want you to do nothing. The time is almost out and so I'm sending Thomas."

"Thomas, are you serious?" Joe Asked

"Yes, he will get the job done at any cost. He will be there tomorrow before that ship sails. You need to meet him at the rondavue spot." Angus said then he hung up.

Great, Thomas, thought Joe. He knew that Thomas would kill Beatrice just as he killed her father and mother. Joe didn't want that for Beatrice. He knew that he messed up big time. He just couldn't be a killer. He just wanted to get the necklace and be done with it. Now, things have changed. He had feelings for Beatrice. Joe paced back and forth in his room trying to think what he could do to salvage this situation. After his third whiskey, he knew just what he was going to do.

* * *

"How do you feel today?" Amanda Asked Beatrice

"Better thank you. I'm sorry about yesterday and last night. I think I just needed some time and some sleep." Beatrice said as she climbed down from her bunk and headed for the bathroom.

"We only have to work half day today then we get to party." Amanda said as she started dancing with Beatrice.

Beatrice danced right along laughing with Amanda. It made her feel better knowing that she had Amanda with her. "How did it go last night with Carl? I didn't even hear you come in last night." Beatrice said

"He kissed me." Amanda said, her face turning red.

Both Amanda and Beatrice busted out laughing. "Where do you think this is going to go with him?" Beatrice asked

"I don't know but I am going to ride this ride as long as I can." Amanda said

"Well, I'm ready to go are you?" Beatrice asked

"Sure am, let's roll." Amanda said closing the door

"Hey, I will meet you back here right after work so we can get ready for the party" Beatrice said as she parted with Amanda to get to work.

After work both Beatrice and Amanda got ready for the party. Beatrice in her usual jeans, this time she choose to wear one of Amanda's silk blouses. A pale green with a low neckline showing some decent cleavage. Amanda donned a bright blue knee length dress with heels.

The party was already under way when Beatrice, Amanda and Felicia arrived. Dinner was being served buffet style with an open bar. A dance floor was set up in the middle of the room. First stop was the buffet then the bar. Once they all had their plates full and drinks, they headed off to find a place to sit with three places together.

"Over there, look, I think that table is open" Felicia said pointing as best she could with her drink in her hand.

Once everyone was seated, Beatrice lifted up her Margarita and said "here's to us and our first cruise"

"Do you mind if I get in on this ladies?" Carl asked taking a seat next to Amanda

"Sure, please joins us" Beatrice said smiling

"Sounds like you are feeling better" Carl said to Beatrice

"Yes thank you. I just needed some rest" Beatrice replied

"Sounds like they have started the music, can I talk you into a dance?" Carl asked Amanda

"Yea sure, I'd love to" Amanda said as she put her hand into Carl's

"I think we have the beginnings of a love story, don't you think?" Felicia said to Beatrice as she gave her a nudge with her elbow

Beatrice thought how great it would be to be in love. To have someone in her life. To talk to and take care of her. Beatrice pictured herself walking down the beach holding hands with a handsome man. Her feet touching the water coming in with a wave. "Excuse me" a masculine voice said bringing Beatrice back from fantasy land. "Would you care to dance?" Beatrice looked up to see a very handsome man ask Felicia to dance.

"Um.... sure" Felicia said as she stood up and took the man's hand. He led her off to the dance floor and started moving Felicia around the floor.

Beatrice sat watching the two couples moving around the dance floor, hand in hand, body to body swaying back and forth to the music. It almost brought tears to her eyes.

"Looks like fun doesn't it?" A voice said from behind Beatrice. She turned to see a man standing there leaning against a decorated pole, drink in hand, smile on his face.

"I suppose, I'm not much of a dancer. Two left feet" Beatrice said returning the smile.

"Would you do me the honor of letting me be the judge of that?" He asked

"Judge of what?" Beatrice asked

The man put his drink down on the table and extended his hand to Beatrice "Your two left feet."

Hesitantly, Beatrice took the man's hand, stood and allowed him to lead her onto the dance floor. She placed her right hand in his and her left hand on his shoulder. He graciously put his hand at the small of Beatrice's back and began to move her around the dance floor slowly. "Now that you have me out here, are you going to tell me your name?" Asked Beatrice

The man smiled, never breaking eye contact with Beatrice "My name is Ron. And what is your name?"

"Beatrice" she said

"A beautiful name for a beautiful woman" He said as he spun Beatrice around.

Amanda caught a glimpse of Beatrice on the dance floor. It touched her heart to see Beatrice smiling and dancing with someone. "Who is that guy dancing with Beatrice" Amanda asked Carl.

Turning Amanda around on the dance floor so he could see, "Oh, that's Ron. He is the head of security here on the ship. Rather nice guy. After the break in of your room, I had him keeping an eye on things for me. So far no other rooms were broken into and nothing out of the ordinary has come up. I've never seen him being this social. Usually he's standing to the back of the room keeping an eye on things."

"I'm so glad she found someone to dance with. I've been so worried about her" Said Amanda

"He's a good guy with decent principles, he will be good to her" Carl said spinning Amanda around once more.

After two dances Ron asked Beatrice "Would you like to get a drink?"

"Sure that would be great." Beatrice responded walking towards the bar with Ron right behind her.

"What would you like?" He asked

"Um… beer please" Beatrice said smiling. It felt good for her to be smiling. "You are a good dancer. Do you do it often? What do you do aboard ship?"

"So many questions from such a lovely lady. No, I don't dance very often anymore. But I used to enjoy it quite a bit years ago and I'm the head of security for the ship," Ron said taking a sip of his beer.

"Is this your first time on a ship?" Beatrice asked

Ron smiled down at Beatrice. "No, I've been doing this type of work for about three years now" Ron said with a small laugh "You know about me now, how about you?"

"What would you like to know?" Beatrice said trying to be coy

Ron laughed then said, "What do you do aboard ship? Is this your first time? Can I persuade you to have dinner with me tomorrow night?"

Before Beatrice had the chance to respond, Amanda, Carl, Felicia and her gentleman friend strolled over to the bar. Carl engaged Ron in conversation. Introducing him to Amanda and Felicia. Beatrice just sat there looking Ron over. He had to be at least six feet taller than Beatrice. He had dark hair cut military style, muscles that stretched his shirt tight and perfectly white teeth when he smiled. Beatrice followed the muscles up from his waist line to his face where she found him staring at her smiling. Beatrice nervously took a drink from her beer, trying to keep her face from turning red.

"Hey Bea, come with me to the dessert buffet. I feel like a snack." Amanda asked "Felicia seems to be busy over there"

Beatrice put her beer down and stood up "Will you excuse me for a minute" Beatrice said to Ron

"Of course, I will be right here waiting for you. Maybe when you get back we could have another dance?" Ron winked at Beatrice as she stepped away.

Beatrice smiled and let Amanda lead her over to the desserts. Chocolate everywhere, tarts, cookies, candies and things with fruit in them. At each end of the table stood tall chocolate fountains. Anything and everything one would want dipped in chocolate was arranged near the fountains. A variety of grapes, strawberries and other exotic fruits. Marshmallows, pretzels and other types of cookies and crackers. Beatrice was sure that she would never get used to all of the food that was served twenty four hours a day.

"I see you have found a friend to dance with" Amanda said to Beatrice while they put odds and ends of goodies on their plates.

"Yes, his name is Ron and he said he is the head of security for the ship. He seems nice enough." Beatrice replied while she put some crackers on her plate to go with the fruit she had chosen.

Amanda on the other hand, had a plate stacked with chocolate everything. "I am so happy for you, and Felicia, have you seen the way she is with that guy? Have you gotten his name from her yet?"

Beatrice laughed at Amanda trying to balance everything she had on her plate. "No not yet but she seems to like him. Don't you think you have enough on your plate?"

"I just can't help it" Amanda said as she and Beatrice headed back to the table.

Arriving back at the table, Beatrice found Carl and Ron sitting engaged in conversation. Ron stood and pulled out the chair next to him when he saw Beatrice arrive. Beatrice sat down and scanned the room for Felicia. Spying her on the dance floor with her new friend made Beatrice smile.

Ron leaned back in his chair, one hand wrapped around his beer resting in his lap, the other hand resting on the back of Beatrice's chair and his eyes on Beatrice.

Beatrice looked up at Ron with a piece of apple halfway to her mouth and froze with her mouth open and her hand almost to her mouth. She found him looking at her with a smile on his face. She kept her mouth open, but moved her hand with the apple in it towards his mouth. To suggest 'do you want some'. Ron leaned down and took a bite of the apple that Beatrice had offered. Slowly, Beatrice put the left over piece of apple in her mouth and chewed slowly, not breaking eye contact with Ron.

"Can I interest you in one more dance?" Ron Asked Beatrice

"Sure I have to work off that apple somehow" Beatrice said as she stood.

Ron laughed, stood and put his hand on the small of Beatrice's back leading her onto the dance floor.

"They look good together don't they?" Amanda said to Carl.

"Yes, they do." He Replied "I've known Ron for close to four years now. A couple of year ago he was in love with a woman. He was going to marry her. On the night before the wedding, she told him she was pregnant with another man's child and she walked out. He was devastated. He really hasn't taken an interest in someone until now."

"What about you, what is your story?" Amanda Asked Carl who gave her a funny look. "You have never been married? Do you have someone else in your life? What exactly do you see happening between us?"

"Wow, straight forward. Well, no I have never been married. No, there is no one else in my life. And I see me walking you back to your room ending with a good night kiss. That is if you don't mind" Said Carl "I am attracted to you and would like to get to know you better. I haven't met anyone that has made me feel the way you do. Is that honest enough for you?"

Amanda just starred at Carl smiling a goofy smile. "Will you dance with me one more time before you take me for that kiss?" Amanda asked taking his hand in hers leading him to the dance floor. On her way to the dance floor, Amanda spotted Beatrice and Ron exiting the room laughing.

Beatrice let Ron lead her out of the dining hall and up a flight of stairs. His hand at the small of her back the whole time. He held open the door that led to the upper deck and let Beatrice step out ahead of him. Beatrice took in a nice long breath and let it out slowly.

"Thank you for taking a walk with me. I can't get enough of the ocean air." Ron said.

"You're welcome and thank you for asking me." Beatrice said trying to keep herself calm.

"So tell me about yourself. Where are you from and why did you chose this as a career?" Ron asked Beatrice.

"I was born and raised in Stockton California. Both of my parents are dead. And I chose this as a career because I wanted something different that had some adventure and travel attached to it" Beatrice said as she shrugged her shoulders. Walking along next to Ron she could feel her heart racing.

"I'm sorry to hear about your parents. Would you like to sit for a little while?" he asked Beatrice pointing to a bench.

* * *

Amanda checked on Felicia before she left the dining room in route to her room with Carl. Amanda wondered about Beatrice, if she was all right and what she was doing. At the room door, Carl gave Amanda a good night kiss. One that Amanda would not soon forget. One she intended on telling Beatrice about once she got in the room. "Hey Bea, are you still awake? I need to talk to you." Amanda called to Beatrice. Silence was what she got in return.

Ron looked at his watch "it's after midnight, I should be getting you back to your room" he said standing and reaching out to take Beatrice's hand.

Placing her hand in his, Beatrice stood from the bench. Ron intertwined his fingers with Beatrice's and led her inside to the elevator instead of the stairs. Ron squeezed her hand ever so gently several times during the elevator ride and along the way to her room door. Beatrice turned to face Ron and that's when he slowly reached up and placed his hand on the side of Beatrice's face, stroking her cheek with his thumb. "Tomorrow night for dinner?" Ron asked as he starred into Beatrice's eyes.

"Yes, I can't wait" Beatrice whispered

"Until then" Ron said as he skimmed his hand down Beatrice's neck to her shoulder and all the way down her arm to her hand. He brought her hand up to his lips and very gently kissed the back of her hand before walking away.

Beatrice opened the door to her room and screamed when she bumped into Amanda. "What the hell, you scared the hell out of me." Beatrice said putting her hand over her heart.

"I was just going out to look for you. I was worried" Amanda said sitting down on the edge of her bunk. "Sit down right now and tell me everything. Don't leave anything out." Amanda patted the space next to her.

A half an hour of filling each other in on the evenings events while getting ready for bed went by quickly. Beatrice climbed up into her bunk, lay her head on her pillow and thought of Ron as she drifted off to sleep.

Chapter Nine

Joe set his plan in motion and was already at the spot to meet Thomas. He arrived one hour early to scout the environment. Thomas was not going to be pleased to find out that he was not going to get on the ship. The only way that was going to happen was over Joe's dead body. Joe knew that once this meeting was over, he would be at the top of the hit list along with Beatrice. "I failed once, I will not fail a second time." Joe said out loud as he stood waiting for Thomas.

Knowing that he would be no match for Thomas, a full on fight was out of the question. Standing against a tree with a full view of the bench that was designated for the meeting spot, Joe checked his watch. His heart started to race and the hair on his arms stood up as Joe realized what happened. He took off at lightning speed for his SUV, jumped in and sped off for the ship. Slamming his fist on the steering wheel and letting curse words fly at every stop light. One more light he was thinking when a small car pulled out in front of him from a parking lot, jumping the curb to avoid the car pulling out, he almost ran over two ladies on the sidewalk. He sped along as fast as he could thinking of one thing, he had to get to Beatrice before Thomas.

*   *   *

Beatrice was awake before the alarm went off. Climbing down from her bunk, she turned toward the door to the bathroom, and spotted a piece of paper on the floor. Slowly she moved to the paper and picked it up. She checked the lock on the door before opening it up.

Beatrice,
I enjoyed getting to know you last night.
Have a wonderful day. Until Dinner tonight.
Ron

Beatrice backed up until she hit Amanda's bunk and sat down on her leg. "Hey what's wrong? You scared the hell out of me." Amanda said as she woke up and turned to see Beatrice. All Amanda saw was Beatrice sitting there starring at a piece of paper smiling. "Bea what is it?"

Beatrice just handed over the note and went into the bathroom smiling. Amanda read the note, stood up and banged on the bathroom door. "What did you do with this guy that you didn't tell me about last night? It must have been something to deserve a note hand written and delivered." Amanda shouted at the closed bathroom door.

Beatrice emerged from the bathroom with a smug look on her face. She stopped and batted her lashes at Amanda.

"Oh don't try to be coy with me missy, you better start talking right now." Amanda demanded with her arms crossed and her foot tapping on the floor.

"Oh, would you stop? Nothing more happened than what I told you last night" Beatrice said laughing. "Go get ready, we don't have much time and I want breakfast before we have to be at work."

"I know, we are setting sail today. I can't wait, I'm so excited." Amanda exclaimed clapping her hands.

Both Beatrice and Amanda exited their room in time to see Felicia coming down the hall. "Hey, you guys ready for today?" Felicia asked

"Well, it's nice to see you. What's been going on and are you all right?" Amanda asked

Felicia smiled and started to laugh putting her hands up to her mouth "Oh my, I just don't know where to begin. He is so great."

"Let's start with his name." Beatrice chimed in smiling

"His name is Peter and he asked me to dinner tonight. He even kissed me last night." Felicia said as she walked to breakfast with Beatrice and Amanda

"Maybe they should re-name this ship *The Love Boat*." Amanda said

Beatrice, Amanda and Felicia laughed and talked all the way to the breakfast area. Amanda choosing her waffles and syrup, Felicia had an omelet with toast and Beatrice went with fruit and toast.

The loud speaker came on and Carl's voice started "Ladies and gentlemen, I would like to take this time and thank all of you for your hard work and efforts to get this ship under way. Everyone has their itinerary for the day. We set sail at 6:00 pm, the guest start boarding at 2:30. Good luck and have a wonderful day." Carl said. Turning his attention to Amanda once he stepped away from the mic, he strolled over to where she was sitting.

"Ladies, have a wonderful day" he said as he winked at Amanda before stepping away.

"If we are all done with breakfast, let's get started. I want to get done with enough time to get changed for dinner." Beatrice said standing up and heading for her work station. Amanda and Felicia followed.

Beatrice's mind was not on her work, pulling her equipment out of the storage area, she dropped the cleaning caddy in the floor. "Shit" Beatrice said as she got down on her knees to pick up the cleaning bottles and towels.

"Here, let me help you with that" a voice said from behind Beatrice.

Before Beatrice could respond, the voice kneeled down next to her and when Beatrice looked up at the voice, she froze as her mouth dropped open. Blinking and starring, but nothing would come out of her mouth.

"It's okay, I'm not going to hurt you. But we need to talk. My name is Joe. Please trust me when I tell you I'm not going to hurt you. Go about your business, I will catch up to you later. Don't tell anyone about me" Joe said as he pulled Beatrice to her feet, handed her the caddy and then walked away.

Beatrice stood there in the hall starring in the direction Joe went. Mouth open, caddy in hand, unable to move. A hand touched Beatrice's shoulder, she jumped, screamed and dropped the caddy again. Turning she saw Ron standing there.

"I'm sorry, I didn't mean to scare you" Ron said smiling down at Beatrice "let me help you with that."

"Okay, it's okay, thank you" Beatrice said forcing a smile. She tried to concentrate on picking up the cleaning items again, but she just couldn't stop looking down the hall for Joe. Standing, Beatrice looked up at Ron and tried to smile. Her heart was just not in it.

"You okay? You look a little frazzled." Ron said putting his hands on Beatrice's shoulders.

"Yes, I'm fine. Just a little tired I guess. Thanks for helping me pick all this stuff up." Beatrice tried to sound convincing.

"All right, I won't detain you any longer. Are you still up for dinner tonight?" Ron Asked

"Yes, of course. I can't wait. What time and where?" Beatrice asked

"I will be at your door around 7:30 tonight. Is that all right?" Asked Ron

"Sure, I will be waiting for you then?" Beatrice said, relaxing a little bit.

Ron leaned down and kissed Beatrice on her cheek "Until later tonight" he whispered into her ear before walking down the hall in the same direction as Joe.

Beatrice stood and watched him go. Once he was out of site, Beatrice headed for her first room. Looking around for Joe as she went. By the time Beatrice reached her last room, she had a head ache from trying to do her job and keep an eye out for Joe. Everytime someone walked by or approached her, she jumped. Beatrice finally made it to the storage unit to put her cleaning equipment away when she saw Amanda.

"Hi, good we are done with this. The guest are starting to come aboard. Now we get to meet and greet them." Amanda said with a small sigh. "What's up with you? You look like a deer caught in head lights."

"I think I am just tired" Beatrice responded

"I will meet you back at the room at five? I want to be up on deck when we set sail. Are you still having dinner with Ron?" Amanda asked Beatrice

"Yes, but I hate to leave you. What are you going to do?" Beatrice asked

"Oh don't worry about me. Carl is supposed to meet up with me later. Don't worry if I come in late." Amanda said with a smile on her face

"Alright then, I will meet you back at the room by five." Beatrice responded before parting to her section of the ship to assist the guests coming aboard.

The next two hours kept Beatrice busy enough she hardly thought about Joe. She could not figure out what he would need to talk to her about. Why was he on the ship? Beatrice was helping an older couple find their room and get them settled in. One her way out of their room,

Beatrice ran into Joe. He grabbed her hand and led her into an empty room two doors down.

"What the hell do you think you're doing? Why are you following me? You had better start talking right now" Beatrice shouted at Joe as she yanked her arm out of his grip.

"Look, I don't have much time right now. I will tell you that I am not the only one following you now. There is another man. His name is Thomas although I do not know what name he is using to get on the ship. I will tell you that I am the good guy he is not. The last time I saw him, he had red hair sporting a mustache. Please try and stay away from him until later when I can get back to you. Right now he is after me too. That is why I have to go. Meet me outside of the casino at midnight." Joe tried to explain as much as he could while he peeked out the door.

"Hell no, you tell me right now" Beatrice yelled

"Stop yelling or you are going to cause attention to us." Joe pressed his message by putting his finger up to his lips.

"Forget this" Beatrice said as she shoved Joe hard in the middle of his back. Causing him to jerk forward, closing the door on his hand. He stepped back to release his hand and turned in time to duck when Beatrice took a swing at him with her right hand. He stood and grabbed her hands trying to keep her from hitting him.

Joe's grip was firm but not harming. Beatrice slowly stopped flailing her arms about when she noticed the grip he had. "Beatrice please stop. I'm not going to hurt you. I am trying to keep you from getting hurt or even killed. Will you please just meet me tonight? I promise I will tell you everything then." Joe pleaded with Beatrice.

"Yes I will meet you" Beatrice said shaking her head yes.

Joe loosened his grip on Beatrice's hands but didn't let go. He stood there holding her hands starring into her eyes. He was close enough to smell her. He felt the electricity between them. He slowly let go of her hands, he held her gaze a moment more and exited the room.

Beatrice sat down in the desk chair in the room for a moment gathering her thoughts before stepping out into the hall. She looked both ways and then bolted to her room. No one will miss me for a half an hour she thought as she practically ran to the stairs, down four flights and ten rooms down. Once inside, she picked up her phone and called Kristy.

Beatrice was highly disappointed when Kristy didn't answer. Beatrice's message was short, "Hi, it's me, I need to talk to you" She tried to sound casual as to not call too much alarm. "A nice long hot shower night calm my nerves" Beatrice said out loud. Gathering her things and heading to the bathroom, Beatrice stopped when she heard the door knob jiggle. Thinking it was Amanda, she opened the door. There stood a man, tall, muscular with red hair and a mustache. Beatrice attempted to slam the door shut. The man stopped it with his hand and took a step forward. Beatrice opened her mouth to scream.

"Excuse me" Amanda said from behind the man

He stopped, turned and looked at Amanda "Oh sorry, I must have the wrong room" he said. Thomas stepped back taking one more look at Beatrice and went down the hall.

"Who was that?" Amanda asked as she entered and closed the door.

"I... um... don't know" Beatrice said as she reached behind Amanda and locked the door.

"Things are crazy out there. The halls are crowded and people are everywhere. We set sail in an hour and a half. Aren't you excited?" Amanda asked Beatrice who was still starring at the door.

"Hello, Bea? Hey are you all right? What's going on with you?" Amanda asked as she touched Beatrice's shoulder.

Beatrice jumped when Amanda touched her. She turned and broke down crying. Dropping everything in her hands to the floor and cupping her face in her hands. Amanda wrapped her hands around Beatrice and guided her over to her bunk and sat her down. "Beatrice tell me what is going on. I can't help if you don't tell me." Amanda pleaded with Beatrice

Beatrice calmed down after a few minutes. Whipping her tears with one hand and her nose with the back of the other hand, she took a deep breath in and began explaining.

"Remember when I told you about the letter from that Uncle? Well what I didn't tell you about is the money that came with it. $300,000 worth of money. I had a lawyer check it out and he said that it was all on the up and up. Then there was that guy, the one I chased down the street. He is here on the ship. He said his name is Joe."

"Wait just a minute, he is here? You actually talked to him?" Amanda said interrupting Beatrice

Beatrice stood up to grab a tissue for her nose, turned to face Amanda and continued "This morning, I dropped my caddy and he helped me pick things up. He said that he was there to keep me safe and to warn me about this other man that was on board. The man that was at the door was him. The other man here to hurt me" Beatrice said as she blew her nose.

"That's it, I'm not going to just sit here and let you get abducted or killed or whatever." Amanda said as she picked up the room phone and called Carl.

Five minutes later, Carl and Ron came busting through the door. In two steps, he was at Beatrice kneeling down placing his hands on hers.

"Are you all right?" He asked Beatrice

Beatrice shook her head yes as her tears started falling again. Carl produced a handkerchief from inside his suit jacket and handed to Beatrice. Ron took it and wiped Beatrice's tears from her face.

"Come on Bea, they are here to help. Tell them what has been happening." Amanda said sitting down on her bunk. "Please"

Beatrice took a deep breath in and let it out slowly. She started talking, filling them all in from the beginning. Telling them about her mother, living in foster care and Kristy. She didn't stop until she saw the redheaded man at the door. Thirty minutes later she said "And that's it. Everything I know, you all know now"

"You don't know either of these men or what they want?" Carl Asked

"No, but I am supposed to meet Joe tonight at midnight outside the casino. He said he would explain everything then"

"Hell no. I am not letting you do that." Ron exclaimed getting to his feet.

"I need to find out something. If this Joe person wanted to hurt me he would have done so already. He has had plenty of opportunity to do so. What scares me is this other man. The one at the door. He scares me and he is on this ship. I don't know where either one of them are or how they got on board." Beatrice stood up and crossed her arms over her chest. "I'm going to meet him tonight"

Carl and Ron exchanged looks and stepped outside the room to talk. Amanda reached over and took Amanda's hand "It's going to be okay Bea. And if you think that I am going to let you meet this guy alone, you're out of your mind."

Ron and Carl stepped back in and closed the door. Ron spoke first "I have some things I need to do before we sail. I want you two" Ron pointed to Amanda and Beatrice "to stay in this room until either Carl or myself has returned. Neither of you are to go anywhere alone for right now. Understand?"

"Yes we understand" Amanda said giving Beatrice a nudge with her elbow "isn't that right Bea?"

"Yes, I understand" Beatrice said, arms crossed over her chest head looking at the floor.

Ron stepped over to Beatrice, cupped her chin with his hand and lifted her face up to look at him. "Promise me you will wait here until I come get you?" Ron's voice was barley over a whisper.

Beatrice smiled a small smile and whispered back "Yes"

Ron bent down and placed a very soft light kiss on Beatrice's lips. When their lips parted, Beatrice's eyes opened and she found him starring at her. He smiled, turned and walk out of the room with Carl right behind him. After the door closed, Amanda reached over and locked the door.

Chapter Ten

THE SHIP WAS MOVING SLOWLY away from the dock via the tug boats and so far Joe had not seen Thomas nor has he been able to find Beatrice. He wasn't even sure he made it on board. Walking through the throng of people up on deck, Joe kept an eye out for Thomas while searching for Beatrice. He was sure that she would be out to see the ship leave port. On his second go round walking the deck, Joe spotted Beatrice. She was standing at the stern of the ship next to a man who had his arm around her shoulders. She was talking with the brunette that he had seen her with before. Joe stood rooted to his spot starring at them. Not happy that she had some guy touching her like that.

Deciding to keep an eye on Beatrice until their meeting that night, Joe stepped aside to let a group of people walk by and that's when he saw Thomas. Leaning against the side of the ship watching Beatrice. "Shit" Joe thought. "He made it. At least he shouldn't know that I am on board as well" Going rogue was not as easy as he thought it would be. But he was not going to let them get their hands on Beatrice.

* * *

Carl set up an intimate dinner for four in his suit. Salad, Lobster with shrimp pesto and chocolate lava cake for dessert. "I thought a bottle of champagne would be in order for this evening." Carl said opening the bottle and pouring a glass for everyone.

"Wow, this is some room" Amanda said as she and Beatrice looked around.

"It even has a balcony" Beatrice said stepping out in the evening air.

Ron brought a glass of Champaign out and handed it to her. "Enjoying yourself" Ron asked taking a sip of the bubbly liquid.

"Yes I am thank you. I'm so excited to get away from land right now. I just want to be free you know? Let the wind blow my hair and live. Does that sound crazy?" Beatrice said smiling as she took a drink herself.

"Not at all. I feel the same way. Sometimes I feel like I have been standing still for so long. I am glad Carl talked me into joining him on another run. I was going to take a job in Texas" Ron said. "But this ship was a new one and I got to do the hiring of the security staff"

"Hey you two, get in here and eat" Amanda called

Ron and Beatrice joined Carl and Amanda for dinner.

"Did everyone enjoy their dinner?" Carl asked

"I sure did. I could get used to eating like this" Amanda said "How about you Bea? You were awfully quiet"

"Yes, thank you very much. I was just thinking about later." Beatrice said

"I know, I was thinking about the same thing. I don't feel comfortable with this plan." Ron Chimed in.

"Look I know how you feel about all of this, but I need to be able to talk to him to find out why and what is going on. I have agreed to taking Amanda with me and you and Carl will be close by incase something goes wrong" Beatrice said getting up from the table and walking to the balcony door looking out.

Ron stepped to her side and opened the door, placing his hand on the small of her back guiding her outside and closing the door behind them. Beatrice stepped to the railing placing her hands on it and closing her eyes. When she opened them, Ron was looking at her. The expression on his face was serious. He reached up and placed his hand on her face. Placing his thumb under her chin, he tilted her head back so he could look into her eyes.

"I hope you don't think that I am being too forward with you?" Ron said

Beatrice smiled and whispered "No I don't"

"Are you sure about this plan?" Ron asked

"Yes, if he has any information regarding my life or past that involves my parents I have to talk to him. Like I said, if he was going to hurt me, he could have several different times. It is the other guy that scares me." Beatrice said.

"Alright then, we will go with this as scheduled. I have my team keeping an eye out for this other man according to your description. And I will be watching. Do you remember the signal to give if you need any help?" Ron asked

"Yes, I do. You are so cute, I've never had anyone fuss over me like this. Well no one except Kristy and Amanda" Beatrice said giggling.

Ron looked at his watch "It's almost eleven. We should get going soon. I want to get into position before midnight."

"Okay, let's get this done and over with." Beatrice said pushing herself off of the railing.

Ron grabbed Beatrice's arm stopping her from going any further to the door. He gently pulled Beatrice to him. He put both of his hands on the sides of her face and tilted her head back. Beatrice put her hands on his forearms and looked into his eyes. His deep chocolate brown eyes. Slowly Ron leaned down and put his lips on hers. Slow and soft at first, then he moved to hot and demanding. Teeth and tongues clashing. He moved one hand to the back of her head and the other to the small of her back. Beatrice had one hand around his neck and the other around his waist. Ron broke from the kiss placing his forehead against hers attempting to catch his breath.

"I'm sorry" was all Ron could say

"Sorry for what?" Beatrice responded matching his whisper.

"I have you in my arms and I don't want to let you go" He said

Beatrice took a moment contemplating her response "Then don't" Beatrice decided to take the bull by the horns, so to speak and live. What did she have to loose she thought.

Ron smiled and started to laugh. "Here I thought I was going to scare you away"

"There is no place for me to go and I'm happy right here with you," Beatrice said giggling.

"Come on we should get going" Ron said taking Beatrice's hand leading her inside.

When they stepped inside they found Amanda and Carl in an extreme lip lock of their own on the sofa. "Are we interrupting anything?" Beatrice asked

Amanda broke from the kiss "No" she responded

"Yes" said Carl laughing

Amanda hit his chest with the back of her hand "Come in. Is it time to go?"

"Yes, we should get going, get into place before midnight" Ron chimed in

"Well, let's rock and roll" Beatrice said heading for the door.

Beatrice sat in a chair just outside the casino, cocktail in hand. Amanda was inside the casino sitting at a slot machine that let her have a good view of Beatrice. Carl was wondering around the casino chatting and checking on things. Ron was nowhere in sight. He told Beatrice she would not be able to see him but he would be watching. Beatrice tried to look casual but that was an impossible task she decided. Keeping her eyes scanning the people looking for Joe.

"Sorry I'm late, I had to make sure Thomas was not following me" Joe said as he took the chair next to Beatrice.

Beatrice slowly turned to look at Joe "You have two seconds to start talking or I'm done with this and you both are getting turned into the authorities. Oh and this is Amanda and she is sitting in on this little meeting whether you like it or not" Beatrice said pointing to Amanda who walked up to them.

"So be it then" Joe said "I was hoping to go somewhere less public"

"No, but we can move to that spot over there in the corner" Amanda said pointing across to the windows

"That's fine, let's go" Joe said has he stood scanning the area.

Joe sat with his back to the windows so he could see the area around them. Beatrice and Amanda took the seats adjacent to him on either side.

"Talk" Beatrice said to Joe

"I'm going to tell you all that I know. Unfortunately I came into a job working for the Cassidy family in Ireland. They are the family responsible for your parent's deaths. They sent me to retrieve the necklace that you are wearing." Joe started

Beatrice reached in and grabbed the necklace. Holding the small heart and key in her hand. "Why my necklace?" She asked

"I'm not sure exactly. They are supposed to open something. A box or safe or something like that. I don't know what is inside or why they would kill for it. I'm the one that went through your room. I was hoping to just go in, get it and be gone."

"But I wear it" Beatrice said interrupting

"That's my problem, I didn't get it and the time limit is running out so they labeled me a failure and sent Thomas. I knew he would kill you for the necklace and I just could not let that happen" Joe said has he sat back in his chair "Apparently I'm no good at this job. I tried to detour Thomas from getting on the ship but failed"

"And what's your plan from here?" Amanda Asked Joe

"I don't have one. That's my problem. If I don't retrieve the key and the heart, Thomas will at any cost. If I stop Thomas, they will send someone else. They won't stop until it's recovered." Joe Said

"I need some time to think this through" Beatrice said as she stood up from her chair. Looking at Joe, "Excuse me" she said and walked off down the corridor towards the elevator.

Amanda left Joe sitting there starring at Beatrice as she walked away and went over to Carl. Ron jogged to catch up with Beatrice who had just entered an elevator. Beatrice stood in the middle of the elevator holding onto her necklace. When Ron entered the elevator, she looked up at him at starred him in the face. Ron reached over and gathered her in his arms. Holding her tight against his chest. Beatrice laid her head against him and closed her eyes. They stayed like that in silence until the elevator stopped on Beatrice's floor.

Ron stopped just outside the elevator, looked at Beatrice "I want you to gather your things and stay in my room tonight. I need to keep an eye on you." He said

Beatrice back in thought mode, just shook her head 'yes'

Ron escorted Beatrice to her room, took her key and opened the door for her. He stepped inside to check the room. Beatrice stood in the door way waiting for him to finish. Ron stepped out of the bathroom to give Beatrice the all clear and froze, Beatrice was gone. He stepped out into the hall way and looked both ways. He heard a woman attempt a scream in the direction of the elevators and ran that way.

Beatrice fought and kicked her attacker. His big hand was trying to keep her mouth covered while the other one held her tight around her waist. Opening her mouth to scream, one of the man's fingers slipped into her mouth. Biting down hard caused the man to yell and then curse at her. She knew then that it was Thomas that had a hold of her. Reaching the elevator, Beatrice let go of her hold on his arms and struggled to get the necklace undone. The elevator doors opened, he dragged her inside and the doors closed.

Several people had stepped out in the hall to see what was going on effectively slowing Ron down on his way to the sound of the scream. Once he reached the elevator he looked to see which way it was headed. The numbers indicated it was going down.

"Excuse me, sir?" A feminine voice said behind Ron "I've seen you before, do you work here?"

He turned to see a very scared woman standing there. "Yes, I'm with security" He said "I'm in a hurry"

"A man dragged a woman into the elevator. Before the doors closed all the way, this came flying out and landed on the floor" the woman said holding out Beatrice's necklace.

"Did you see the man?" Ron asked

"Yes, he had red hair with a red mustache. He looked to be taller than the woman. I've seen the woman before. She work's on the ship, yes?" the woman said

"Thank you for your information. Go back into your room and lock the door." Ron said

The Elevator doors opened and Ron stepped in hitting the down button. He pulled out his phone and called Carl. "He took Beatrice, she's gone. I'm going down to look for her. Find that Joe person, I will call you shortly." And he hung up.

All the blood drained from Carl's face as he hung up. "Beatrice has been taken" He said as he looked at Amanda.

"What the hell do you mean taken?" Amanda shouted

"Look I don't have time to explain" Carl said holding Amanda's shoulder with his hands. "I need you to try and find that guy you were talking with earlier. Whether you find him or not, meet me at my cabin in twenty minutes. And be careful." Carl said to Amanda before stalking away.

Ron went down to the engine room searching for Beatrice. Not knowing where he would have taken her made him worry more. They were still out at sea so exiting the ship wasn't an option. Ron saw a group of men standing up ahead inspecting a door.

"What's going on?" Ron asked the men flashing his badge.

"We received a message that this door had been breached and we cannot figure out how or why at this moment." One of the men said

"Hello sir, my men here said they heard someone coming through that corridor about five minutes ago, but when he got there he saw no one" Another said

"There has been a woman abducted. The man that took her is large in size with red hair. I need you two to come with me to search. You two keep watch here." Ron said as he entered the engine room.

"Yes sir, my name is Aaron. Take one of the radios, it's loud in here. Makes it easier to communicate" He said to Ron

"Thanks" Ron said taking off in search for Beatrice

*   *   *

"Hi, Kristy?" Amanda said into the phone "I know it's late and all but…"

"What happened?" Kristy said interrupting Amanda as she sat straight up from her bed. "Where's Beatrice?"

"I don't know how much you know, but Beatrice has been taken…."

"What do you mean taken?" Kristy interrupted again.

"Long story short, Beatrice and I talked to Joe tonight. Do you know who he is?"

"Oh My God yes, go on" Kristy said

"Well he said that another man has been sent to retrieve her necklace. That he was supposed to do it but failed. Now this guy he called Thomas was going to do it. Now we can't find her." Amanda explained

"When did this happen?" Kristy asked

"We talked to Joe at midnight and she went missing after that. It's been about twenty minutes or so" Amanda said trying to keep from crying

"Oh, honey don't cry. I am going to make a phone call and I will call you back on this phone. Give me a few minutes." Kristy said and hung up.

Amanda wiped her tears away with a tissue, blew her nose and excited the room for Carl's cabin. Two back pack's packed, one for her and one for Beatrice.

"I know what time it is, just wake him up" Kristy shouted in the phone "They have Beatrice" Kristy waited until Angus came on the line.

"Hello, Kristy?" Angus said "What's happened?"

"The Bastard sent Thomas and now he took her. That's what happened" Kristy yelled

"Oh my Lord, are you sure? How did you find this out? What happened to Joe?" Angus asked

"All I know, is that Beatrice and her friend talked to Joe. He said that since he failed, they sent Thomas. Now she is missing. He took her

Angus. So help me if he hurts her I'm going to kill him myself" Kristy said still yelling. She took up pacing in the garage as to not wake up the kids in the house.

"Where is everyone now? Didn't she get on a cruise ship?" Angus asked

"Yes, they are on the way to Ensenada. They should be arriving in a few hours. That senile old bastard Charles screwed our plans up." Kristy said

"Stay by the phone, I will be in touch" Angus said before hanging up.

Kristy stepped inside the house, got a pot of coffee going for herself. She went upstairs to check on the children sleeping, grabbed her robe and settled in for an early morning. Once she got some coffee in her, she called Amanda back.

"Hi Amanda, is there any news?" Kristy asked

"Hi, no we have not heard anything. I can't find Joe either. Look there is someone hear that wants to talk to you. His name is Carl" Amanda responded

"Hello Mrs.......?" Carl paused

"Hi, sorry. O'Riley, Kristy O'Riley. And who are you?" Kristy asked

"My name is Carl Masters. I am one of the ship's directors. I have my best security member and his team looking for Beatrice as we speak. Can you tell me anything about this Thomas fellow?" Carl asked

"He is ruthless, horrible and gets what he wants by any means he thinks is necessary. Please go find Beatrice, I can't have anything happen to her please" Kristy begged as the tears started

"Mrs. O'Riley we are doing everything we can. There are people searching as we speak. We are even keeping watch for bodies going overboard." Carl stated

"Oh My God, bodies? Are you serious?" Kristy shrieked

"I'm sorry, I'll give you back to Amanda now" Carl said handing the phone to Amanda.

Amanda gave Carl a look as she took the phone. "Hi Kristy?"

"Amanda, I can't take much more of this. We have gone through a lot of trouble keeping Beatrice hidden from these people"

"I don't understand. What are you talking about?" Amanda asked

"I'm sorry, this is something I am not ready to talk about just yet. Please keep me informed okay?" Kristy said

"Yes sure, I will call as soon as I know anything" Amanda said

Amanda saw Carl pacing out on the balcony, phone to his ear. Stepping closer, she deduced he was talking with Ron. She stood in the door way leaning on the doorjamb hands clasped together watching, waiting and listening.

Chapter Eleven

Ron cut his conversation with Carl short when he heard some commotion over the radio. He closed his phone, put it in his pocket and ran in the direction of the commotion. Upon arrival, he saw three men looking at the ground.

"What's going on?" Ron asked

"Blood on the ground sir." One man said pointing to the ground.

Fear spiking through his veins, Ron thought the worst for Beatrice. Glancing around the area, Ron heard more commotion over the radio, this time in Spanish. "What the hell are they saying?" Ron shouted at the men standing near him.

"Hurry Senor this way hurry" One man said as he ran

When Ron and the others reached the end of the corridor, he saw a man pulling a body out from between the wall and a set of pipes. Ron froze for a fraction of a second before reality set in. "Move I'll do it, get out of my way" Ron shouted shoving men to the left and right making his way to the body. Kneeling down he gently pulled Beatrice out and checked her vitals. Breathing out a sigh once he found a pulse. He quickly checked for broken bones and yelled out instructions for the men standing near. One ran off to retrieve the doctor, two men cleared the way. Ron scooped Beatrice up off the ground and carried her out of the engine room to the service elevator.

Two security members met them at the elevator door and assisted Ron with taking Beatrice to his room. He laid her down on his bed as Amanda and Carl busted through the door followed by the doctor and Joe.

Ron turned to let the doctor get to Beatrice and spotted Joe standing by the door. "This is your fault" Ron yelled strutting over and giving Joe a mean right hook.

Joe's head flew to the left and his body hit the wall. Ron pinned him to the wall with his fore arm pushing his neck. Joe didn't fight back, he just stood there starring Ron in the eye. Carl touched Ron's arm.

"Hey man, she's alive and she is safe now. Don't do this here. We need to talk let's step outside" Carl told Ron

Ron slowly let go of Joe, he stepped back and followed Carl outside on the balcony. Joe stood looking at Beatrice's unresponsive body before following Ron and Carl outside.

Ron pinned a look at Joe "Start talking" he told him

"What do you want to know?" Joe asked

"I want to know just what the hell is going on. That's what I want to know" Ron said taking a step toward Joe.

"Look, all I know is that I was supposed to retrieve the heart and the key on the necklace she wears. It is important to the people that hired me. No, I don't know why or what for. Since I failed and their time line is running out, they sent Thomas. And since Beatrice is still alive means that he didn't retrieve the items. Something tells me that he was interrupted when torturing her for the location." Joe said

"We will be pulling into port in about three hours. There is only one way off of the ship. We are planning extra security as passengers get off and on the ship today. But we are limited as to the amount of man power to search the entire ship." Carl said

"I'm not leaving Beatrice until she wakes up" Ron said "this Thomas bastard can't get anywhere until we stop. That leaves three hours to search"

"I will help with the search. If I find him I will let you know." Joe said

"Here is my number. Call me when you find him" Carl said to Joe

Joe stepped inside to check on Beatrice before he left. Standing at the foot of the bed, Joe just watched the doctor and Amanda tending to the cuts on her face. His heart went out to her, feeling that Ron was right, this was his fault. If he had only talked to her before, things might have turned out different. He slowly exited the room before anyone saw the tears forming in his eyes.

"How is she doing doc?" Ron asked stepping up to the edge of the bed.

"She has a slight concussion. Cuts and bruises all over her body. None that need stitches though. She needs to be monitored closely for the next few hours. I will be back, if you need me before than just call me." He explained

"I'm not leaving her until she wakes up so I will call if I need you." Ron said

"I'm not leaving her either." Amanda said "Carl, tell whomever you need to that I will not be returning to work until she is okay"

Carl scooped Amanda into his arms and hugged her tight. "Don't worry about any of that. I will take care of everything. I am going to have everything in your room brought here. You can separate your things from Beatrice's while you sit with her." Carl told her

"Why? Am I leaving the ship?" She asked Carl

Carl chuckled and said "I am moving you into my cabin and Beatrice will stay here with Ron until we get things figured out anyway. Is that okay with you?"

"Oh, sure that's okay thank you" Amanda said burying her face into his chest. Amanda pulled away "I'm going to call Kristy and let her know that we found her"

"I want to speak to her when you are finished" Ron told Amanda as he stepped over to sit down on the bed next to Beatrice. He gently put her hand in his. Lifting it up to kiss a bruise on the back of her hand. Just being so close to her made Ron come alive. He had felt like he wasn't living the last four years. Not until he met Beatrice.

"Ron" Amanda called holding the phone out to let him know that it was his turn with Kristy.

He gently put her hand down on the bed and joined Amanda outside on the balcony taking the phone from her. "Hello?" he said into the phone.

"Hello, Amanda filled me in a little bit. Who are you? If you don't mind be asking." Kristy asked Ron

"No ma'am I don't mind. My name is Ron Peterson, I am the head of security. And I just wanted to tell you that I have Beatrice here with me and I won't let anything else happen to her." Ron said feeling silly with what just came out of his mouth.

"Well, that's very noble of you Mr. Peterson. But I think enough has happened to her already. I would like to make plans to come and pick her up from where ever you stop at."

Kristy said

"I understand your feelings ma'am. I will talk to the doctor on board and see what arrangements I can make for you." Ron said trying to get the nerve to say what was really one his mind.

"Thank you I would appreciate that" Kristy replied

"Excuse me ma'am, um…… I would like to let you know my intensions with Beatrice if you don't mind." Ron stumbled the words out the best he could

"Intensions?" Kristy asked

"Yes, I would like to date Beatrice as long as she says yes that is" Ron told Kristy. He was glad that she was not able to see his face.

"Well, we will have to see how things go in the next couple of days" Kristy said trying to keep the smile on her face from showing in her words.

"Thank you. I will be in touch with you soon. Good bye" Ron said before handing the phone back to Amanda.

"You know, Beatrice has not had a serious boyfriend before. She has concentrated on her school work and extra activities. We used to joke that she was much older than her years. Guys her age never impressed her. Just be good to her okay?" Amanda told Ron while they sat outside.

"She told me a little bit the other night while I walked her to her room. Something about her makes me … I don't know….. happy I guess." Ron said smiling.

* * *

Beatrice opened her eyes just in time to see Thomas deliver another blow to the side of her face. He was shouting at her, but the ringing in her ears made it difficult to hear what he was saying. Heat, where was the heat coming from she wondered. Her arms and legs where burning. She faintly saw him stand, then she felt pain in her stomach, her back and her legs. She opened her mouth and tried to scream but nothing came out. She felt someone touch her shoulders, someone was calling her name.

"Beatrice wake up. Wake up your safe. I'm here. Beatrice" Amanda was calling as she gently touched her shoulders

Ron stood at the foot of the bed watching Amanda talk to Beatrice as she thrashed around on the bed. His eyes were wide with alarm "What's wrong with her?" He whispered

"She has night mares. Get me a cool cloth for her head please" Amanda asked Ron

Ron returned with the cloth, he leaned down on the other side of Beatrice placing the cloth on her fore head. "Beatrice please wake up" he said close to her ear "It's me, I'm here wake up for me please"

Beatrice slowly stop screaming and thrashing around but her eyes didn't open. "Talk to her some more" Amanda said to Ron

"Hey, I'm right here. I've got you and I won't let you go." Ron whispered in her ear taking her hand in his.

Beatrice slowly blinked her eyes. Her lips parted but nothing came out. Amanda got a bottle of water and put a cap full into her mouth. Beatrice started to moan. Amanda did it again with the water.

"It's working keep going" Ron said to Amanda

"I don't want to choke her" Amanda said

A knock at the door brought Ron's finger up to his mouth in a 'shhh' action for Amanda. Ron moved to the door with his gun at his side. He opened the door to find a porter with Amanda and Beatrice's belongings. Ron stepped aside to allow him to enter the room. Ron instructed him to leave the cart. The porter inclined his head and backed out of the room.

"I'm too tired to go through all of that right now" Amanda said

"Don't worry about this now, we dock in two and half hours so why don't you get some sleep. I'll keep an eye on her" Ron said. He went to the closet and retrieved an extra blanket for Amanda and covered her up. Amanda lay down in the bed next to Beatrice holding her hand.

Ron stepped out onto the balcony, pulling a chair over to the railing to relax a bit. He crossed his legs at the ankles and propped them up on the railing, crossing his arms over his chest. Starring out at the water, Ron's thoughts drifted to Beatrice. He had shut himself off emotionally after Emily left him. Could he go through that again? Was he willing to take the chance on having his heart broken yet again. The sun rising sprayed orange, red and yellow colors on the horizon. "Hi" a female voice whispered from behind Ron. He turned to see Beatrice standing, one hand on the door and one hand wrapped around her middle.

Ron jumped up to assist Beatrice into a chair. "You shouldn't be up. How are you feeling?" Ron asked as he eased her down into a chair.

"I am so sore all over and I feel like my head is going to explode. All in all like shit" Beatrice said producing a laugh that made her wince and grab her ribs.

"I'm so glad that you have such a good sense of humor but I'm glad you're awake" Ron said pulling a chair up next to Beatrice and sitting down. "Why the good mood?"

"Because it's over" Beatrice said smiling

"What do you mean it's over?"

"I threw my necklace out of the elevator before the doors closed. And unless there is a really good Samaritan out there, who knows who picked it up. What's with all the boxes stacked on the cart and whose room are we in?" Beatrice asked trying to situate herself in the chair.

At that point, Ron decided to keep it to himself as to the where a bouts of the necklace. Ron smiled "This is my cabin and those are yours and Amanda's things from your room. Carl thought it would be better that both of you stay with us until we get this situation resolved. Is that all right with you?"

"If it's not going to cause a problem. What about work?" Beatrice asked

"Not for me, Carl is taking care of the work aspect of things. We still need to find Thomas before he hurts anyone else." Ron said "I'm sorry I didn't protect you Beatrice. I just about died when I turned and you were gone"

"It's okay, I don't want to talk about it right now. Maybe later. Look we are coming closer to land." Beatrice pointed out across the water. "Did you even sleep last night?"

"No, I'm doing okay." Ron smiled a full on smile

"I'm kind of hungry and I would like to take a shower. Is that possible?" Beatrice asked

"Sure, sure, I will call for food and I can help you take a shower" Ron said standing to give Beatrice a hand standing up and escorted her into the bathroom. He sat her down on the toilet while he started the water running. He turned to find her looking at him. "Let's get these clothes off shall we?"

"Um…. I'll be okay thank you" Beatrice said blushing

"Okay, do you want me to wake up Amanda?" Ron asked

"No, let her sleep, I'm fine" Beatrice said standing up to undo the button on her pants.

"I will get breakfast ordered, call me if you need any help" and he stepped out of the bathroom leaving the door open a crack.

Beatrice was able to get her pants and underwear down to her knees, sitting down on the toilet she got them the rest of the way off. She tried to get her left arm out of her shirt, no luck. She tried her right arm, no luck. Every time she tried to raise her arms pain shot through her ribs. Contemplating what to do, she didn't want to disturb Amanda, she took a deep breath and called Ron. After she did, a big smile crossed her lips.

Ron approached the door but didn't enter "I'm here, what do you need?"

"I can't get my shirt off. It hurts to bad. I have everything else off. Do you think you could help me with your eyes closed?" Beatrice said through the crack in the door.

Ron slowly opened the door "I can help, but not with my eyes closed" he entered with a smile. He stood looking at her in just her shirt and bra. Her legs long, tan and bruised. He wanted to take her in his arms and never let go. He stepped over to her and reached down for the hem of her shirt.

Beatrice hesitated for a moment, then looked up into his eyes. "Maybe we could just cut it off, I can't raise my hands over my head it hurts too much. I don't know how I'm going to wash my hair."

"Don't worry about anything, I've got you covered. Don't move I'll be right back" he said as he exited the bathroom. He returned with a pair of scissors in one hand and closed the door with the other.

Ron did a circular motion with his hand in the air, indicating he wanted Beatrice to turn around. She obliged him slowly. He reached down, grabbed the hem of her shirt and applied the scissors to her shirt working is way up to the neck of the shirt. Beatrice bent her head as far forward as she could to allow him to finish cutting. He laid open the sides of the shirt and reached out to undo the hooks of her bra. The first thing he noticed was that it wasn't white, it was purple. He slid both items off her shoulders and down her arms until they fell on the floor.

At that moment, his front was pressed against her back. He gently wrapped his arms around her. Beatrice leaned her head back against his chest. Ron leaned his head down and gently kissed her neck. Soft, warm kisses from her ear down to her shoulder. "I'm so happy you're okay" he whispered into her ear.

At that moment, Beatrice decided to grab life by the horns and be happy. "I'm glad I'm okay too." She said smiling "Help me wash my hair?"

"I'll be happy to help wash everything" Ron said smiling

Beatrice tried to laugh, but the pain made her wince. "Now let's not get carried away." She said stepping into the shower with Ron's assistance.

Chapter Twelve

CARL KNOCKED AND ENTERED THE room pushing a food cart. He was clean and dressed in his usual suit. Today it was navy blue, white shirt and a red tie with white stars. He smiled when he saw Amanda. She was pacing in the small cabin. "I brought breakfast. What are you doing? Where is everyone else?"

"I'm pacing because I have to use the bathroom and right now it is being used by everyone else" Amanda said pointing to the bathroom.

"Why don't you just knock on the door?" Carl asked

"Because if Beatrice has finally decided to be up close and personal with someone, I'm not going interrupt" Amanda said picking up her pacing again.

Carl laughed "You're right. If Ron has decided to get up close and personal, as you say, than I'm not interrupting either. Come I will get you to a restroom" He said taking her hand and escorting her down the hall to one of the public restrooms. Carl waited outside for her than escorted her back to Ron's cabin.

There they found both Beatrice and Ron coming out of the bathroom. Ron still clothed and Beatrice wrapped in a bath robe Ron had hanging on the back of the door, both were smiling.

"Bea" Amanda squeaked running over to embrace her best friend.

"Easy, easy, still in pain." Beatrice said

"Come on you two let's get something to eat and do some catching up" Carl called from the balcony "So far as I know, we are unable to find

Thomas or Joe. The search continues and we have upped the security at the gateway for the passengers coming and going today. They both could have changed their appearances. Anyone else?"

"Like I told Ron earlier, it's okay. It's over, I threw my necklace out of the elevator before the doors closed. Anyone could have it by now. I told that to Thomas when he was......" Beatrice paused "Anyways, he left me alive because I couldn't tell him where it is. I'm sure of it."

"It's not that easy Bea. They still need to find them and get them off of the ship or in prison or whatever" Amanda said "and before we do anything else, I think you need to call Kristy. She is probable going out of her mind by now."

"You called her? When did you do that?" Beatrice asked

"Last might when we couldn't find you. She talked to Carl and Ron as well. I told her that we found you and that you were resting and that I would call her with an update. I will get you the phone." Amanda got up to retrieve the phone.

Beatrice drank a glass of orange juice while nibbling on toast with butter and jam. Ron stood behind her gently rubbing her back. Beatrice smiled thinking about him touching her. The way he gently washed her body, skimming over every inch of her body. Massaging her scalp while washing her hair. The sound of Amanda's voice brought her back from her thoughts.

"I have Kristy on the line for you" Amanda said handing her the phone

"Kristy?" Beatrice said walking away from the group

Carl looked at Ron giving him a look of 'well'. He didn't want to say anything in front of Amanda.

"No Carl, I'm not going to tell her, not yet. If this means that she can relax and have a life without looking over her shoulder I'm going to give it to her" Ron tried to stress his urgency home for Carl.

"As long as you think you know what you're doing. I will go along with it for now. You like her don't you? Do you think she's a little young for you?" Carl said

"She's twenty one and I am twenty six. It's only a five year difference. And yes, I like her. I think she likes me too but I'm just letting her lead for right now." Ron responded with a great big smile on his face.

Beatrice stepped back out on the balcony "I know it has been hectic lately, but I would really like to get off the ship for a while. Do you think that might be possible?" Beatrice asked

Ron looked at Carl "Yes I don't see what harm it would do. Are you sure you feel up to it?" Carl asked her

"I think so as long as I take it slow" Beatrice said

"I have some things to do here. Maybe I can catch up with you later." Carl said to Amanda

Amanda smiled "That sounds great, I'll be waiting for you." She stepped over to Carl, placed her hands on his chest, stood up on her tip toes and kissed him. "Come Bea, let's go get ready"

"I'm going to need some help putting clothes on" Beatrice said following Amanda inside

"Let me know if you need my help" Ron yelled at Beatrice's back

She stopped, turned slowly, smiled and winked at Ron before continuing on.

"Something happened on the phone between Beatrice and Kristy." Ron said

"How can you tell, she didn't say anything." Carl said watching Ron's face

"I don't know it's just a hunch." Ron said "So how are things going on the search?"

"I can't find either of those scum. I am bringing in two more guys today. They are coming aboard while we are at port. I'm on the fence about this Joe." Carl said

"I will escort the women off the ship today. My goal is to be back by five." Ron said gathering the food cart and pushing it to the door.

"Sounds good, wish I could go with you today, I am working an arrangement to meet up with you later. Keep your phone on and I will keep in touch," Carl told Ron

Beatrice and Amanda dragged Ron in and out of every store. Being the gentleman that he was, he carried the majority of Beatrice's bags. She bought a shirt for all of the children at Kristy's including one for Kristy. Twice Ron noticed Joe lurking around. Beatrice was oblivious to her surroundings and seemed happy so Ron didn't say anything to her. Just before lunch, Beatrice talked Amanda into going for a walk on the beach.

Beatrice chose jeans due to the bruises on her legs. Amanda was in a short swirly skirt and sandals. Ron agreed to sit with the bags on a bench as long as the girls promised to stay where he could see them. Beatrice rolled her jeans up and removed her shoes. Ron watched both of them walk out into the water and run back laughing when a wave came too close. Amanda was bending over picking up seashells for Beatrice.

"What did Kristy have to say?" Amanda Asked Beatrice

"Oh you know how she is. One question after another." Beatrice said

"Did you tell her anything that Joe said? You know about Thomas killing your parents? About your necklace unlocking something? Did she tell you anything at all?" Amanda asked

"Basically all she said was that she and I need to sit down and have a serious conversation. That I need to take care of myself, call her every day and keep her informed of anything that happens." Beatrice said

Amanda could tell that she was keeping something from her. "Is that all she said?"

"No, she said that I needed to find the necklace" Beatrice said

"How on earth are you supposed to do that?" Amanda asked

"I don't know. I've been thinking about that since I got off the phone. I thought about talking to Ron or Carl about it. I kind of want to wait until Thomas is out of the picture" Beatrice said

"I don't know what is going on but I'm dying to find out. Hey look Carl is here" Amanda pointed as she started walking his way.

Beatrice shook her head and followed along. Looking around as she walked, Beatrice noticed Joe. He was standing under a tree watching her. Beatrice wanted to talk to him about what Kristy told her but she wanted to do it alone. A conversation left for a later date she thought. Reaching Ron, Carl and Amanda, Beatrice slowly sat on the bench next to Ron.

"How are you feeling? You noticed him too?" Ron questioned Beatrice

"I'm doing ok. It feels good to sit down for a minute and yes I saw him" Beatrice said leaning back on the bench.

Ron put his arm on the back of the bench. "Tonight is the formal dinner with the Captain, would you like to go?" Ron Asked

"I'd love to but I don't have anything to where. I thought I would be working for that dinner so I didn't bring anything." Beatrice said

"That's alright, I saw a store over there with a nice outfit in the window. After we get some lunch would you like to check it out?" Ron asked

"Sure" Beatrice said smiling.

Ron leaned over and planted a gentle kiss on Beatrice's lips. When their lips parted, he put his fore head against Beatrice's as she put her hand on the side of his face. They both looked into each other's eyes and smiled.

"Hey you two love birds, I'm hungry. Let's get some lunch" Amanda said interrupting Ron and Amanda.

At the lunch table, Ron looked at Beatrice over his drink "Hey, how are you feeling" He asked her

"I'm a little tired. Maybe we could head back soon?" Beatrice said

"I was thinking the same thing. I have some work to do before dinner tonight. Shall we go?" Carl said standing, reaching for his wallet, putting money down on the table.

Joe stood to the back of the restaurant watching Beatrice and her friends gather their things and head for the door. He gave them a thirty second head start before following. He knew he was taking a risk getting back on the ship, but there was as instinct he could not pin point to protect Beatrice. He was sure that Thomas was still on board searching for the necklace. He had to find him and stop him before Ron and his men stopped him. Joe stood on the dock and waited for the last shuttle back to the ship.

* * *

"You look lovely" Ron said to Beatrice when she stepped out of the bathroom wearing the dress he had bought for her. A black knee length dress that had a short sleeve to it to help hide the bruises.

Beatrice wore a gold watch she had brought with her. A birthday present from Kristy. "Thank you" She replied with a dip of her hip and a wince from the pain. "You look pretty good yourself"

A series of knocks on the door interrupted their conversation. Ron stepped to the door and opened it to find Carl in a black tuxedo with a young woman dressed in a long red gown, brunette hair in a half up and half down hair style smiling. "Oh Bea, you look wonderful" Amanda squeaked stepping to Beatrice taking her hands in hers and kissing her cheek. "My shoes look great with that dress"

"Yeah, you should have seen me putting on these pantyhose, that was a sight let me tell you" Beatrice said

"I asked if you wanted any help from me but you said no and kept the door locked." Ron said laughing.

"I think we should get going before we are late." Carl said holding the door open.

Carl arranged for a table for four to be set up for the group. Dinner consisted of Cucumber soup, Escargot, Caesar salad, Steak, roasted potatoes and vegetables. Beatrice and Amanda laughed over trying the cold cucumber soup and talked each other into attempting the Escargot. Ron sat with his back to the room. Scanning the dining area every few minutes. Towards the end of the meal, Ron spotted Joe. He seemed to be pre-occupied with a waiter standing in the middle of the room. Ron kept his eye one him as well when he noticed Joe's target.

The waiter stood near the middle of the room scanning the crowd. Ron put his napkin down on the table and leaned forward sitting on the edge of his chair. He spied Joe moving closer to the waiter hiding behind plants and poles in the room. Carl noticed Ron's body language, he watched Ron waiting for him to give him a clue as to what was going on. The waiter slowly turned and spotted Joe standing too close. Joe and the waiter starred at each other for a fraction of a second until the waiter started moving toward the doors. Joe started after him weaving in and out of the crowd.

"It's him" Ron whispered as he stood up and followed Joe and the waiter through the double doors.

"Who, where are you going?" Beatrice said as she got up and started to follow Ron.

Carl up and moving first and was now closing in on Ron. Beatrice and Amanda chucked their high heeled shoes and ran in their stocking feet. Beatrice felt the motion of the ship moving, lost her balance and fell into a potted plant. "Amanda, help" She shouted

Amanda back tracked, assisted Beatrice and they took off again towards the back of the ship. Amanda spotted a group of employees gathered by the doors leading out to the deck. Beatrice pushed her way through and rounded the corner. Arriving just I time to see Joe and Thomas fall over the edge of the ship into the water. Beatrice and Amanda ran to the railing and looked over. All Beatrice saw was dark water moving due to the engines roaring.

"What the hell" Asked Ron as he and Carl joined them at the railing

"Joe" Beatrice shouted leaning over the edge. "You have to save him"

"Why, that guy he was fighting with was Thomas. I feel bad but at least he's gone" Carl said

"You don't understand, he's my brother" Beatrice shouted with tears forming in her eyes.

Ron looked at Beatrice, chucked his jacket and shoes, jumped over the edge and was gone into the dark water.

"What the fuck, Ron" Carl shouted. Turning he ran inside.

"Beatrice are you sure?" Amanda shouted to her

"Yes, it's one of the things Kristy told me when we were on the phone earlier." Beatrice replied.

Chapter Thirteen

Beatrice sat with a blanket wrapped around her drinking coffee in Ron's cabin. Amanda had helped her change out of the dress and into a grey sweat suit. Thank full for her company, Beatrice still felt numb inside. "I'm done, done with all of this. At the next port I'm getting off of the ship and going home. I guess I should say Kristy's because I don't have a home." Beatrice said starring at the television.

"Bea, they are going to be alright. The Coast Guard are looking for them. Ron and Joe are smart capable men. Just have a little faith" Amanda said coming to kneel down at Beatrice's feet.

"I've got family coming out of the wood works and I finally fall for a guy and he kills himself trying to save one of them." Beatrice scoffed

"Come on let's get in bed and cuddle up and I will order a movie for us to watch. Some sort of comedy. I know that's your favorite." Amanda pleaded trying to do anything to get her mind off of everything.

"Sure, I'll try anything at this point" Beatrice said getting into the bed.

Amanda got a movie playing and laid down next to Beatrice. She watched Beatrice's eyes slowly close as she drifted off to sleep. Amanda left the movie playing and settled into sleep with Beatrice.

Beatrice gasped when she opened her eyes at the sight of Joe sitting in a chair next to the bed watching her. "How did you get here and where is Ron?" Beatrice asked

"Shh" Joe said putting his finger up to his mouth "Ron is asleep over there in the chair" pointing across the room.

"What time is it" Beatrice asked

"It's about 5:30 in the morning. We got in a couple of hours ago. The Coast Guard picked us up and brought us to the ship." Joe said with a small smile on his lips

"What about Thomas?" Beatrice asked

"The Coast Guard took him with them. I am not sure what will happen to him. Ron filled them in on all of the things he was doing on the ship and told them he wanted them to take him. Make sure he gets to the proper authorities." He replied

"He brought you back here? Why?" Beatrice asked

"He said that you said that I am your brother. Where would you get information like that?" Joe asked

"It was told by a reliable source that we had the same father, different mothers" Beatrice said shrugging her shoulders. "I'm thinking about getting off of the ship at the next port and going to find out more information about all of this. I was under the impression that I didn't have any family. That is why I was brought up in foster care. Now I seem to have family everywhere and people want me dead."

"I would be interested in hearing what this source has to say as well. I grew up not knowing my father. When I was fourteen, my mother passed away. I went to live with an Uncle who died three years later. I have been on my own ever since. And if our father was the same person, I'm going to be pissed that I didn't kill that bastard Thomas when I had the chance" Joe said

Ron cleared his throat and sat up in his chair interrupting Beatrice and Joe's conversation. Joe smiled and stood up walking out to the balcony to give them some privacy. Ron sat down on the bed next to Beatrice. She reached up and put her hand on the side of his face feeling the stubble on his cheek. Ron reached up and put his hand on top of hers leaning into her caress.

"I thought I would never see you again" Beatrice whispered

"I'm sorry, I don't know what came over me, but you seemed so scared and screamed my brother and I just acted" Ron whispered back and leaned in to kiss her

"You two want me to leave?" Amanda asked

Ron and Beatrice busted out laughing at the same time "No" Beatrice said hitting Amanda with her pillow.

Carl came in pushing a food cart "I brought breakfast, thought you people might be hungry" he said

"Good lord, the food just doesn't stop around here does it?" Beatrice said getting up off of the bed.

"And look who I found" Carl stated

"Felicia" Amanda and Beatrice shouted at the same time running over for a group hug.

Breakfast consisted of pastries, bagels, eggs, bacon, orange juice and coffee. The sun was coming up over the horizon as the girls caught up on the recent events over breakfast on the balcony. Joe sat with them so Beatrice could introduce him to Felicia. Ron and Carl stayed inside talking with a cup of coffee.

"I heard Beatrice tell Joe that she was planning on leaving the ship when we reach our next port to investigate all the things that have been happening to her" Ron told Carl

"You are not going to let her do that are you?" Carl asked

"How can I stop her?" Ron said

"I don't know, but she is the best thing to happen to you in a long time. I've known you for what, five years now or so? Finally you have let things go and allowed Beatrice to get close. I suggest you find out her feelings before you let her go." Carl said

"That's kind of hard to do since we are never alone. I have work and she wants off of the ship." Ron said

"Look, I will take Amanda to my cabin, Felicia can go to work and Joe, well he said he has a cabin on the ship somewhere. He can go there. Take some time to just talk to her." Carl suggested

"Yeah I guess" Ron said leaning back in his chair watching Beatrice talk and laugh with the group outside.

Carl stepped onto the balcony, "alright everyone, how about we let Beatrice get some rest for a while?" Carl stated to the group

"I have to be getting to work anyways" Felicia said as she got up "Will I see you guys later today?" She asked

"Sure we can make plans for later tonight" Amanda said

"I'm going to head out to my room and freshen up" Joe said standing up

Ron closed the door after everyone left.

Beatrice lay down on the bed and put her arm over her eyes. "I don't know what to do" She said out loud

"I can't tell you what to do but I can tell you what I want to do" Ron said putting his hand out to help her sit up. "I want to spend more time with you. Get to know all I can about you. I heard you tell Joe that you wanted to leave the ship at our next port. Which we will be pulling into in about an hour."

"I don't know what to do. But I will agree with you getting to know more of me." Beatrice smiled pulling Ron down on the bed with her.

"I could get used to this" Ron said kissing Beatrice soft and gentle at first then moving to demanding, putting his hand under her shirt against her skin rubbing gently.

A series of knocks on the door brought a grunt out of Ron "I'm going to kill whoever is at the door" he said getting up.

"Good Morning, I thought I would stop by and check on my patient before I head to the clinic" The doctor said when Ron opened the door.

"Come on in" Ron said opening the door and moving to the side

"How are we feeling today? Any headaches, nausea, vomiting?" the doctor asked

"No, none of that. I'm just sore but it's getting better" Beatrice said smiling.

"It looks like things are healing pretty good. Just take it easy for a couple more days." He said putting his instruments back in his bag. "Call me if you need me"

"Thanks I will" Beatrice said

"Now where were we?" Ron said pulling his shirt up over his head and tossing it to the floor. He crawled up the bed to Beatrice, placing his lips on hers, reaching his hand up under her shirt.

Beatrice helped pull her sweat shirt up and over her head before placing her hands on Ron's back. Sliding her fingers just under the waist band of his pants bringing a moan from Ron who stopped and looked Beatrice in the eye. "Are you sure you're up for this?" Ron asked "I don't want to push you"

"Shut up and kiss me" Beatrice said smiling

Laying with her head on his chest, Beatrice closed her eyes and drifted off to sleep. Ron with one arm around Beatrice slowly stroking her hair and back could not keep his eyes off of her. Wondering what it was about Beatrice that made him put his guard down. Whatever it was, he decided to relax and let it happen. At some point in his thinking Beatrice started moaning and kicking in her sleep.

"Hey baby, wake up." Ron said stroking her back. "Beatrice I'm here it's okay" Ron said louder this time giving Beatrice a small shake.

Beatrice opened her eyes and scanned her surroundings. Once she realized she was in Ron's arms, she relaxed replacing her head on his chest.

"How are you doing?" Ron asked "what were you dreaming about?"

"He was just hitting and hitting me. I tried to stand but I kept falling. The last time I fell down, he started kicking me." Beatrice whispered "I'm not sure exactly what made him stop. Maybe he believed me about throwing the necklace out the elevator doors."

"I'm am just sick that you got hurt. That I couldn't stop it or prevent it. I'm so sorry Beatrice" Ron said

"What's done is done. I'm feeling better and you shouldn't be sorry for anything. It's over, the necklace is gone and so is Thomas. All I have to do now is go home and find out what all this is about" Beatrice said

"So you're going to leave then?" Ron asked shifting Beatrice off of him, removing the sheet and reaching for his pants.

"Well, I think I have to don't you think?" Beatrice said propping herself up on her elbow.

Ron started shutting down yet again. She was leaving and there wasn't anything he could do about it. "I'll have your luggage brought here from storage after I take a shower." He said walking into the bathroom.

Beatrice reached for her phone and called Kristy. "Hi it's just me." Beatrice said when Kristy answered

"Hi honey, how are you feeling?" Kristy asked

"Better thanks. Just thought I would check in with you. Um…. is it alright if I come to stay with you for a little while? Just until I figure all of this out?" Beatrice asked

"You know you are always welcome here for as long as you want."

"Kristy, I just can't wrap my head around all of this. And well you said you had some answers but not over the phone. What else can I do?"

Kristy wanted to hug Beatrice and tell her everything but scared at the same time that Beatrice would hate her for it. "There is time for that. Honey just have some fun, finish your cruise first. Do something for yourself for once. What about this guy Ron? Is he still in the picture?" Kristy asked

Beatrice smiled at the way he was in the picture this morning. "Yes he is still in the picture." Beatrice said glad that Kristy could not see the red in her cheeks.

"Great, go have some fun would you. I don't want to see you here until another three to five days" Kristy said laughing

"Okay, okay, okay I'll stay here and see what I can get into for a couple of days. I'll check in with you tomorrow or so, bye" Beatrice said hanging up.

Stretching made Beatrice wince from the pain. Something she had to get used to for a couple more days. Although she was feeling better than before. Ron was taking a long time in the bathroom Beatrice thought. She got up and put the robe on from the chair near the bed and knocked on the bathroom door. Ron didn't open the door, he stood starring into the mirror holding the necklace in his hand trying to decide what to do.

"Ron, are you still in there" Beatrice called out as she knocked again

Ron opened the door "Sorry, the bathroom's all yours. I will call for your luggage while you freshen up." Ron said stepping past Beatrice

"Wait, can you hold off on calling for the luggage? I think I am going to stick around for a little bit. That is if you don't mind?" Beatrice asked

Ron stopped but didn't turn around to face Beatrice "Yeah sure I don't mind" Ron said before continuing on to the balcony.

Frowning, Beatrice followed Ron out to the balcony "What's wrong"

"Nothing" Ron said not turning to face her

"Don't give me that I can tell. Did I do something?" Beatrice asked

Ron turned to face Beatrice "I have spent a long time keeping myself from getting close to anyone, then comes you."

"Bea, Bea" Amanda shouted busting in to Ron's cabin with Carl right behind her.

"Right here, what's going on?" Beatrice announced from the balcony

"Look, just look what Carl gave me" Amanda said holding out her left hand

Beatrice took her hand to see a large diamond ring with little diamond clusters on each side. She brought her eyes up to meet with Amanda's "Does this mean what I think it means?"

Amanda started shaking her head up and down as tears started coming. "He asked me and I said yes"

Both Beatrice and Amanda hugged while Ron and Carl watched them. "Are you sure about his man? It's only been a few days." Ron asked Carl

"Yes, I've never met anyone like her. I'm not getting any younger, she makes me happier than I have ever been and I think I make her happy" Carl said smiling watching Amanda and Beatrice hugging, laughing and talking.

"Beatrice told me that she wants to stay around a little bit longer but what good is that going to do, she's just going to leave" Ron said

"Does she make you happy?" Carl asked

"Of course she does. But……" Ron said

"But what? You need to let go of the past and grab a hold of the now. It could lead to the future. One that might last a life time. Look, we both joined this cruise thinking it was going to be our last and look what happened, we both met someone. Talk to her, she might say something good." Carl said grabbing Ron's shoulder and directing him inside.

"Bea you have to be there. Promise me you will be there." Amanda pleaded with Beatrice

"Of course I will be there. When are you thinking about doing this?" Beatrice asked

"I don't know, we didn't talk about a date but you will be the first to know." Amanda said smiling clapping her hands.

"Come on Amanda, let's let these people get going with their day" Carl said holding his hand out for Amanda to take it.

"We will catch up with you guys after Beatrice gets dressed for the day. What are you plans?" Ron asked

"I think we are going to go ashore for a while, Catalina awaits." Carl said standing at the open door.

"I'll call you in a little bit" Ron said

Chapter Fourteen

"Look, I told you that I am through with the lies. I am done with all of this, I am going to do what I think is right. First and foremost, I am going to find out if Beatrice and I are really related." Joe shouted into the phone

"You will do no such thing. Get yourself back on track and find that necklace. Someone on that ship has to know what happened to it." Aengus shouted back and disconnected

Joe thought for a minute and stormed out of his room in search for Beatrice. He was not going to take this anymore. He was solving this mess if it was the last thing he did. Knocking on Ron's cabin door Joe received silence. "Shit" he said out loud walking away.

Beatrice and Ron caught up with Amanda and Carl for lunch. Sitting at a table outside so Beatrice could smell the ocean, Ron sat watching Beatrice smile and laugh with Amanda. Twice she reached over and touched his knee without looking at him. Each time chills ran up his spine.

"Hello, Ron are you here?" Carl asked

Ron brought his head out of the clouds and looked at Carl "Yeah?"

"I was asking you if you would be my best man when I get hitched." Carl said laughing

"Of course I will. I wouldn't miss this for the world" Ron said

"Hey Felicia, over here" Beatrice called. "Amanda has something to show you" Beatrice stood up when she saw Felicia and her friend walking towards them.

Beatrice let Amanda fill Felicia in on all the good news. Turning her head, Beatrice caught sight of Joe walking down the street. She got up and ran to catch up with him.

"Hey Joe, wait" Beatrice shouted to get his attention

Joe turned and smiled when he saw Beatrice coming. "You stalking me now?" He asked laughing.

Beatrice stunned by the sound of his laugh took a second to answer. "No, I tried to find you on the ship earlier but didn't know how. I thought that we could talk for a little bit. I don't know exchange information?"

"What kind of information?"

"You know, phone numbers, addresses. Things like that. I just find out that we very possibly could be related and I don't want to lose contact. You know?" Beatrice said getting shy all of a sudden.

"I know what you mean. Look I have something's to take care of right now, can we get together later tonight back on the ship?" Joe asked

"Sure, how do I get in touch with you?"

"I will find you" Joe said smiling. He winked at her and turned on his heels.

Beatrice slowly walked back to the restaurant. She was thinking that Joe was up to something but what? She did not know him very well, not at all actually. Stepping into the seating area, she looked up to see everyone starring at her. "What" Beatrice asked sitting down in her chair.

The entire group started laughing "Nothing Bea, nothing. What did Joe have to say?" Amanda asked

Beatrice was sure that she was missing something but no one was talking. "I asked if we could do some talking later. He said that he would find me later on the ship. I have this feeling he is up to something,"

"It's okay baby, we will find him later" Ron said putting his arm around Beatrice's shoulder gently caressing it.

Beatrice felt his touch and butterflies fluttered in her stomach. She had only had one serious relationship in her life and that was two years ago. Granted she was only twenty one now, but she felt older than that. Her thought drifted off to earlier this morning. The passion she shared with Ron is not something she would easily forget. Closing her eyes she could still feel his kisses on her neck, his hands on her thighs.

"Beatrice" Ron whispered in her ear

This shocked Beatrice out of her revere. "Uh? What?" She said opening her eyes to find everyone looking at her.

"You started moaning. You feeling alright?" Ron asked. Still whispering close to her ear.

Beatrice felt the heat in her cheeks. "Oh, yes I'm fine" She said reaching for her iced tea.

Beatrice walked back to the ship with her hand intertwined with Ron's. Listening to Amanda go on and on about her wedding plans. She wanted to get married on the last day of the cruise. Somewhere by the pool having the Captain performing the ceremony.

"Ron, when we get back can we see if anyone has turned in my necklace? Maybe ask around to see if anyone comes forward with it?" Beatrice asked

"I think we can arrange something" Ron said bringing her hand up to kiss the back of her hand.

Carl arranged a special dinner for the six of them to celebrate Amanda saying yes. Ron was dressed in a pair of black jeans, white shirt unbuttoned at the collar and a black dinner jacket. Beatrice wore a lavender ankle length dress with a pair of matching heels.

"You look lovely" Ron said talking Beatrice's hand leading her over to a chair "sit down, I want to talk to you before we go"

"Sure, is there anything wrong? Did you find my necklace? Do you want me to....."

Ron reached down and took her chin lifting it up to meet his eyes and cut off her question's with a kiss "Just listen for a minute will you?" He asked "I've been doing some thinking, when you go to investigate this business of your family, the necklace and Joe, I want to go with you. That is if you'll let me." Ron said getting down on one knee in front of Beatrice so they were eye to eye.

"You would do that? Don't you have to work? What about the ship? Why?" Beatrice asked

"Good Lord woman you ask a lot of question's" Ron said smiling "Yes, I would do that, No I don't need to work, the ship will do just fine without me and because I love you and don't want to lose you"

Beatrice brought her hands up to her mouth then threw herself at him wrapping her arms around his neck knocking him back onto the floor. Beatrice landed on top of him laughing. "Yes, I would love for you to come with me" Beatrice said kissing him. Ron grabbed the back of her head and depended the kiss.

"I think we should get going before we don't make it at all" Beatrice said breaking from the kiss.

"Then I want to get you back here so I can hear more of those moaning noises you were making at lunch" Ron said smacking her behind causing her to yelp. Ron rolled her off of him, stood and helped Beatrice up off of the floor. "Before we go, I want to give you something" Ron said taking her hand palm side up, he reached into his jacket pocket and produced her necklace. Slowly he laid it in her hand.

"You found it" Beatrice whispered as tears started forming in her eyes

"I got to the elevator just after the doors closed. The woman in the room by the elevators picked it up and gave it to me when she saw me." Ron explained

Beatrice took the chain, unlatched to clasp and attempted to put it on when Ron took it from her "turn around" Ron told her. She did as instructed, lifting her hair to allow him easier access.

"Thank you" Beatrice whispered moving to the mirror.

"Beautiful" Ron said stepping behind her placing a kiss on her neck "Let's go party shall we?"

*   *   *

"So it's all set then? Day after tomorrow by the pool. I called my mother and she is going to meet us when we get back to Long Beach. She said she almost fainted on the floor when I told her. She was sure she would never unload me" Amanda said laughing

"What about the dress?" Felicia asked

"I saw this dress in the shop on the fifth floor. I want to check it out tomorrow. Bea you will come with me?" Amanda asked

"I wouldn't miss it. I should get a dress too and Felicia has to get one too" Beatrice said

"We'll make arrangements to meet later in the afternoon when Felicia gets done. Sound good Felicia?" Amanda asked

"Sure I can't wait. I think we are going to get going now. Just let me know what time tomorrow" Felicia said standing, hugging Beatrice and Amanda before taking Paul's out stretched hand.

Joining the men, Beatrice sat down next to Ron and Amanda sat on Carl's lap. "After tomorrow you won't be able to get rid of me" Amanda said to Carl kissing him.

"Come on baby, let's leave them to their planning" Ron said standing and holding his hand out for Beatrice. "I want to hear more of those sounds you make"

Beatrice punched Ron's chest "I can't believe you said that" she said laughing

*   *   *

Ron had his arm draped over Beatrice holding her close to him sleeping. Beatrice lay awake thinking that she wanted travel and adventure and that is just what she got. Trying to imagine what kind of adventure she was going to have when she went home, Beatrice realized that Joe had not come to find her since they spoke last. She drifted off to sleep thinking about finding him in the morning.

Beatrice stood trying to see the water at the bottom of the cliff. Wondering what she was doing there in the first place. Turning towards a noise behind her she noticed a large rock illuminated by the moon. Someone grabbed her arm and pulled her away from the edge of the cliff causing Beatrice to scream.

Beatrice faintly heard her name being called and pressure on her shoulders. "Get off me" Beatrice shouted

"Beatrice it's me. Wake up, you're having a bad dream" Ron said gently shacking her shoulders.

Beatrice opened her eyes to see Ron sitting next to her with his hands on her shoulders. "What happened?" She asked

"You started thrashing around and screaming in your sleep. What was that all about?" Ron explained

"I has dreaming I guess. It was weird, this is the second time I dreamt about this one cliff area." Beatrice said

Ron retrieved a glass of water and handed it to Beatrice as he sat down next to her on the bed. "Thanks" she said taking a drink.

"As a child I had night terrors the doctors called it. They stopped when I got older but since my last birthday they have come back." Beatrice explained

Ron turned off the bed side light and laid back down taking Beatrice in his arms kissing her softly. Then moved to demanding, teeth clashing and tongue searching. Shifting Beatrice underneath him, Ron placed kisses along her jaw and down her neck. Just like magic Beatrice's body responded and before she knew it, he was between her legs bringing the moans and the sound of his name to her lips.

Beatrice yawned and stretched, feeling the soreness in muscles she didn't even know she had. Rolling over, she tried go get up without disturbing Ron and headed for the bathroom. Showering and dressing for the day was getting easier as her injuries healed. Finding Joe was first on her list of things to do. Ron was awake but still in bed when Beatrice came out dressed in jeans and a light pink blouse.

"Hi, how are you feeling today and just where do you think you're going?" Ron asked

"I'm feeling much better thank you and I am going to try and find Joe today. What are you doing today?" Beatrice retorted

"I'm hanging out with you today and you don't need to look very far for Joe. He stopped by already and we are to meet him by the pool in half an hour" Ron said getting up and heading for the bathroom.

Beatrice noticed that there was an assortment of beagles, cream cheese and fruit set out on the table along with coffee and juice. She fixed a plate and went to the balcony to wait for Ron. Looking out at the water, she thought she saw a whale come up for air. Standing and starring out at the water she saw the whale come up again, This brought a smile to her lips and an excited feeling to her soul.

"What so interesting out there?" Ron asked joining her with a cup of coffee.

"I saw a whale. It came up twice" Beatrice said smiling

Ron smiled, reached over and kissed the top of her head "You ready to do this?" Ron asked smacking her behind.

"You like doing that don't you?" Beatrice said following him in while rubbing her right cheek.

"Yes I do. Ready?" Ron replied

"Yes, let's get this over with" Beatrice said heading for the door.

The ship was rocking due to the waves forcing Beatrice to hang onto Ron's arm for support. In the elevator, Beatrice lost her balance and slammed into Ron forcing him to hit the wall of the elevator. "I will never tire of having you in my arms" Ron said kissing Beatrice. The ding announcing the doors where opening didn't persuade Ron to let go of her.

The elderly couple that stepped on smiled "What it is to be young" The woman said

"Tell me about it" Ron replied causing everyone to laugh

The ding came again announcing the end of the ride. Ron held the door open for all to exit. "Have a wonderful day" Ron said to the couple

"Thank you, and please do the same" the man said assisting his wife out of the elevator.

Beatrice and Ron found Joe standing with his hip against the bar by the pool. It wasn't even noon and he had a drink in his hand. Coming closer, Joe made eye contact with Ron and indicated to a table off to the side.

Ron sat with his back to the railing facing the pool area. Beatrice took the chair to his right and Joe to his left. "Morning" Ron said

"Yeah" Joe said

"Okay now that we have the testosterone on the table, can we get down to business please" Beatrice asked

Joe smiled his full on smile "Sure"

"Tell me what you know and why you were sent and why my necklace and who is behind this?" Beatrice asked

"Wow all at once huh? All I know is that I was supposed to retrieve your necklace. That the key and the heart open a box. I don't know what is in the box or why it is so important. A man named Aengus sent me." Joe explained

"Who is this Aengus person? And why did he send you?" Beatrice asked persisting with her questioning

"After my mother died, I was sent to live with my uncle in Ireland. I was told that my father died when I was young. My Uncle was in the business of making people disappear and I was put to work at a young age. Doing errands and things. My Uncle moved us to the United States five years ago when a deal went wrong and we had to run. He died last year and I traveled back to Ireland to try and hunt down any family I had left." Joe paused to take a drink

"So how do I fit into all of this?" Beatrice prompted

"That is when Aengus brought me on with him when I was looking for work. That is how I ended up looking for you and your necklace. It was my first mission on my own," Joe said

"Okay, then what is your last name?" Ron asked

"My Uncle changed my last name to Carrick but the last name I was given was O'Riley" Joe said

Beatrice gasped "O'Riley really?"

"Yes why, do you know that name?" Joe asked

"Yes, it is the last name of the woman who has raised me" Beatrice said leaning back in her chair. "Kristy said to enjoy the rest of my time here and that we needed to talk when I went back there. She also told me that you were my brother. She knows more than she would tell me over the phone. She seemed relieved when I told her that I lost my necklace." Beatrice's voice was barely a whisper.

"What are your plans now?" Ron asked Joe

"I was planning on sticking with Beatrice and trying to find out what is going on. Obviously there is more going on here than either of us knows" Joe said

"I think you should come with me to meet Kristy. That is if I can trust you?" Beatrice said

"Well, I am hoping my sending Thomas over the edge might have proven something" Joe shrugged his shoulders "I'm not working for Aengus anymore, he doesn't know that yet though. I want to find out what is going on myself. Obviously there is a story and I want to find out what it is"

Beatrice looked at Ron for a second then to Joe "Well, I guess we can talk to Kristy together then"

"I would really appreciate that. I think it would also help if we can locate the necklace before everyone leaves as well. Thomas told me that you ditched it somewhere in your struggle." Joe said

"Yes you could be right. I can ask around" Beatrice said

"That is what I am going to be doing today. Trying to track down the necklace" Joe said

"Okay, you do that and then we can meet up later?" Beatrice asked

"Sounds like a plan. I will catch up with you later this evening" Joe said as he stood and departed the table.

"You didn't tell him about the necklace. Why?" Ron asked

"I don't know. I just don't trust him completely yet. Sound weird?" Beatrice said

"No not at all. It was a smart move. Come, let's find Amanda. This wedding is supposed to be happening some time tomorrow" Ron said holding out his hand for Beatrice

Chapter Fifteen

THE DRESS THAT AMANDA PICKED out was floor length, cream colored and strapless. Beatrice picked out a short dress the color of mint. Bringing out the color of her emerald eyes. Felicia went with a soft pink floor length dress with a high neck. A sheet of glass had been laid over the pool with a laddish work arch laced with flowers at one end. Ron and Carl wore black tuxedoes with white roses in their lapels. Joe, Paul and Amanda's mother were the only other attendees. Beatrice and Felicia stood by Amanda with Ron next to Carl. During the entire ceremony, Ron and Beatrice starred at each other.

"You may now kiss the bride" The Captain announced

Everyone clapped and whistled when Carl took Amanda in his arms and kissed her. Beatrice and Felicia reached for their tissues that were tucked into their bouquet of flowers to catch the tears.

Cake and Champaign was served on the deck. "To my wife" Carl said raising his glass in a toast

"To my wife" everyone said in Unisom raising their glasses.

"I'm very happy for you" Beatrice said embracing Amanda for what might be the last time.

"Thanks Bea" Amanda said dabbing at the tears on her face with her tissue

"Why the tears? You should be happy" Beatrice asked

"I'm just going to miss you. I feel like I'm ditching you." Amanda said tossing her arms in the air.

"Listen, you need to get your life started. I'll by just fine. Ron and I talked last night and he is coming with me and Joe to talk with Kristy. He said that he was not going to let me go alone. I will talk to you when you get back." Beatrice said

"Hey you two, what's with the tears? This is supposed to be a party" Ron said approaching Beatrice and Amanda.

"It's a girl thing" Beatrice said smiling through her tears

"We should get going soon. They need to get their honey moon started and we have a long drive ahead of us" Ron said stepping away to join Carl and the others.

"Come on let's go say good bye" Beatrice said taking Amanda by the arm leading her over to the others.

*   *   *

One last hug and a wave good bye and Beatrice parted from Amanda. Ron had rented a SUV to drive her and Joe to Stockton. Amanda and Carl left for their hotel before heading off to Hawaii for a week. Beatrice settled into the front seat while Joe and Ron loaded their luggage into the back.

Once Ron got in the driver's seat, he reached over and caressed Beatrice's face. Rubbing her cheek with his thumb. "Ready?" He asked

Beatrice placed her hand on top of his, leaned into his touch and shook her head yes.

Half an hour into the ride and she heard Joe softly snoring in the back seat "I'm scared Ron." Beatrice said

"I can only imagine baby. But we are going to figure this out and then you can relax" Ron said

"What if we can't figure this out? Everything that I've been told just sounds ridiculous. And the fact that Kristy has something to do with this is even worse. I trusted her. I even called her Mom" Beatrice said looking out her window.

"Why don't you close your eyes and relax. It will make the drive go by faster" Ron said

"Yeah, perhaps you're right" Beatrice said settling down in her seat and closing her eyes.

Ron just couldn't imagine what Beatrice was going through. This situation is one he had never heard of before. He was happy that he took

Carl's advice and followed his heart. His wish was that Beatrice would not get hurt in all of this drama that had followed her.

"Hey, I could use a drink or something. Can we stop somewhere?" Joe said from the back seat interrupting Ron's thoughts.

"Sure, there is a gas station in about five miles. Will that be good?" Ron asked

"Yeah, I could go for some food as well." Joe said stretching "She asleep?"

"Yes, she's been out for over an hour now" Ron said

"You don't trust me do?" Joe asked Ron

"To be honest, no I don't. I don't trust anyone involved with this mess" Ron said

"I guess I can't blame you. I'm not sure what is going on or who I can believe myself. I appreciate you letting come along" Joe said

"You're here because it's important to Beatrice. If it were up to me you would be on your way to being Thomas's cell mate" Ron said

Ron turned to glance at Beatrice when she started to stir. He reached out and touched her shoulder. "Hey, we are stopping for gas and food. You hungry?" He asked

"Not really hungry, but I could use the bathroom?" She answered

"We are almost there now" Ron said

Beatrice turned in her seat to take a look at Joe. "Hi" she said

"Hi, feeling better?" Joe asked.

"Some" Beatrice said turning back to face front.

"Okay, everyone out" Ron said reaching his hand out to Beatrice "Here"

Beatrice reached out and took the money Ron handed her. "Thanks" She said with a smile.

Snacks, a full tank of gas and they were back on the road. An hour left to go and Beatrice was getting nervous. She had no idea what she was going to encounter once she saw Kristy. The one good thing is that she was going to get to see Billy. It seemed like forever since she got to talk to him.

"It's going to be alright. Just relax and enjoy the rest of the ride" Ron said reaching out for Beatrice's hand.

Beatrice reached out, took his hand and intertwined her fingers with his. "Thank you for being so nice to me." She said to Ron

"No sweat baby" Ron said laughing

Beatrice loved how he can lighten her mood with just a touch and a smile. Coming into town made Beatrice smile as well. Rolling down her window and taking in the air that only Stockton was known for made her laugh.

"What's so funny?" Ron asked

"It's nothing, just feeling like I'm home is all" Beatrice said

"What's that smell?" Ron asked

"The sewer" Joe said

"Hey" Beatrice said turning around to look at Joe "It is a certain odor that only Stockton has. It's home to me"

Tapping Beatrice on the shoulder Ron asked "What exit did you say to take?"

"Oh sorry, Hammer Lane, go right on the off ramp. Down a few lights then we are turning left." Beatrice said

"What street do I turn left? Ron asked laughing

"I'm sorry I'm just a little excited. Don Avenue turn left and then take your second right. It will be the third house on the right" Beatrice said

Pulling up to the house, Beatrice froze with her hand on the door handle starring out the window. She didn't move until she saw Kristy step out onto the porch. Slowly Beatrice opened the car door, stepped onto the sidewalk and walked towards Kristy.

Kristy staring at Beatrice walked towards her not sure what kind of reception she was going to get. The closer Kristy got to Beatrice, she could see the tears streaming down her face. Kristy wrapped her in her arms and hugged her tight. Beatrice and Kristy stood like that until Beatrice pulled away.

"I'm sorry, I don't know what came over me" Beatrice said wiping her tears.

"It's fine honey, why don't you and your friends come inside for a spell?" Kristy said "I've got a lasagna in the oven with garlic cheese bread"

Beatrice made the proper introductions with Ron, Joe and Kristy then led Ron and Joe into the living room. Ron and Beatrice sat next to each other on the love seat and Joe sat in one of the nearby chairs.

"Is anyone thirsty? Can I get anyone a beer?" Kristy asked trying to stall the conversation.

"A beer would be great, thank you" Ron said

"Yes please" Joe said

"I'll help you" Beatrice said following Kristy into the kitchen

"Ron seems nice and he's handsome. How are things between you? How old is he? Is he nice to you?" Kristy asked

Beatrice laughed "I forgot how much I missed you and your questions. In answer, things between us are good, he's twenty six and yes he's very nice to me" Beatrice said taking two of the beers from her.

"Bea, do me a favor. Can you please be open minded about the things I'm going to tell you tonight? I've dreaded this moment for so many years. I just don't want you to hate me" Kristy said

"Yes, I promise to be open minded" Beatrice said doing her best at a smile. Following Kristy into the living room.

"Dinner has about another thirty minutes left. So why don't I get started" Kristy said sitting down taking a deep breath "Beatrice, Joe is your brother. I am your Aunt. Your father was my brother. Our family originated in Ireland. That is where your father met Joe's mother. There has always been a feud between the O'Riley and the Cassidy families. Bea, your father had to flee Ireland. That is how he ended up here" Kristy paused and reached under the sofa and produced a small wooden box. "This was your father's. In here are some pictures of you, Joe with your father"

Joe took one of the pictures Kristy produced from the box. He stood and started to pace in the room. "I don't understand. I was always told that my father died when I was young." Joe said.

"He tried to get you and your mother out of Ireland, but your grandfather wouldn't allow it. He took you and your mother away. He could not find you. That is when he found your mother Beatrice" Kristy said

"All that sounds semi normal, but what do I have to do with all that and how does my mother's necklace fit into all of this?" Beatrice asked "Wait, then why isn't my last name O'Riley?"

"Your father and mother decided to give you your mother's last name as a way to protect you. We thought it worked too. That is until your mother's death, you coming to live with me was our backup plan" Kristy said

"You mentioned this feud? What is that all about?" Ron asked interrupting

"It's been about land in Ireland. As far back as I can remember, my family has talked about this land. The story goes that my great grandfather lost this land because of a deal gone bad. But before anyone could take control of the land they needed the deed. My great grandfather supposedly hid the deed. He died before he could tell anyone where he hid it. The search has been on going since." Kristy said "I think dinner is ready, excuse me while I check"

"This seems too unreal. Feuds over land and deeds. This is just crazy" Beatrice said standing and stalking into the kitchen

Beatrice entered into the kitchen and picked up the plates and utensils for the table. Picking up as if she never left, as if any of this never happened. Carting her items to the table, Beatrice set them out.

"Come on everyone let's eat" Kristy called

Kristy passed the bread first then the lasagna. Once everyone had what they needed Kristy began again "So tell me Joe, how are you involved in all of this?"

"After my mother died, I went to live with my Uncle, he brought us to the United States. We lived here for a few years until he died. After that I went back to Ireland to try and find some of my family. That is when I met up with Aengus. He took me under his wing. Retrieving the necklace was my first assignment." Joe explained

Kristy froze with her fork half way to her mouth at the sound of Aengus's name. "Excuse me, did you say Aengus?" Kristy asked "Are you absolutely sure?"

"Yes, why do you know him?" Joe asked

"This is starting to make more sense to me now" Kristy said putting her napkin down on the table and getting up. She walked out of the room leaving everyone else looking at each other. Kristy returned with the telephone. "Everyone be quiet for a minute, I'm going to make a call"

"Who are you calling?" Beatrice asked

"Aengus" Kristy said

In an instant you heard the clank of silverware hitting plates. Everyone's jaw dropped to the floor at the same time. Beatrice put down her fork and leaned back in her chair waiting to hear this conversation.

"Aengus, it's Kristy" She said into the phone

"Yes, have you heard from Beatrice?" He asked

"Yes, she said that she wanted to come here for a while. Do you think that is wise? What should I tell her?" Kristy asked

"Did she locate the necklace?" Aengus asked

"Not that I know of. You wouldn't know who sent Joe out here do you?" Kristy asked

"No not yet. See if you can find out if she has the necklace. I will call you back shortly." Aengus said hanging up

As soon as Kristy put the phone down, Joe's phone rang. "It's Aengus" Joe said

"Answer but don't tell him that you are here" Kristy said

"Yeah" Joe said answering the phone

"Beatrice has plans to travel back to Stockton. Find out what they are and have you recovered the necklace?" Aengus asked

"I told you I'm done with this. You are going to have find someone else to do your dirty work" Joe said

"And I'm telling you that if you value your life, you will do as I say" Aengus yelled. Loud enough for the rest to hear.

Kristy and Ron started shaking their heads in a 'yes' motion trying to get Joe to agree with him. That would prevent him from sending someone else for the moment.

"Fine" Joe said into the phone and hung up.

Ron, who had been listening and watching everything spoke up before anyone else could. "This Aengus person has been playing both sides of the fence. He knew where Beatrice was all these years and that she had the necklace. Why didn't he just take it years ago? Why wait until now?" Ron asked

"Because he found out the box containing the deed to the land can only be opened by the necklace. He played me by getting information from me about the where a bouts of Beatrice and the necklace. I didn't even know about that part until you showed up here, Joe. He has been acting like he wanted to keep her safe" Kristy explained

"And does he know where this box is?" Ron asked

"Not that I know of" Kristy said

"Not that I know of either" Joe added "He has been telling me that he doesn't have it but at the rate we are going he could be lying about that too"

"I don't get it. Who is this Aengus?" Beatrice asked

"He is my Uncle" Kristy said "And if he sent Thomas, then this is all bad"

"What do we do from here?" Beatrice asked looking from Kristy to Ron

"Let's start with finishing this fine meal and we can talk after" Ron said reaching over and squeezing Beatrice's hand.

"Yes, lets. Tell me what you did on the cruise. How was it? Where is Amanda?" Kristy asked

It took Beatrice thirty minutes to fill Kristy in on everything that happened. The cleaning and the vacuum incident had everyone laughing. She told Kristy about the food on the ship and at the ports they stopped at. Tears started for Kristy when Beatrice told her about Thomas. Beatrice decided to keep her information rated 'G' when it came to Ron. She told her all about Carl and Amanda including the wedding and the dress.

"I'm am so excited for Amanda. Is this Carl a good guy?" Kristy asked

"One of the best" Beatrice added "They went to Hawaii for a week on a honey moon"

"Wow that's great" Kristy said "Why don't we go into the living room?" Kristy suggested

"You two ladies retire to the living room and leave the dishes to the men" Ron said stacking the dishes

"You don't have to do that" Kristy said

"No, you two do some catching up. This won't take us long" Ron said smiling as he headed into the kitchen with Joe on his heels carrying the rest of the lasagna and bread.

Once in the kitchen, Joe started looking for something to put the leftover food into. Ron started the water for the dishes.

"How on the up and up are you with all of this?" Ron asked Joe

Joe paused and looked at Ron, "The moment I saw her, I felt something between us. Now, I find out that that bastard Aengus had my parents killed. I'm totally on the up and up. I'm in this till the end"

"I'm going to need to count on you for the plan that I'm going to suggest. If I can't count on you than let me know now and we will do this without you" Ron said

"You can count on me" Joe said stressing his statement by getting close to Ron's face

In the living room, Beatrice filled Kristy in on the 'R' rated version to the Ron story. Kristy was happy for her.

"Oh Bea, I just wanted to tell you how sorry I am for all of this. We were just trying to keep you safe from those people. We didn't want what happened to your parents to happen to you" Kristy said getting close to Beatrice and taking her hand.

"I understand that. I wish I knew why? Why now I mean. You know? And what do I do about it?" Beatrice said.

"Don't you worry about that, I have a plan." Ron said coming into the room with Joe on his heels.

Chapter Sixteen

RON AND JOE TOOK SEATS on the couch. Joe leaned back in his spot and crossed his legs. Ron sat on the edge of his cushion, elbows on his knees, hands clasped together. Beatrice and Kristy leaned back in their chairs, crossed their legs, right over left and put their hands in their laps.

"'I think that we should go to Ireland, do our own investigation. See what we can find out. Maybe we can confront this Aengus directly." Ron began

"I can't leave the children" Kristy said

"The three of us can go. Beatrice, Joe and myself." Ron said pointing at them in turn.

"I don't know about that. What do you think Bea?" Kristy asked

"Shoot, I'm game. I would love to get this over with so I can just live. You know?" Beatrice said

"I will make the reservations" Ron said getting out his phone

"Isn't that going to be expensive?" Kristy asked

"Don't worry about the cost. I've got it" Ron said

Beatrice stood and started to pace in the room. Joe sat back, legs crossed, his left arm resting on the arm of the couch watching Beatrice pace. Kristy watched him watching Beatrice.

"What's your take on all of this?" Kristy asked Joe

"I think it's wise to do this. I can play Aengus. He doesn't know I'm with Beatrice. This could work" Joe said

"I don't want anything to happen to Beatrice" Kristy paused when she realized her mistake "And of course you too" she added

Joe chuckled "Yeah, I get it. You don't trust me?" he said to Kristy

"No I don't. I'm sorry to say that, but it's the truth. And let me tell you, that if you have anything to do with Bea getting hurt, I will come for you' Kristy said

Joe smiled as he put his hands up in an 'I give up' fashion "I get it, I get it. I will do my best to protect her" Joe said

Kristy wanted to believe him but she just wasn't quite sure of him yet. Ron, she didn't know any more than Joe. She looked at both of them and shook her head "More liquor, I need more liquor if I'm going to get through this" Kristy said heading for the kitchen.

Beatrice watched and listened to Ron while he was on the phone making the reservations. He took out his wallet from his back pocket produced a credit card and read off the numbers. Beatrice couldn't understand why he would be doing this for her. They've only known each other for a week and a day. Yet he was right here with her. Beatrice thought why? Does he have a stake in this too? Doubt clouded her mind, fear started to take over. Turning to go find Kristy, Beatrice ran into Ron's chest.

"Oh Sorry" Beatrice said backing up, putting some distance between them.

Ron reached out for her and she took a step back "What's wrong?" Ron asked frowning.

"Why? Why are you doing all of this? I've only know you for a short time" Beatrice asked

Ron reached out and took Beatrice's hand, pulled her to him and wrapped her in his arms. "Baby, because of the way I feel when I'm with you. You have brought me back to life. And if you'll let me, I'm with you to the end." He said

"Ron, I just don't know who to trust. Who to be afraid of and I'm scared" Beatrice said leaning into his chest wrapping her arms around his waist.

Standing like they were glued together, neither Beatrice nor Ron heard Joe enter "Hey you two, I think Kristy's downing the liquor" Joe said laughing "Maybe we should finish setting our plan before she can't remember her own name"

"Hey, what's everyone doing in the entry way? Come on back to the living room and join me" Kristy called to them

Beatrice, Ron and Joe all looked at each other, shook their heads and started laughing. "We're coming" Beatrice called as she, Ron and Joe re-entered the living room.

Ron directed Beatrice to sit on the love seat next to him. Joe chose a chair and Kristy sat on the couch with her glass.

"I have us booked on a flight to Ireland, leaving the day after tomorrow. We fly out of Sacramento at 6 am. We have one lay over at Lax then landing in Dublin Ireland. I got three round trip tickets. We are due to return in three weeks. If it takes us that long" Ron said. "The tickets are under my name. I figure Beatrice and I can take separate transportation, and sit separate from Joe on the plane just in case someone spots us. What do you think, Joe" Ron said

"Yeah that sounds good. As it is I don't think I should stay here just in case as well" Joe said

"Once we get to Ireland, where should we meet up? Is there some place safe?" Ron asked

"There is a hotel at the airport. Check in there and I will find you roughly two hours after we land" Joe said

"What are you going to do until we fly?" Beatrice asked Joe

"You can stay here" Kristy said

"No, I've got some place to stay and things to get ready to go." Joe said standing up

"Here take the rental" Ron said handing Joe the keys.

"Thanks, I'll see you at the airport" Joe said heading for the door.

"It's late and I'm done drinking. With the kids gone tonight, I'm not getting up until noon" Kristy said heading for the stairs

"You're sure you don't mind that I stay here?" Ron asked Kristy

"Shoot from what I here, you're almost family. And family's always welcome here" Kristy said heading up the stairs.

Ron looked at Beatrice who was shaking her head while looking at the floor. When she picked her head up, she saw Ron standing with his hands in his pockets. Rocking back and forth on his heals smiling. "Family huh?" He said

"Don't listen to her, she's three sheets to the wind" Beatrice said

"Is your bed big enough for me?" Ron asked taking Beatrice's hand leading her up stairs

"My bed? You're sleeping on the floor." Beatrice said laughing

"Don't bet your sweet ass honey" Ron said slapping Beatrice on the behind.

*   *   *

The bed side clock read 5:25 am when Ron opened his eyes. Beatrice was snuggled up against him with her arm draped over his waist. How he hated to disturb her, she looked like an angel, his angel. Taking a deep breath, he smelled coffee. Slowly he removed her arm and slid out of bed. Locating his clothes from the floor, he followed the smell of the coffee. Entering the Kitchen, Ron found Kristy pouring herself a mug. "Morning" Ron said

Kristy jumped, turned and smiled "Morning, you startled me. Want some coffee?" Kristy asked

"Sorry I didn't mean to scare you. Yes I would love some. I woke up to the smell" Ron said watching Kristy pour some coffee into a mug for him.

"The cream and sugar are on the kitchen table" Kristy said pointing

"Black for me. Thanks Mrs. O'Riley" Ron said

"Oh call me Kristy please. Sit down won't you?" Kristy asked

"Thank you" Ron said taking a chair

"Tell me about yourself" Kristy said

"There's not much to tell. What would you like to know?" Ron asked

"I don't know. You've only known Beatrice for a short time and you are willing to do all of this for her. I was just wondering is all" Kristy said

Ron smiled "I joined the Marines when I was eighteen. Got discharged at twenty two due to a knee injury. Almost got married once, no children. What is left of my family lives on the east coast. Now I'm here with Beatrice" Ron said smiling over his coffee mug.

"What do you mean almost married?" Kristy asked

"The woman I was going to marry told me she was pregnant with another man's child and left me." Ron said shrugging his shoulders

"Oh my, that's terrible" Kristy said frowning

A hard series of knocks on the back door, made Kristy jump and spill her coffee. She opened her mouth to speak, Ron held up his finger to silence her. He stood and stepped to the door yanking it open to surprise who was there. Who he found was Joe in a black sweat shirt with the hood pulled up.

"I have news" Joe said

Ron opened the door and stepped aside to allow him entry. "What's going on?" Ron asked

"I talked to Aengus last night and this morning. He can't believe it takes all this just to retrieve one simple necklace. He says the time is running out whatever that means. He said that he is sending reinforcements. He wants that necklace at any cost" Joe said taking a seat at the kitchen table

"This is just getting out of hand" Ron said

"You bet it has" Kristy said reaching for the phone "I'm calling Aengus and putting an end to this right now"

"I don't think that's a good idea" Joe said "He's old and gone over the edge. I'm telling you he is obsessed with this. He says that land belongs to him and he's going to get it no matter what. Whatever that means"

"I think he's right" Ron said

"Well what am I supposed to do? Just sit here and let him hurt Beatrice?" Kristy yelled.

"I'm not going to let that happen" Ron said

"Our flight leaves in twenty three hours. I'm going to lay low until then. I will see you at the airport. You have my number just in case" Joe said

"I think you're right. I am going to keep a low profile here. If that's okay with you Kristy?" Ron said

"I think that's a great idea. The kids come back today and they would love to see Beatrice before you leave." Kristy said

"I'm going up and get Beatrice" Ron said

Ron found Beatrice sleeping, curled up holding her pillow. He pulled the desk chair up to the bed and sat down. He couldn't believe he let his guard down just enough to let her in. Let her in his heart, let her stir his feelings up from the dead. How far would she be willing to go with him? That was the question hanging over his head. He put his elbows on his knees clasping his fingers together and bowed his head.

Beatrice opened her eyes to see Ron sitting next to the bed. She reached out and touched his head. When he lifted his head, Beatrice saw worry and sadness in his face. "What's wrong? Is everything alright?" Beatrice asked Ron

"Everything is just fine baby. Move over" Ron said laying down next to Beatrice and pulling her into his arms.

"Everything's alright as long as I have you" Ron said trailing kisses from her neck to Beatrice's lips. Reaching up under her night shirt attempting to lift it up over her head.

Beatrice reached out to stop him. "Ron, I can't do this here" she said smiling.

"Why not?" he asked in between kisses.

"Kristy is here, she will know" Beatrice said trying to squirm out from underneath him.

"She's down stairs and the way I'm feeling this won't take long" Ron said in her ear.

Beatrice gave in to his advances returning his kisses. Slowly, Ron slid off her night shirt and shorts. Beatrice reached out to undo his button and zipper on his pants while he removed his shirt. His hands skimmed her waits up to her breasts before his mouth found hers. And all thoughts of complaints were forgotten as she found the type of bliss only he could bring.

"You smell that?" Ron asked Beatrice who had her head on his chest

"Bacon, Kristy must be making breakfast. I'm starving" Beatrice said getting up.

"She must have known I worked up an appetite" Ron said getting up himself and reaching for his pants.

Beatrice threw a pillow at him hitting him in the head "I can't believe you sometimes" Beatrice said laughing.

Beatrice and Ron followed the smell of bacon cooking and hot coffee. Beatrice gave Kristy a hug and a kiss on the cheek as she was cooking eggs.

"I've missed the breakfast that you would cook. I'm starving" Beatrice said taking a mug for coffee.

"Since when do you drink coffee?" Kristy asked

"Since I do, I guess" Beatrice said shrugging her shoulders

Ron walked passed Beatrice smacking her behind as he went. Beatrice yelped, grabbed her left cheek and gave Ron a look.

Both Ron and Kristy started laughing "Oh what it is to be young and in love" Kristy said putting the platter of eggs and bacon on the table.

"In love, what makes you say that?" Beatrice asked taking a plate and passing it to Ron

"Honey, trust me. I've only seen that look once in my life and he has it. It's written all over his face" Kristy said

Ron didn't say anything. He went about filling his plate with a great big smile on his face. Beatrice thought about it and wondered about love. She'd never been in love before. And was Ron in love with her? It certainly seemed that way this morning. He is still with her and doesn't seem to be leaving anytime soon.

"Beatrice" Ron said reaching over and taking the serving spoon from her hand. "Let me help you with this" spooning eggs onto her plate

"Huh? Oh, thank you" Beatrice said smiling coming out of her thought cloud.

"Like I said, young and in love" Kristy said

Beatrice and Ron did the dishes while Kristy showered and dressed for the day. Beatrice showed Ron all the pictures Kristy had hanging on the walls as they made their way to the stairs to shower and dress themselves. They were three steps up when the doorbell rang.

"I'll get it" Kristy said coming down the stairs

"It's okay, I'm here I'll get it" Beatrice said stepping down to the door.

Opening the door, Beatrice came face to face with Thomas. He reached out, grabbed Beatrice and threw her over his shoulder. He turned and ran back to the SUV waiting at the curb. He threw her into the back seat and climbed in after her shutting the door. The driver of the SUV took off with Beatrice screaming.

Ron and Kristy saw the door open and Beatrice disappear. They both ran to the door. Ron ran after the SUV not reaching it in time. Kristy ran back inside to get the keys to the minivan. Handing them to Ron upon meeting him at the door. Ron took the keys yelling back to Kirsty "Call Joe now, I'll be back"

Chapter Seventeen

"He took her he just took her. Right from my front door even" Kristy yelled into the phone when Joe answered

"Slow down and tell me again" Joe said

"Beatrice, she answered the door and a man took her right from the front door" Kristy said slower

"Where's Ron?" Joe asked

"He took my van to follow the SUV" Kristy said with tears starting.

"I'm on my way" Joe said hanging up

Kristy paced in the living room wringing her hands waiting for someone to come. On her tenth pass in the room, she decided to call Aengus. He just can't go around kidnapping people, especially not family. Not her Beatrice. As she was about to dial the phone, Ron and Joe came in the front door. Kristy ran to the door, looking at both of them. They both shook their heads 'no'. Kristy hit the floor on her knees crying. Joe went to help her up and into a chair.

"Call Aengus and see what he has to say about all of this. I'm going to change, I'll be right back" Ron said running up the stairs.

Kristy picked up the phone and dialed Aengus. "They took her. From my front door. What the hell is going on Aengus? I'm not going to sit here and listen to your lies. Start talking and do it now" Kristy yelled into the phone.

"Who took who?" Aengus said

"Beatrice, he took her." Kristy yelled

"Slow down and stop yelling. Are you saying I have something to do with Beatrice being taken?" Aengus said

"So help me, if something happens to her….." Kristy yelled

"I told you we had to be careful. I will check on my end and get back to you" Aengus said and disconnected.

A second later Joe's phone rang. He put up his finger to silence Kristy when he answered. "Yeah?" Joe said into the phone

"It's done. You're off the hook. Have a nice life." Aengus said. He then disconnected

Ron came down the stairs as Joe hung up the phone "Well?" Ron asked

"He denied having anything to do with it to Kristy and told me I'm done and to have a nice life" Joe said "Did she have the necklace on her?"

"No, she took it off last night, put it in a dish thing on the night stand" Ron said producing the necklace from his pocket.

"I think that's the only thing that is going to save her life" Joe said

"Where would he take her?" Ron asked Joe

"I have no idea, he could take her anywhere" Joe said

"Well, I'm not just going to sit here and wait for him to do what he did to her already" Ron said heading for the door.

"Wait up I'm going with you" Joe said heading out after Ron

"We can take your car, I don't want to leave Kristy without one" Ron said climbing in the passenger seat

Joe got behind the wheel and took off. "Do you have any suggestions?" Joe asked

"I followed them down the main street we came in on but going away from the freeway. They turned left up at that light and then wound around down there" Ron said pointing

"They're heading to the country area" Joe said

*　　*　　*

"I told you I don't have it" Beatrice said to Thomas

Thomas back handed Beatrice again. Her nose and lip were bleeding, the blood running down her face and onto her shirt. Unable to wipe the blood with her hands tied behind her back. She tried to turn enough to get the door open in the SUV as they drove.

"Bitch don't lie to me. The woman on the ship told me she gave it to that boyfriend of yours. She picked it up when you threw it" Thomas yelled

"I don't know, maybe she lied" Beatrice yelled back spitting blood at Thomas. Which brought another blow this time to the side of the head causing Beatrice to fly back hitting her head on the window cracking the glass. After that, everything went black.

*　*　*

"I'm going to kill that bastard" Ron said checking his gun one more time

"Not if I get to him first" Joe replied

Ron jumped when his phone rang. "Slow down and start again, I'm putting you on speaker phone" Ron said

"Beatrice called me from some truck stop on Highway 12 and I-5. She said she got thrown out the car while that were driving. She had to walk to get there." Kristy said

"I know where that is if she calls back tell her we're on our way" Joe said

"Someone is trying to come in" Kristy whispered into the phone "Oh shit......

"Hello? Kristy? Hello?" Ron yelled into the phone

"What the hell do we do?" Joe asked

"Who are we closer to?" Ron asked

"Beatrice is just up here, Kristy about 15 minutes" Joe said

"Get Beatrice first. Drive faster" Ron said

Joe stepped on the gas and the car took off. Joe passed a car on the wrong side of the road barely missing a tractor pulling out of the field. Speeding all the way to the truck stop. Joe pulled in to the pump area searching for Beatrice.

"Over there" Ron said

Joe pulled up to the curb outside the store entrance. Ron jumped out of the car before Joe had stopped all the way. He scooped Beatrice up in his arms and ushered her to the car. Joe had opened the back door for them and ran around to the driver's side. Ron helped Beatrice in and slid in next to her. Joe took off like a shot out of the parking lot.

"Baby are you okay?" Ron asked Beatrice

"No" Beatrice said crying putting her head in her hands

"I'm killing that bastard" Ron said hanging onto Beatrice when Joe hit a bump in the road.

Joe ran the red light and sped along the road towards Kristy's house praying she was alright. Nine minutes later they screeched up in front of the house. Joe flew to the front door that was open while Ron assisted Beatrice out of the car and up to the house.

Joe found Kristy tied up and gagged in one of the chairs in the living room. She had a bloody nose and was crying. The room had been tossed. Furniture turned over with papers thrown all over the floor. Joe took the gag off and untied her as Beatrice and Ron entered the room. Beatrice ran over to Kristy and they embraced both crying.

"They said that they were going to come back" Kirsty said through her tears. "They said to tell you Ron that they want the necklace and they know that you have it"

"Come on let's get you both up stairs and cleaned up" Ron said "Then we are taking you to the hospital" Ron said to Beatrice

"No, I'm not going to the hospital. I'm not leaving Kristy. I've dealt with the head injuries before, there is nothing they can do. I'm not letting them beat me" Beatrice said following Kristy into her bathroom.

"The kids will be back here in an hour or so. I can't let them see the house like this. Can't have them here when and if they come back" Kristy said to Beatrice

"Let's get cleaned up and we will help you put the house back together. Then we can figure out something with Ron and Joe" Beatrice said stepping into the shower. "Can you please go to my room and see if you can find me a pair of jeans, a shirt, a bra and some underwear"

"Yes, I'll be right back" Kristy said

Kristy found Ron in Beatrice's room putting the bed back together "Joe is down stairs putting things together and picking up" Ron said

"Beatrice wants me to bring her some clothes" Kristy told Ron

"Here I have them, let me take them to her. You go down stairs and help Joe. You alright?" He asked

Kristy put her hands up to her mouth and shook her head 'no' as the tears started again. Ron pulled her into his arms "I will make this right, he took her twice. He will never take her again" He told her

Kristy pulled away, wiped her tears with her finger, shook her head 'yes' and went down stairs.

Ron heard a loud bang as he entered the bathroom. Rushing in he saw Beatrice struggling to stand in the shower. He ran over, slide the shower door open and caught Beatrice just as her eyes rolled back in her head and she passed out. He carried her over and placed her naked body on Kristy's bed. He covered her up and ran down the stairs.

"I think Beatrice has a concussion. I caught her as she passed out in the shower, she's in your bed" He said to Kristy "I think she needs to rest, but could you keep an eye on her for me?"

"Holly shit" Kristy said bolting up the stairs

"Get that sick bastard on the phone" Ron said to Joe

"Which one?" Joe asked

"Let's start with Thomas" Ron said

"I will see if he answers or has the same number I have" Joe said reaching for his phone

Joe passed Ron the phone when Thomas answered, "Consider yourself warned, don't you ever touch her again" Ron said then disconnected. He handed the phone back to Joe "Now Aengus"

Joe handed the phone to Ron when he answered "I'm coming for you old man" Ron said handing the phone back to Joe.

"Let's get this place put back together then we are leaving" Ron said to Joe

"I'm on it" Joe said

It took both men twenty minutes to pick up all of the papers which they stacked on the dining room table for Kristy to go through at a later date. The furniture was put back to the spot it belonged.

"I know that you can't watch both the front and the back, but keep an eye out and do the best you can. I'm heading up stairs. I'll be back shortly" Ron said heading for the stairs

"I'm on it" Joe said

Upstairs, Ron went to Beatrice's room in search for his bag. There he donned his black cargo pants, black t-shirt and his black boots. He packed his bag and had it ready to go by the door. Next he went to check on Beatrice. There he found Kristy sitting on the edge of the bed calling Beatrice's name and not getting a response.

"May I sit with her for a moment please?" Ron asked stepping closer to the bed

Kristy, with tears in her eyes stood and walked out of the room. Ron stepped over and sat next to Beatrice gently taking her hand in his.

"Oh baby, please wake up. I don't want to leave you like this. Or have to put you in the hospital where he can get to you. Please wake up." Ron said bending over kissing her still lips.

Ron left Beatrice to retrieve his bag and head down stairs. "If she doesn't wake up in the next thirty minutes I'm calling an ambulance" Ron said to Kristy and Joe when he got down stairs.

"Shouldn't we call now?" Kristy asked

"I don't want to unless we have to. It will be too easy for them to get her in the hospital" Ron said

"In the hospital or here doesn't seem to matter. He took her right from my front door" Kristy snapped

Ron didn't look at Kristy, he just hung his head and walked into the kitchen to make a pot of coffee.

"I'm sorry I didn't mean anything" Kristy said to Joe

"I know, he just feels it's his fault that they got to her both times" Joe said "And he loves her"

"I can see that. I'm going to sit with her" Kristy said heading up stairs.

Joe went to find Ron. He found him sharpening his knife in the kitchen looking out the window. "She didn't mean anything" Joe said to Ron

"She's right. I let my feelings cloud my ability to do my job" Ron said

"Beatrice is not a job man, she's your girlfriend" Joe said

"If she is ever to be my girlfriend, I need to treat her as a job. Are you still interested in traveling to Ireland with me?" Ron asked

"Of course. I'm in this until the end" Joe said

"I'm calling in some reinforcements. One is a medic and he can tend to Beatrice. The others will stand guard over the house, Kristy and the kids until we get back" Ron said

"I'm ready to go any time. I have a bag packed in the car" Joe said

Ron got out his phone and dialed Harvey Watson, his right hand man. "Harvey, you up to some work?" Ron asked him

"Sure buddy, what's going on?" Harvey asked

Ron filled him in on Beatrice, the necklace and the recent events leading up to the phone call to him.

"Yes, I love her" Ron said smiling into the phone.

"I'm happy for you. It's about time you moved on and found someone worth your time" Harvey said

"Yeah, can you call Fred and Mike? See if they are available as well. I'm not taking any chances with this. And how soon can you get here? I have a flight out of Sac at 0600." Ron asked

"We will be there in six to seven hours or less" Harvey said

"Copy that" Ron said disconnecting.

Feeling a little better about the way things were going, Ron went upstairs to check on Beatrice. Kristy was sitting on the bed reading to Beatrice. Ron stood in the doorway leaning on the doorjamb watching and listening. Looking around the room, Ron noticed the flowered paper high up on the wall. It matched the flower bed spread on the four poster bed. The whole room reminded him of the room he would have for his wife. He softly knocked on the door interrupting Kristy and her reading.

"Can I talk to you for a moment?" Ron asked Kristy

"Sure, come in and sit down" Kristy said clearing the chair for him.

Ron sat down in the chair next to the bed. I wasn't sure how Kristy would handle hearing the plan Ron set up with all of his men, but he had to tell her.

"I'm not sure how you are going to react, but I am having some of my men from my unit come here to help. One is a medic that can help take care of Beatrice. The other two will be taking turns guarding the house, you and the kids. If Thomas believes the necklace is still here, he will be back. I'm going to go to Ireland with Joe in the morning and solve this issue myself." Ron said

Kristy sat quiet considering this information before answering.

"Ron, Beatrice is the only family I have left. The only family I can trust and care about that is. I will support you and your decisions until this is over and she is safe. Please do what you have to do to ensure this. She is my life." Kristy said

"Thank you, the men should be arriving in the next six hours" Ron said

"Well, then I had better get cooking…….." Kristy's words got cut off when Beatrice started moving and whining.

Both Ron and Kristy went to the bed side. Beatrice stopped moving and whining forming a frown on her face.

"Bea it's me honey. Can you hear me? Open your eyes please." Kristy said

"I'll sit with her for a while. You can take a break. Joe's on point down stairs" Ron said squeezing Kristy's hand

Kristy wiped at her tears with her fingers. She kissed Beatrice's forehead and left the room. She decided that if she were going to have a gaggle of men in the house along with three children, she had better do what she did best, cook. She planned to fix a large pot of vegetable soup to keep on hand with homemade bread. She put a pork roast and beans in the crockpot and started a block of cheese defrosting for grilled cheese sandwiches. Those were the children's favorite.

Ron sat with Beatrice holding her hand and calling her name. He rubbed her arms with his hands. Feeling her skin on his skin made him stronger inside. He stayed with her until he heard the doorbell down stairs. Instantly he was on alert. Leaving the bedroom with his gun in his hand, he stopped at the bottom of the stairs so Joe could open the door.

Chapter Eighteen

Joe swung open the door as Ron brought his gun up and ready for the worst. Breathing out a sigh of relief and lowering his weapon when he saw Harvey standing in the doorway.

"Wow man, don't do that to me. This situation really that bad?" Harvey said stepping in carrying his bags.

"You have no idea. This is Joe, he's on the team" Ron said by way of introduction

"Glad to meet you" Harvey said to Joe reaching out to shake his hand

"Same here" Joe said reaching out his hand

"Joe has point down here, your patient is up stairs. Follow me" Ron said climbing the stairs.

Harvey followed on his heels. Ron opened the bedroom door and saw Beatrice kicking her legs and frowning with her eyes closed. He rushed over to her calling her name.

"This is a good sign Ron. Keep calling her name and touching her arm and hand" Harvey said opening his bag "Ron fill me in on her situation"

Ron spent the next thirty minutes filling Harvey in on everything starting with the first moment he laid his eyes on Beatrice. Ron told Harvey about her first experience with Thomas and this last one.

"Can you help her? Is she going to be alright?" Ron asked

"She has a cut and a bump on her head over here. Most likely from the window. She has cuts and bruises here, here and here. In conclusion, she has another concussion. How bad I can't tell you without doing a scan. Her moving and making noises like she was doing earlier is a good sign. The brain is trying to recover" Harvey explained

"She had better come out of this alive and well or the body counts are going to rise" Ron said

"Easy now. She is resting comfortably, lets head down and you can fill me in on the plan" Harvey said

Ron kissed Beatrice's temple "Come back to me baby" He whispered into her ear. She twitched at the sound of his voice in her ear.

"See, good sign. Give her some time" Harvey said

Down in the kitchen, Joe was talking with Kristy while she cut vegetables. She turned when Ron and Harvey walked in.

"Kristy, this is Harvey Watson. He just examined Beatrice" Ron said

"Hello ma'am. Thank you for letting me into your home" Harvey said holding out his hand for hers.

"Hello, and its Kristy please" She said sliding her hand into his.

Harvey brought her hand up to his lips and kissed the back of her hand. He kept a smile on his face while never breaking eye contact

Ron noticed Kristy turning fourteen shades of red. Ron smiled and laughed remembering how Harvey had a way with the ladies.

Ron, Joe, and Harvey sat around the kitchen table talking out Ron's plans to protect Beatrice, Kristy and the kids; and to oust Aengus and this overwhelming need for Beatrice's necklace.

Kristy had already had the crockpot going with the meat and the beans. The vegetables were almost done being chopped for the soup and the bread was rising. Kristy enjoyed having them in her kitchen, she felt like she was part of the planning, listening to them plan out time schedules and instructions for the men that were due to show up at any time.

"Smells good in here ma'am. Um…. I mean Kristy. Thanks for being so accommodating" Harvey said standing up from his chair. "I'm going to check on Beatrice"

"May I come with you?" Kristy asked

"Yes, that would be nice" Harvey said with a great big smile

Ron chuckled and shook his head. Knowing full well what Harvey was smiling for.

Harvey fancies himself a ladies man. Ron put in a thought to talk with Harvey about putting the movies on Kristy. Kristy screaming his name brought him to his feet and flying up the stairs. Where he found Beatrice sitting up in the bed, her green eyes glossy but open. He smiled when he saw her. Crossing the room, he put a soft kiss on her lips.

"Hi baby, I'm so glad you're back" Ron said

Beatrice smiled but didn't say anything. She was sitting up in the bed holding the blanket up as to not show everyone her naked body. Harvey was checking her vitals and her breathing. A quick check of her eyes showed that she still had some swelling behind her eyes.

"How's your vision?" Harvey asked Beatrice

"Blurry" was all Beatrice could squeak out.

"You're showing improvement but you still need to stay in bed for a while longer" Harvey said

"No" Beatrice squeaked out

"Awe..... a stubborn woman. Now how did you know I love a challenge" Harvey said giving Beatrice a wink. "I've got three men coming here and I will put them on Beatrice detail if I have to. Now you just relax and stay put. Oh and I would advise putting some clothes on before they get here. And make sure it is something easy for me to get around the next time I check you" Harvey said standing with his hands on his hips.

Ron, Kristy and Joe laughed hard hardy laughs. Beatrice pouted with her arms crossed over her chest. And because she was feeling every bit of an adult she stuck her tongue out.

"I will get you some clothes. Be right back" Kristy said

"I'm going back down stairs. I'm glad you're doing better" Joe told Beatrice touching her arm.

"I want to take a shower" Beatrice said, her voice barely over a whisper

"Will it be alright if I help her?" Ron asked Harvey

"I think that will be alright. As long as you go slow and then right back to bed. Don't make me come up here and put some Special Forces moves on you" Harvey said

Beatrice gave Harvey a look and rolled her eyes. "Okay" Beatrice said

Kristy brought some clothes in for Beatrice and laid them in the bed. "Do you need any help?" she asked

"I think we got this" Ron said helping Beatrice stand and keep herself covered

"Why don't we go down and check on that soup and bread?" Harvey said to Kristy

"Oh my the bread" Kristy said running out of the room and down the stairs

Harvey put his hands in his pockets and gave Ron a look and a smile before heading down stairs to the kitchen.

Ron just shook his head "Come on baby, let's get in the shower. I mean get you in the shower" Ron said smiling

Beatrice rolled her eyes again. This time smiling remembering the last time he helped her out in the shower.

Down in the kitchen Harvey and Joe were put to work helping Kristy. Harvey was chopping onions and Joe was kneading bread. Kristy and Harvey kept looking at each other and smiling. Kristy couldn't remember the last time she even went out on a date none the less had some sort of relationship. After her husband left her, she tried to date once she became a foster parent, but with the young children it was difficult. Now that the children she has are spending time with their parents, maybe a social life could be possible.

Ron entered the kitchen interrupting her revere "Beatrice says she's hungry" Ron announced

"Hey, another good sign. Did she say how her vision was doing?" Harvey asked as he scrapped the onions into the pot on the stove.

"She said she can see a little bit better, still a little fuzzy" Ron said

"Great, after she eats I will check her again." Harvey said

Knocks on the front door made Kristy jump. Harvey put his hand on her shoulder and put his finger up to his mouth to silence her. Ron and Joe went to the door. When Joe opened it there stood Fred and Mike with their bags over their shoulders wearing the same style black cargo pants, black t-shirt and boots as Ron. A smile and an incline of their heads was the only greeting necessary. Both Fred and Mike entered and put their things down in the living room. Ron introduced Kristy to Fred and Mike as she was on her way bringing Beatrice a sandwich and some soup.

"Very nice to meet you both. Please make yourselves at home. I will be right back" Kristy said on her way up the stairs.

Ron guided Fred and Mike into the dining room. He and the others took seats around the table. As he started filling them in on his plan Kristy came in.

"Guess who's sleeping?" She said smiling sidling up to Harvey's chair and putting her hand on the back of it.

"Oh Thank God" Ron said

"Who's sleeping?" Fred asked

"The love of his life" Harvey snickered

"Wow, congrats man. I thought you were destine to be a bachelor" Mike said

"So when do we get to meet this woman that stole your heart?" Fred asked

"As soon as she is feeling up to it and her medic says she can get out of bed. Now can we get on with this?" Ron asked

"Yes sir" Fred said giving Ron a sloppy salute and laughing along with everyone else.

"There's a man that goes by Aengus. He is supposedly based out of Dublin Ireland. He is after Beatrice and the charms on her necklace. They are supposed to unlock some sort of box. This box is said to contain the deed to some land in Ireland. So far he has sent two different men to retrieve these charms. One has taken and beaten Beatrice twice. I want to leave two men here to guard Beatrice, Kristy and the children that Kristy cares for and to take one of you with me and Joe to Ireland to confront this Aengus. I have three of us booked on a flight out of Sacramento at 0600 tomorrow" Ron said

"I'll stay behind with the women and children" Harvey said

"Count me in to stay behind with Harvey" Fred said

"Shoot I'm ready right now. When are we leaving" Mike said

"You're not going anywhere without me" Beatrice said standing in the entry to the dining room leaning on the wall for support.

Everyone's head turned at the sound of her voice. Ron jumped up and assisted her into a chair that Joe had pulled out for her.

"You shouldn't be up and out of bed" Ron scolded

"I knew you were up to something leaving me alone for so long. Planning to leave me here are you? I don't think so" Beatrice sitting in the chair that was pulled out for her

Ron smiled and put his arm around her shoulders. "Harvey, I think we have a volunteer for some of those Special Forces moves" Ron said

"You wouldn't dare" Beatrice said eyes wide as the moon

"Don't try me. Beatrice this is Fred and Mike. They have been dying to meet you. And yes we are going without you. I am not taking a chance on anything happening to you again. Besides, you are in no shape to travel" Ron said

"Over my dead body are you going without me" Beatrice yelled as she stood up.

She lost her balance and fell to the floor. Ron and Harvey knelt down at her side. Harvey shined his light in her eyes checking her vision.

"Get that light out of my eyes and help me up off the floor would you?" Beatrice snapped

"You got yourself a wild one there Ron" Fred said laughing

Ron and Harvey helped Beatrice up into a chair at the table. Beatrice put her head in her hands trying to calm the throbbing going on in her head. Ron stood next to her rubbing her back.

"Here take these" Harvey said handing Beatrice a couple of pills and a glass of water "It should help with the throbbing"

"How did you know my head is throbbing?" Beatrice asked taking the pills.

"Just take them and don't worry about that" Ron said

"Ron please don't leave me behind. I have to go with you" Beatrice pleaded

"The kids will be here in an hour" Kristy said coming into the dining room. "I just wanted to let you all know so you're all aware. Dinner is just about ready as well. Can I get anyone anything?"

"Food, yes ma'am" Fred and Mike said in unison standing and heading into the kitchen.

Ron knelt down next to Beatrice's chair "You should really be resting baby. I'm worried about you" He said close to her ear

"Ron, I have to go with you. I'm not going to stay here" Beatrice said

"We can talk about this later. You need to rest" Ron said scooping her up in his arms grooms' style and carrying her to the couch in the living room. Laying her down and sitting next to her, Ron caressed her face looking deep into her mesmerizing green eyes. Stroking her long blonde hair, he leant down and kissed her lips. Moving to her cheek and then her temple, moving his way up to her forehead. "I'm so sorry you're hurt baby" he whispered as he put his forehead against hers.

Beatrice reached up to caress his cheek and felt the tears streaming down. She reached both her arms around his neck and pulled him down to her. She held him close and whispered "don't cry. I'm fine really I am"

Ron picked his head up to meet Beatrice's eyes "I love you" he said

Beatrice smiled "I love you too" she said pulling him down for a kiss. One long slow kiss.

Kristy watched from the doorway to the kitchen. She hoped that this thing with Ron would last a life time for Beatrice. Give her the chance that she and her mother never got. The chance to love and have children and watch them grow up healthy and happy with no worries.

"They make quit a pair don't they?" Harvey said touching Kristy's shoulder startling her.

"You scared me. Yes they do. I hope that it will last" Kristy said

"You and me both. Ron has been hurting for a long time. It's great to see him like this. He really loves her" Harvey said

"I sure hope so" Kristy whispered

"Come on let me help you in the kitchen" Harvey said taking her hand and leading her away from Beatrice and Ron.

Kristy went about the business of setting the table. The soup was done and the bread was just about ready to be taken out of the oven. The pork and beans in the crock pot were almost done. Kristy loved taking care of the men. It made her happy to taking care of people.

The first to come through the door was Billy. He bound into the living room and spotted Ron leaning over Beatrice. "What the hell?" Billy said

"Billy" Beatrice said sitting up with Ron's help.

"Hey Bea" Billy said stepping closer slowly eyeing Ron sitting next to Beatrice

"Sit down, I want you to meet Ron" Beatrice said patting the space next to her

"Hi Billy, Beatrice has told me a lot about you" Ron said reaching his hand out

"Hi" Billy said taking his out reached hand

Kristy heard the front door open and slam shut. She and Harvey peek their heads out of the kitchen and she spotted Billy sitting on the couch next to Beatrice and Ron "Billy" Kristy called "Come here please"

Billy stood and gave Ron one last look before heading into the kitchen. He stopped just inside the kitchen door and froze at the site of the four men standing there. Three of them in black outfits with buzz haircuts and one in jeans and a t-shirt.

"Billy, I want you to meet some people. This is Joe, Fred, Mike and Harvey. They are going to be staying with us for a while." Kristy said

"Why? What's going on?" Billy asked

"Listen, there is some things going on that you don't need to worry about. But as long as these gentlemen are here, you will do as they tell you. Do you understand?" Kristy said

"I guess" Billy said

"Good, now go wash up for dinner. I'm expecting the others any time now. Chop, chop now" Kristy said clapping her hands

Chapter Nineteen

Dinner went off without a hitch. Kristy had Fred and Mike pull out the table and put in the leaf so there would be enough room for everyone. Billy relaxed once everyone was around the table. Beatrice filled everyone in on her cruise adventures. The things she saw and the things she got to do. Leaving out the Thomas fiasco of course. Beatrice noticed that Billy was quiet and starring at Ron for most of the meal.

After dinner, Kristy had Billy and the other children help with the dishes. Ron assisted Beatrice to the living room couch and turned on the television for her. Ron, Joe, Fred, Mike and Harvey stepped out onto the front porch. There, Ron called and got the last remaining seat on the plane to Ireland. Deciding he wasn't going to go without Beatrice.

Billy took this opportunity to visit with Beatrice "So tell me what's going on? Why are these guys here?" he asked

Beatrice smiled a small smile and began "Remember the money and the letter that I got on my birthday? Well since then someone has been following me trying to get my necklace. I guess it has to do with my Mom and Dad. I was attacked twice and beaten up pretty bad. I have to go to Ireland and see if I can figure all this out. Ron wants to leave Fred and Harvey here to make sure they don't try to hurt anyone here." Beatrice explained

"This Ron guy, is he your boyfriend?" Billy asked

Beatrice looked down at her lap before answering "Yes, he is. I met him on the cruise"

"Oh, I see" Billy said

"While I'm gone I'm going to need you to help out around here" Beatrice said

"Yeah, I can do that. When you get back, will you tell me everything?" Billy asked

"Sure I will" Beatrice said

"So you're coming back then?" Billy said

"Of course I am" Beatrice said reaching for Billy's hand

Billy pulled his hand away when he heard the front door open. Ron and the others entered the living room. Ron sat next to Beatrice and the others sat around the television arguing about what to watch.

"How are you feeling?" Ron asked

"Better now that I've eaten and taken those pills Harvey gave me. Things aren't so fuzzy anymore" Beatrice said

"Good, I'm glad to hear it because I just booked another seat for the flight. You should pack as light as you can" Ron said smiling

"Yes" Beatrice said hugging Ron

"What's going on in here?" Kristy asked sitting in the chair next to Harvey

Beatrice laughed "Well, let's see. The guys are fighting over the T.V., Ron said I get to go and I'm feeling better" Beatrice said

"I have the girls bunking together so you guys will have a room to stay in. I can show you where it is later. Does anyone want some popcorn?" Kristy said

"Actually, could you show me the room now? I would like to catch some shut eye so I can take the night shift" Fred said

"Sure, follow me" Kristy said

"And you should be packing and getting some sleep young lady. We have to get up early in the morning" Ron said

"Yes sir" Beatrice said taking Ron's hand

Ron assisted Beatrice up stairs to her room. She got a bag out of the closet and filled it with three pairs of jeans, six t-shirts, eight pairs of underwear, a spare set of tennis shoes and a sweat shirt. A smaller bag contained her toiletries.

"That's it. If I am missing anything or need anything else, I will just buy it. Does this packing job suit you sir?" Beatrice asked

"Yes, it does" Ron said pulling her into his arms

Beatrice put her hands on his face standing on her tip toes to kiss him. The kiss was soft and tender.

Breaking from the kiss, Ron whispered "I love you baby" bringing her in for a deeper more demanding kiss.

Breaking away from the kiss before they got carried away "You had better get some sleep. I will wake you soon" Ron said

"You're not coming to bed with me?" Beatrice asked

Ron chuckled "No baby, I've got things to organize and you still aren't one hundred percent yet. I will tuck you in though. I will come lay down with you if there is time" Ron said

"Alright, I will behave because I get to go" Beatrice said giving him a peck on the cheek

Ron smiled, kissed her forehead and tucked her in. He walked out into the hall closing the door behind him. The checking of his watch let him know it was 9:15 pm. Time to get going he thought.

Kristy made sure there was a hot pot of coffee for the men as they sat around the kitchen table doing there planning. She placed a tray of crackers, cheese and salami out for them to snack on. At 11:00, Kristy laid down on the couch. Trying to stay awake long enough to see them off. She lost the fight and her eyes closed.

Harvey looked up and from his seat, he could see Kristy sleeping on the couch. He went over and covered her with a blanket that was on a chair. Carefully moving a stray piece of her blonde hair away from her face before returning to the group.

"Well, as long as we are all on the same page here, I'm going to lay down for a bit. Meet at the front door at 0300" Ron said

Ron sat on the bed next to Beatrice stretching his legs out on the bed. As if on cue, Beatrice snuggled up to him putting her head in his lap, draping her arm over his legs. He spent the next hour stroking her hair and back. "Hey Beatrice" he started calling her name trying to wake her up.

Beatrice stretched and opened her eyes. Tilting her head up, she looked into Ron's eyes. He was not smiling nor did he say anything. He leaned down and kissed Beatrice. Not soft and gentle but demanding. Tongues and teeth clashing, twice Ron took her lip in his teeth. He kissed and nibbled down her neck to her collar bone and back up. He loved her like it was his last. "Oh baby" was what Beatrice heard at the climax he brought her to.

"I would love to stay here and relax with you forever baby, but we have a job to do. When we are through and home, I promise to take the time with you. Every day for the rest of my life" Ron said

"You spoil me, Ron Peterson. Now get off me so I can get ready" Beatrice said slapping Ron's behind

Ron smiled and rolled off to the side to allow Beatrice to stand. "You feeling alright? Do I need to get Harvey?" Ron asked

"No, I think I'm fine. Nothing is blurry and my head barely hurts. I will take a shower in Kristy's room so you can take the hall bathroom" Beatrice said with her clothes in her hand.

"Okay, sure you don't want me to join you?" Ron asked

"I don't think Kristy would appreciate the both of us in her shower while she is sleeping Beatrice said

"She isn't in there. She is down stairs on the couch. Well the last time I saw her anyway" Ron said following Beatrice into Kristy's bathroom.

Kristy woke to the sound of talking. Stretching, she opened her eyes and sat up. "What time is it?" Kristy asked Fred

"It's 2:15 ma'am" Fred said

"Oh my, I had better get going. I need to make breakfast for those leaving" Kristy said

"Don't hurry yourself. Harvey has been cooking for the last hour ma'am" Fred said

"Call my Kristy please" Kristy said smiling

"Yes ma'am" Fred said looking out the front window

Kristy stood in the door way to the kitchen watching Harvey move around like he lived there. He had potatoes in one pan, bacon in another and he was scrambling eggs in a bowl.

"Can I help?" Kristy asked

Harvey looked up from his bowl and smiled. "Sure, can you finish cutting the onions and bell peppers for the eggs please? I thought I would make burritos for them to take with them for their journey" he said

"That sounds great" Kristy said smiling and picking up the knife

Ron and Beatrice bound down the stairs together at 2:30 carrying their bags and laughing.

Kristy came out of the kitchen to see what was going on, she spied Ron and Beatrice kissing at the bottom of the stairs. "You two want to wake the entire house?" Kristy asked

They both jumped "Oh sorry" Beatrice whispered

"We're in the kitchen" Kristy said turning towards the kitchen

Ron and Beatrice followed. "Have you been up all night?" Beatrice asked Kristy,

"No, I napped on the couch for a couple of hours. All of this is Harvey. I am just assisting the chef" Kristy said giving Harvey a smile

"How are you feeling?" Harvey asked Beatrice

"Much better thank you. My head is not pounding, it only aches a little and I can see with no blurriness" Beatrice said helping herself to a piece of bacon

"That all sounds great, but I'm checking anyway" Harvey said reaching for his bag

"Yes sir" Beatrice said snapping a salute and laughing

"Smart ass" Harvey said joining in on the laughing.

Harvey checked Beatrice out and gave her a clean bill of health. As long as she promised to take it easy another day. Kristy finished the burritos and had them wrapped and packed to go. She also filled two thermoses with coffee for the ride to the airport.

At exactly 2:50 Joe and Mike came down the stairs. Dropping their bags next to Beatrice and Ron's and going into the kitchen.

"I'm going out to start the car" Joe said

"Right behind you" Mike said

Kristy hugged Beatrice and Ron and kissed their cheeks "Good luck and come home safe" She told them

"I'll be back soon, take care and don't let Harvey push you around" Beatrice said winking at Harvey who was standing next to Kristy.

Harvey reached out to grab Beatrice. She jumped back laughing and ran to the car. She turned and waved one last time as she got in and closed the car door.

Beatrice sat in the back with Mike. Joe drove and Ron sat in the passenger side. Beatrice sat string out the window into the darkness. Excited and scared at the same time. Scared mostly at what she might find. Did she still have family? Were they bad or good people? The one thing she wanted to avoid was another run in with Thomas.

Ron, Joe and Mike talked the entire ride to the airport. Joe parked in the extended parking. Everyone except Joe got out of the car and grabbed their bags. Joe's instruction were hang back and scan the area for Thomas or anyone following.

Going through the security was crazy. Beatrice got separated from Ron and Mike when she came up as the random person to get searched. An officer took her aside and searched her and her bag. Ron stood off to the side watching, getting agitated the longer it took.

Mike put his hand on Ron's shoulder "Easy now, she's fine. Look, here she comes" Mike pointed

Once Beatrice was through the security check point, Ron gathered her in his arms and kissed the top of her head.

"That man just wanted to play with my panties" Beatrice said

Mike laughed "Can't blame him" he said walking towards their gate.

Ron and Beatrice followed along carrying their bags. Gate six was just a few feet more. Ron got his phone out and called Harvey.

"Checking in. We got through security and we are waiting at the gate. How are things there?" Ron asked

"Good and quiet. Fred is sleeping and Kristy and I are talking till she has to get the kids up for school" Harvey said

"Yeah talking" Ron said laughing and he disconnected

"How are things at home?" Beatrice asked

"Great, just great" Ron said

Upon boarding the plane, Ron guided Beatrice to the seats in the middle of the plane next to an exit. Mike took a seat directly across the aisle from them. Joe was one of the last to board a few minutes later. He walked by and made eye contact with Ron and shook his head no on his way by. Joe took a seat to the back of the plane.

"What was that all about?" Beatrice asked

"As far as he can tell, no one has followed" Ron whispered

"Well that's good. Right?" Beatrice said

"Just because he didn't see anyone, doesn't mean there isn't one" Ron said leaning close to Beatrice

Beatrice leaned in close to Ron and said "This is my second time on a plane"

Ron smiled and took her hand. He squeezed lightly when the engines started and the doors closed. Trying to make Beatrice calm and comfortable was difficult when he was on high alert. Locked in a plane was not the place to be if someone was there to harm Beatrice.

"Ron, why are you doing all this for me?" Beatrice asked

"Baby, I told you already. I came alive again when I met you. I spent the last five years keeping everyone at a distance. Carl tried to get me to date, but no one interested me. I was doing fine on my own. Then comes you, seeing you sitting there watching everyone else dance. Something called to me to ask you to dance. And then when you put your hand in mine, my heart skipped a beat. Looking into your eyes while we danced, my blood started to boil. The way you flipped your hair out of your face, I was just mesmerized" Ron said kissing the back of her hand.

Joe walked by them and talked to the stewardess for a minute than he walked back by clearing his throat when he reached Mike. Mike looked at Ron. Ron held up his hand in a stay motion. Two minutes went by and Ron put his hand down. Mike got up and went to the back of the plane.

"What's going on?" Beatrice said turning in her seat

"No" Ron said turning Beatrice around to face the front

"What?" Beatrice asked

"Joe is going to pass Mike a note as they pass in the aisle and you don't need to watch" Ron said

"Oh, is this part of your plan?" Beatrice asked

"No, Joe must have some information to share" Ron said "Must be important for him to do it on the plane"

"Now I'm really scared" Beatrice said

"Not to worry. Now, I need you to turn to talk to me and see if Mike is coming" Ron said

Beatrice turned her head and leaned in to kiss Ron glancing down the aisle to check for Mike. She gave him a small peck on his lips and whispered "yes" to him before turning and facing front.

Ron stood and passed Mike in the aisle. Mike reached his seat and sat down keeping his eyes forward. Ron returned to his seat a few minutes later.

"Well, what's going on?" Beatrice asked

"There is a guy that Joe is suspicious of" Ron said

"When we land, you need to do just as I tell you. Don't leave my or Mikes side. Whomever I tell you to go with. Do you understand?" Ron asked

"Yes" Beatrice said "Do you still have the necklace?"

"Yes, I do. It's safe with me. It's you I don't want to lose" Ron said giving Beatrice the eye.

For the rest of the flight, Beatrice rested her head on Ron's shoulder and played with his hand. Checking to see how much bigger his was than hers. She played with the controls up above her head until she heard the put your seat belts on and seat trays in the upright positon.

"Listen, we are going to stay behind and try to force the guy we're watching to exit the plane ahead of us. Don't move until I tell you and stay by my side at all times" Ron said

The doors to the plane opened and the first passengers started standing, reaching for their luggage in the overhead compartments. When the people started filing out, Ron stood and opened the overhead compartment above their seats effectively blocking Beatrice from anyone walking by. Ron waited until the man and Joe exited the plane before allowing Beatrice to stand and exit with him. Mike took up the rear following behind.

Chapter Twenty

When Beatrice and Ron stepped into the airport from the plane, Joe was nowhere to be seen. Ron and Beatrice started walking to their next gate to wait for their connecting flight to Dublin. Mike strolled along behind keeping watch. Ron kept scanning the area keeping an eye out for Joe.

"I'm getting a little bit hungry" Beatrice said "Can we stop and get something to snack on while we wait?"

"Sure, what sounds good to you?" Ron asked

"I don't know, how about that store over there. I can get some stuff to put in my purse to snack on and maybe get a book to read or a word search book. You know to keep me busy on the flight. Otherwise I might drive you crazy" Beatrice said laughing

Ron and Beatrice headed over to the store. Mike stood watch outside. Mike stood and texted his order to Ron. Beef jerky, gum, nuts or trail mix and a dirty magazine. Ron passed the list off to Beatrice to see what she would do. Reading the list that Ron forwarded on to her she smirked and went about shopping. Ron wandered around the little shop keeping an eye out while Beatrice shopped.

"You get everything you needed?" Ron asked when they met up at the register

"Yes and then some" Beatrice said smiling

"Great, our gate is just up here. We have thirty minutes till we board" Ron said

"May I give Mike his items?" Beatrice asked

"Only if I can be there to watch" Ron said

Beatrice and Ron walked to their next gate. Beatrice put her items in her bag and strolled over to Mike.

"Here is your gum, your jerky, your mixed nuts and your magazine" Beatrice said handing Mike his items.

Mike turned beat red in his face and slack jawed when Beatrice handed him the magazine. Ron started laughing out loud. Beatrice smiled and rocked back and forth in her heels.

"Come on, let's sit down and wait for our flight" Ron said

Sitting next to Ron, Beatrice spotted Joe standing off to the side. She tried not to stare at him, but she noticed him watching a man. The same man that was on the previous plane. Beatrice watched the man, he was standing next to a potted plant using the outlet with a device plugged in. Beatrice couldn't tell if it was a phone or a tablet. At one point, Beatrice thought he might be taking pictures with the device. Having pointed it in her direction more than once.

"Ron, there is that guy that was on the previous flight. He is standing over there by that plant. I swear I saw him taking pictures of me. Joe was on the other side watching" Beatrice said leaning in to keep her words low.

Ron didn't look up, he took out his phone and sent Mike a text message. Mike got up from his seat and strolled over towards the guy. Joe took off for the restroom, Mike followed. Ron stood and stretched moving to effectively block Beatrice from this guy.

Ten minutes later, they called for the boarding of their flight. Mike showed up a couple of minutes later. Ron looked at his phone, said a few choice curse words and put his phone away.

"What's wrong?" Beatrice asked

"Mike met Joe in the bathroom. Joe told him that guy is one of Aengus's people. He is taking pictures and sending them to Aengus and giving him reports. He knows we are going to Dublin. This is going to be a long restless flight" Ron said

"This just keeps getting more and more out of hand" Beatrice said

Mike stood in line in front of Beatrice and Ron stood just behind her. Suddenly Ron turned and put Beatrice behind him at the loud sound coming from the end of the line. The flight attendant encouraged the line to keep moving. In a flash, security surrounded the guy that Joe had been watching. Joe stood off to the side smiling at Ron.

"Outstanding" Ron said turning around to face Beatrice "It's clear, lets get on the plane"

"Why, what just happened?" Beatrice asked trying to see over Ron's shoulder

"Joe just proved himself. Come, I will fill you in on the plane" Ron said turning Beatrice around by her shoulders and nudging her forward.

"Okay, we're sitting. Tell me what happened" Beatrice said

Ron laughed "I don't know the details, but Joe came up with a distraction and effectively removed the guy from the flight. Now maybe I can get some shut eye" Ron said

"That's all you know?" Beatrice said eyeing Ron

"Oh woman don't start doubting and questioning me" Ron said "I will always tell you everything I can. Maybe not right away, but I will tell you"

"Alright I'm sorry. I guess I'm just a little jumpy" Beatrice said leaning in to kiss Ron on the cheek.

Settling into her seat, Beatrice was asleep before the plan reached cruising altitude. Leaning her head on Ron's shoulder for support. Ron smiled down at her and kissed the top of her head.

Beautiful rolling hills of grass, tall enough to be swaying in the breeze. Tall trees scattered on the landscape with green leaves rustling in intervals as if they were talking to each other. Down at the bottom of the hill where one meets the other a stream runs through, winding around like a snake. Next to one of the larger trees, sits a bolder. It has three smaller boulders clustered at the bottom. Beatrice wandered closer to the boulder. As she drew closer, Thomas stepped out from behind the tree. Beatrice opened her mouth to scream but nothing came out. She tried to run but her feet wouldn't move. Thomas stepped ever closer to Beatrice. He reached out to grab her.

Beatrice swung her arm and made contact with Ron's jaw. Three people sitting in the row in front of Ron and Beatrice turned to see what was going on. Mike unbuckled his safety belt and made to stand up. Ron put up his hand to let Mike know everything was alright.

Beatrice opened her eyes to see Ron looking at her rubbing his face. "What happened?" Beatrice asked

"You started making noises in your sleep. I tried to wake you up and you swung your arm around and hit me. What were you dreaming about?" Ron asked

"Oh baby, I'm sorry. Are you okay?" Beatrice asked

Ron smiled, "Yes, it takes a lot more than you to knock me down" Ron said

"I was in this field going toward a tree and a rock when Thomas came out from behind the tree and tried to grab me" Beatrice said.

"Don't worry, I'm not going to let anything happen to you. Drink some of your water and relax. We should be landing in about thirty minutes" Ron said

"Wow, did I sleep all that long? Why didn't you wake me?" Beatrice asked

"You needed your sleep. I took a nap while Mike and Joe kept watch. I'm good" Ron said.

*   *   *

De-boarding the plan was a clandestine affair. Joe went first, followed by Ron, Beatrice and then Mike. Joe scouted out the people waiting for the flight. When Ron and Beatrice emerged from the plane, Joe was waiting and gave the signal that all was clear as far as he could tell. Ron Beatrice and Mike headed for the car rental desk. Ron arranged to have a car brought to the loading zone out front and reservations at the hotel for two rooms. From there, Ron, Beatrice and Mike loaded into the car and headed for the hotel to wait for Joe.

The rooms that Ron reserved were joining rooms. One for him and Beatrice and one for Mike and Joe. It was almost eight at night when they finally got to the hotel. Ron ordered room service for everyone. Beatrice went to take a shower.

"How long do you think we are going to wait to hear from Joe?" Mike asked looking out the window.

"I'll give him a couple of hours than I am going out on my own. Someone out there must know about this Aengus and his whereabouts" Ron said

"Where are you going to start?" Mike asked

"I was thinking about that. Maybe we could hit some local bars and pubs. You know, ask around. I'm sure we will hit a nerve somewhere and get some type of response." Ron said

Mike moved to the door, "Looks like our food is here" He said

Mike chuckled, "Joe is pushing the cart" He said laughing.

"What the hell is he up to?" Ron asked

Mike opened the door as he reached the entrance. Joe pushed the cart inside.

"Where would you like the cart sir?" Joe said entering the room.

"What the hell is all of this?" Ron asked

Joe took the tray of food and put it on the table in the room and lifted the table cloth on the cart to reveal a crate. He and Mike pulled the crate out from under the cart. Joe took off the lid to reveal a supply of weapons and ammunition.

"Well I'll be" Mike said sitting on the edge of the bed unloading the crate.

"Way to come through man" Ron said

"What's all this?" Beatrice asked

"Over there is some food for you. You said you were hungry. The rest of this is for us to worry about" Ron said kissing the top of her head.

Beatrice opened the lids to the food on the table. She found four double cheese burgers with French fries and a chicken salad.

"Whose is who's over here?" Beatrice said out loud

"I got everyone a cheese burger even you and just in case you didn't want that, I got a chicken salad. Is that okay?" Ron replied

"Yes, that's fine and very thoughtful of you" Beatrice said sitting down at the table. She cut one of the burgers in half and put some of the salad on a plate.

"I found out that Aengus is aware that we are here. He is also unaware of our whereabouts at this time. Due to the distraction at the airport. I also know that he is nervous. He still has not been able to find the box that the jewelry opens. Every time he gets information, it falls through" Joe explained

"Then why was he in such s hurry for it if he doesn't know where the box is?" Mike asked

"I guess he thought that the last tip he received was going to fall through. Apparently, someone told him it was somewhere near a tree with a rock next to it. But he has not been able to find it." Joe said shrugging his shoulders

"Wait, are you sure of this?" Beatrice asked

"I am almost positive why?" Joe asked moving closer to Beatrice

"On the plane, I had a dream. I was on this grassy hill. There were trees scattered around and one tree had a giant boulder with three or four littler rocks in a cluster at the bottom of the giant one" Beatrice said

"And that's it. There is nothing else?" Mike said

"Um…….. no, there at the bottom of the hill was a small river or creek winding along like a snake. There was another hill next to that one. You know the hill I was on slopped down to the river and the next hill started. Am I making any sense?" Beatrice said

"You've got to be kidding me" Joe said sitting down on the edge of the bed

"What? Does this mean something to you?" Ron asked Joe

"Yes, my Uncle used to take me to a place just like when I was younger. Before we left for the United States" Joe said

"Can you get us there in the morning?" Ron asked

"I'm sure I can. Why, do you think that the box is there?" Joe asked

"It's worth a try. If we can get a hold of that box before Aengus does, then we have the upper hand" Ron said

"Does anyone know what this box looks like or what size it is?" Mike asked "Do you think we night need shovels or digging equipment?"

"I know that it is supposed to contain the deed to some land and money. I don't know just how much money. It can't be very much money, you think?" Joe said

"Well we will see tomorrow of we can find it. I want to get an early start at this. I have a room next door for the two of you. Is that going to work for you Joe?" Ron asked

"Sure that's great. I wasn't looking forward to going out alone with everyone looking for me" Joe said

"Great, let's all eat and get some rest. Is 0700 to early of a start in the morning?" Ron asked

"No sir, we will be ready to go" Joe said

Mike nodded due to the cheese burger he stuffed in his mouth. Everyone laughed at the sight.

Digging in to her salad and burger, Beatrice felt a little bit better. She put the other half of her burger in the refrigerator that was in the room. After Joe and Mike retired to their room, Beatrice slipped into her night wear and crawled into bed while Ron took off his gear and joined her. He pulled her close to him. Beatrice put her head on his chest and they stayed like this until Ron started to snore. Beatrice giggled softly, rolled over and snuggled her back up against Ron's side and closed her eyes.

Beatrice woke up to Ron's hand on her right breast massaging it and his tongue in her ear.

"What time is it? And just what do you think you're doing?" Beatrice asked

"I don't care what time it is and you know what I'm doing" he said into her ear. Suddenly shifting so that she was on her back and he was on his knees between her legs pulling the bottom half of her night clothes off.

Before Beatrice could object to anything, Ron was on top of her and then inside her while he kissed her. The kind of kiss and passion that Beatrice had become to know and love. Beatrice put one hand on his back and one hand on the back of his neck holding him to her. Kissing and biting his neck and ear. Moving in rhythm until she heard "Oh baby" softly in her ear.

Ron slowly slid out and then off of Beatrice, pulling her close to him draping his arm over her waist in a spooning position. And in what seemed like seconds to Beatrice, Ron started to snore, softly this time. She smiled and closed her eyes drifting off to sleep by the sound of the man she loves breathing and his heartbeat.

Chapter Twenty One

BEATRICE WOKE UP AND REACHED out for Ron, but his side of the bed was empty. She got out of bed and checked the bathroom, empty. She put on her clothes and went to the door and looked out the peep hole, she saw nothing. As she put her hand on the door knob, the door to the joining room opened.

"And just where do you think you're going?" Ron asked

"I woke up and you were gone. I was looking for you" Beatrice responded

"I'm sorry, I should have left a note or something but I thought I would be back before you woke up" Ron said

"What were you doing?" Beatrice asked sitting down on the bed.

"Planning out the day. Joe got a message that Aengus wants to see him. I am going with him. Then we can go check out this tree and rock." Ron said getting his equipment strapped on.

"I'm going with you" Beatrice said heading for the bathroom.

"No, I don't think that would be a good idea. I'm leaving you with Mike" Ron said

"I don't think so" Beatrice said standing in the door way to the bathroom.

"Yes, I don't know what the environment looks like and what kind of security is there and who will be there. You are not coming for this" Ron said

"But….." Beatrice started but Ron cut her off with a kiss and a smack on her left butt cheek

"Don't argue with me please. Now go do whatever you're going to do. I will have the boys come to our room while you are in the bathroom so come out with clothes on" Ron said

Beatrice opened her mouth to speak but shut it just as quick. Ron smiled as she shut the door in his face.

Beatrice took a record fast shower and got dressed in jeans and a t-shirt. When she emerged from the bathroom, she found breakfast had been delivered and everyone was in attendance gathered around the small table eating and talking.

"So what's the plan?" Beatrice asked coming up to the table

"I already informed you of the plan for the morning" Ron said in a don't mess with me voice

Beatrice sat down on the bed to put her socks and shoes on. All the while keeping her mouth shut and listening carefully to their planning.

"This is the address to the place we are going to. If you don't hear from one of us in three hours you know what to do?" Ron asked Mike

"Yes, I have the plan down" Mike said

"Good, until then sit on Beatrice. I think she might be the sneaky type" Ron said looking at Beatrice and winking at her.

Beatrice smiled the biggest smile she could. Inside she was scared that something would happen to Ron or Joe.

"While I'm being babysat, I think I will call Kristy and check in. You two need to be careful and I will take could care of Mike" Beatrice said giving Mike a shove with her shoulder.

Ron reached out, put his hand at the back of Beatrice's neck. Causing her head to tilt and look into his eyes for a brief moment before he leaned in to kiss her goodbye.

"We'll be back soon" Ron said and he was gone.

Beatrice watched from the window until she saw the car pull out of the lot. She grabbed her phone and flopped on the bed.

"You know he really loves you don't you?" Mike asked Beatrice

"I guess. I just don't want anything to happen to him. Or Joe for that matter" Beatrice said

"I've known him for years now and I've seen what his last relationship did to him. He was devastated and almost didn't recover. I'm glad he found you. You brought him back to life. Don't worry about him. He's good at what he does" Mike said picking up the remote and switching on the television.

Beatrice picked up her phone and dialed Kristy.

"Kristy? How are things going?" Beatrice asked when Kristy answered

"Great, how are things there. I'm guessing you made it alright" Kristy said

"Yes, we made it. Ron and Joe went to meet Aengus. He knew we were coming and had someone following us. It makes me nervous and mad at the same time" Beatrice said

"Well don't worry. I've been talking to Harvey and Fred, they both say that Ron is good and he will take care of things. Then this will all be over with and you can come home" Kristy said

"Oh my, I forgot about the time change. Did I wake you up?" Beatrice asked

"Oh no, no I was awake" Kristy said

"Well as long as things are going fine there I will let you get to bed. I'll call later and let you know what has happened" Beatrice said

"Ok, honey. Take care of yourself and call me later" Kristy said

"Alright I will, goodnight" Beatrice said as she disconnected

Kristy put her phone on the night stand and rolled over into Harvey's waiting arms. He pulled her to him and kissed her. Breaking from the kiss, Kristy put her head on his chest and closed her eyes.

"So how are things going in their neck of the woods?" Harvey asked

"Beatrice said that Ron and Joe went to meet Aengus. She said that she would call later when they get back. I'm nervous about all of this" Kristy said

Harvey rubbed her back and stroked her hair "Don't worry about it. Ron has things covered, they'll be alright. I bet they're home before you know it" Harvey said

Kristy snuggled closer to Harvey enjoying his affection. It has been too long. Just how far and long was Kristy going to let this go with Harvey she wasn't sure.

Beatrice settled in watching the channel that Mike chose. Her phone ringing startled her. Picking it up and checking the caller I.D said it was Amanda.

"Hi, what are you doing calling me on your honey moon? Are you alright?" Beatrice said not giving Amanda a chance to answer

"Aloha, and how are things on the main land? And yes I'm fine. I just had to tell you that I'm pregnant" Amanda said

"Oh my God. Are you serious? When did that happen? Is Carl excited about that? When are you coming home? How far along are you? I can't wait to see you" Beatrice rambled

"Holy crap, I've missed talking to you" Amanda said laughing "I'm not sure when and yes Carl is ecstatic. Not sure how far along yet. I'm going to see a doctor when we get back. I will be home in three days. What's up with you?" Amanda asked

"Right now I am sitting in a hotel room in Dublin Ireland watching T.V. with Mike" Beatrice said smiling waiting for her response

"Wait just a minute. Who the hell is Mike and what happened to Ron and what's this about Ireland?" Amanda said

Amanda's questions caught Carl's attention.

"Remember all of the mess with Thomas and Joe? Well, Ron called in some of his buddies and two of them stayed back with Kristy and Ron, myself, Joe and Mike flew to Ireland to solve this mess once and for all" Beatrice said giving the short version

"Hold Bea, Carl wants to talk to Mike" Amanda said

"Mike, Carl wants to talk to you" Beatrice said to Mike handing him the phone

Mike reached out and took the phone. Beatrice sat watching and listening to their conversation. From what she heard, Carl wasn't happy that he was not here with us. Mike filled him in on everything. Giving Carl the long version. Some of the phrases she didn't understand. After a few minutes he handed the phone back to Beatrice.

"You still there?" Beatrice said into the phone

"Yes, I don't know what just happened, but Carl is on his phone making reservations to fly to Ireland." Amanda said

"No, don't cut your honey moon short to come here" Beatrice said

"It's too late, he said we have to hang up so we can pack. I guess I'll be seeing you sooner rather than later" Amanda said

"Okay, just be careful. See you soon" Beatrice said hanging up

"What the hell was that all about?" Beatrice asked Mike after she hung up

"Carl wanted to know everything so I filled him in. I guess he doesn't want to miss out on any of the action." Mike said shrugging his shoulders.

"This whole situation just keeps getting more and more out of hand" Beatrice said putting her head on her pillow and covering her eyes with her arm

*   *   *

"He should be at this bar up ahead. He sits in the back right corner booth. Be prepared to have at least two guys blocking the way to get to him" Joe said to Ron

"I'm not worried about the guys. Are you?" Ron asked

"Not with you here no" Joe said with a snort

The bar was a small corner affair. Upon entering, Ron noticed the tables arranged in the center of the room with booths lining both sides of the room with a bar with stools at the back of the room. The walls were painted a deep forest green. The entire room was dimly lit. One bar tender stood cleaning glasses. Two men sat on stools at one end of the bar. Four out of the eight booths had people in them. Ron and Joe strolled in and up to the bar. Ron could see another door to the back of the room and Aengus sitting in the last booth on the right side reading some papers. No other men were close to him. Ron gave Joe the stay here gesture and strolled over to Aingus's booth and sat across from him.

Aengus put down his papers and looked at Ron. "How dare you sit without an invitation" Aengus said

"You have no room to talk, kidnapping and beating young women" Ron said

"Who the hell do you think you are? Do you know who you are talking to?" Aingus said placing both hands on the table.

"I know exactly who you are and I'm the person who's going make sure that doesn't happen again" Ron said

Aengus snapped his fingers and two men appeared from back behind the bar. They went over and took a hold of Joe. Each one taking an arm and holding him still.

"I don't think you know who you are talking to. I will do what I want, when I want. You will leave my country if you know what's good for you" Aengus said waving his hand in the air

The two men holding onto Joe started moving him towards the back door. Joe started resisting, trying to get free from them.

Ron reached inside his jacket and produced his gun. He laid it on the table resting his hand on the gun.

"Let the boy go" Ron said

"I don't think so, he needs to be taught a lesson" Aengus said

Ron picked up the gun and pointed it at Aengus, "I don't ask twice" Ron said

Aengus waved his hand in the air again. Both men let go of Joe and stepped back.

"Good. Now that we understand each other, let me ask if you've found the box yet?" Ron asked

Aengus's face went sheet white. "How do you know about the... oh, I see Joe has been talking too much. See I told you he needs to learn how to keep his mouth shut" Aengus said looking at Joe

"No, you need to learn you can't go around hurting people because you think it will give you personal gain" Joe shouted moving closer to the booth where Aengus and Ron were seated

One of the men standing behind them lunged for Joe. He caught him at the waist and they both went down on top of the table. Ron pushed them both towards Aengus spilling Aengus's beer in his lap. As Ron stood up, the other man that was holding onto Joe stepped forward and took a swing at Ron hitting the left side of his face causing him to land on the floor.

The ruckus in the room caught the attention of the other patrons in the bar. Two men joined in the fight to help protect Aengus. Before Ron could blink, the numbers jumped to four on two and Aengus was leaving out the back door. There was blood on the table and arms swinging left and right. A chair was broke over someone's back. Suddenly everyone froze at the sound of a gun discharging.

Chapter Twenty Two

Beatrice kept checking the bed side clock. It had been two hours since Ron and Joe had left. She hadn't heard a word from either of them.

"What could be taking so long? It's been two hours since they left?" Beatrice said to Mike

"I know, I've been watching the time myself. Ron said three hours so we have an hour to go before we take off ourselves. Are you ready to roll if we have to?" Mike asked

"Yes, I have everything ready to go and I'll use the bathroom now just in case" Beatrice said

Beatrice took up pacing in the room while she waited. Looking out the window each time she paced near it.

"Holly shit it's Thomas" Beatrice said on her fourth time looking out the window

Mike was on his feet and at the window in seconds. "Are you sure?" He asked looking out the window with Beatrice.

"Yes, look he is coming up the steps now" Beatrice said pointing

Mike yanked the curtains closed, grabbed Beatrice's hand and led her through the connecting door to their rooms and closed the door. He pulled out his phone and dialed. Mike moved Beatrice next to the door leading out while he waited.

"Thomas just showed up. Going to plan "B". I repeat plan "B" and he disconnected

"I need you to watch me, follow my signals and stay silent" Mike whispered to Beatrice

Beatrice shook her head in a 'yes' motion as she waited by the door. Having another run in with Thomas was something Beatrice wanted to avoid at all cost.

Mike put his ear to the adjoining door to the rooms and listened. He heard Thomas enter the room via a key card. Followed by lots of rustling and crashing of furniture. Mike moved closer to Beatrice "I'm tired of this bastard. Go in the bathroom, lock the door and get into the bathtub. Don't open the door for anyone except Ron or myself. No matter what you may hear" Mike whispered to Beatrice

Beatrice did what she was told. Locking the door and getting into the bathtub. She closed the shower curtain for extra measure. Beatrice thought she heard the faint sound of the door opening and closing.

Mike made his way to the door to Beatrice and Ron's room. He opened the door quietly and found Thomas going through Beatrice's things. Thomas looked up and saw Mike. Mike took in his large physique and shocked look on his face.

Thomas took four seconds to react to Mike coming in the room and attempted to shove Mike out of the doorway to get out. Mike stood solid, shoved Thomas back two feet, entered the room and shut the door locking it quickly.

Beatrice heard crashing and swearing. Twice the shower walls shook making her jump. She pulled her knees up to her chest wrapping her arms around her legs holding on tight. Praying and hoping Mike would be alright. She knew firsthand what time spent with Thomas could be like. After what seemed like forever, silence ensued. Beatrice waited and waited but nothing. Tears began rolling down her cheeks. Pictures of what could be happening to Mike stated flashing through her head. A series of knocks on the bathroom door brought her back to reality. She stood quiet until she heard the sound of Mike's voice.

"Beatrice it's Mike, open the door it's alright" Mike called through the door.

Beatrice ripped the shower curtain open, jumped out of the bathtub, opened the door and flew into Mikes arms. Throwing her arms around his neck crying on his shoulder.

Mike wrapped his arms around her waist picking her up so her feet left the floor. "It's okay, he won't be hurting you anymore" Mike said laughing

"What's going on in here?" Ron said entering the room

Mike put Beatrice down and they both turned toward the open door. There stood Ron and Joe. Both had scratches and bruises on their faces. Ron had a white bandage with blood seeping through on his left upper arm.

Ron smiled as Beatrice ran to him throwing herself at him. He caught her with his right arm holding onto her the best he could. Beatrice covered his neck and face with soft kisses.

"I was so worried" She said into his neck

Ron loosened his grip so Beatrice would slide down his body effectively putting her feet on the floor. Mike joined the party shaking Joe's hand and then Ron's.

Ron took one look at Mike "It looks like we've all seen some action today" He said

"Yeah we've got company next door" Mike said inkling his head in the direction of the joining door. Mike opened the door and stepped through followed by the others.

"I think he was searching for the necklace. I took him down, he's in the bathtub" Mike said "How are the others on your end? Oh and Carl will be here in about four hours or so"

"Let's just say that they know we mean business. And what is this about Carl" Ron asked

"Beatrice was talking to Amanda when Carl requested to talk to me and I filled him in on the events. He told me to tell you that he is on his way here. He's pretty pissed that you didn't call him" Mike said smiling

"What was I supposed to do, interrupt them playing hide the salami?" Ron said bringing out a round of laughter from the group.

"Why don't you all put this room back together while I pay a visit to our visitor" Ron said heading for the bathroom.

Beatrice started picking up the clothes and putting back the dresser drawers. Mike and Joe put the mattresses back on the frames and straightened the rest of the furniture.

"He's not talking" Ron said when he emerged from the bathroom.

"What's our next move?" Joe asked

"We're going to put this room back together as much as we can. Call room service to fix or replace what was broken. Then we are going to load that jack ass into the trunk and dump him off at the bar for Aengus" Ron said

"Are we going to wait here for Carl and Amanda?" Beatrice asked

"No baby, after we dump our load off, we are going to try and find the whereabouts of that box" Ron said

When they were finished putting the room back together, Beatrice helped Ron change his bandage. Joe went to the hotel desk and retrieved a cart. Mike attempted to contact Carl to check on his E.T.A.

"The office said that they would be sending someone up to check out the room. Anything that is broken will be added to your bill and they will leave an itemized detail of those charges." Joe said returning with the cart.

It took both Joe and Mike to load Thomas onto the cart and into the trunk. Thomas wasn't happy about being tied up and gaged.

The parking lot to the bar was half full. There were a few patrons milling around out front when they pulled up. Ron and Beatrice stayed in the car with it running while Joe and Mike got out and pulled Thomas out of the trunk and dropped him on the ground. Beatrice watched one man standing out front run inside and two others ran to help Thomas. Ron drove off as the two men reached Thomas.

"Can you navigate from the back seat?" Ron asked Joe

"Yup, sure can. Head North on this road. Take the left at the fork and keep going for about ten miles" Joe said

Ron reached out and took Beatrice's hand. Beatrice smiled and let the tingles and warmth from his touch reach the smile on her face. Beatrice watched the beautiful country side go by as Ron drove. Rolling hills of grass with trees scattered around. Farms with horses and cows sporadically placed here and there along with single family homes. When they reached the fork in the road, Ron veered left and off to the right stood the biggest castle that Beatrice had ever seen.

"Who lives in that castle over there?" Beatrice asked

"Not many people live in the castles anymore. Mostly they have been taken over by private companies and made into museums and places to tour" Joe said

"I would like to tour a couple of the castles before we go home. Would that be possible?" Beatrice asked

"I don't see why not. Maybe you and Amanda can take some tours once we get this mess all settled" Ron said

"Did you know that Amanda is pregnant?" Beatrice asked

"Holly shit, Carl's a Dad?" Mike said from the back seat "He didn't tell me that when I was talking to him earlier"

"Wow, good for him" Ron said laughing

"You don't want to have kids?" Beatrice asked

"I didn't say that. I just said that was good for Carl. He's wanted to have a wife and kids for some time now. I'm happy for him is all" Ron said in defense

"You're going to want to pull off the road as far as you can anywhere along here. There isn't a road going where we want to go. From here it's all on foot" Joe said

"How far do we have to walk?" Beatrice asked

"Not too far, maybe a half a mile or so" Joe said

"Then can we get some lunch? I'm hungry and thirsty" Beatrice said

"Yes dear" Ron said

Everyone pilled out of the car and followed Joe off into what looked like a forest to Beatrice. Making their way through some trees and bushes led them into a clearing. Beatrice stood rooted to her spot staring into the area in front of her.

Ron stopped and looked at Beatrice "What's wrong?" He asked

"This is just like my dream" Beatrice answered moving slowly forward

Ron, Joe and Mike stood still watching Beatrice. She slowly started walking forward. They followed her, letting her set the pace. Beatrice walked along reaching down to let the grass run through her fingers. Listening to the tree leaves rustling in the breeze. A few feet in front of her sat a large tree with a giant boulder next to it. So close it looked like they were leaning on each other for support. At the base of the boulder nearest the tree, were three small rocks clustered together.

"Now what?" Mike asked approaching the tree and boulder.

Ron and Joe looked at Beatrice who was walking around the boulder and tree feeling them with her hand as she went.

"Baby, do you have any idea what we do now?" Ron asked

Beatrice stopped walking and looked down at the three rocks. She bent down touching them, trying to get them to move.

"I don't know, but there is something about these rocks. Why won't they move? They don't seem to be connected to or part of the big one" Beatrice said trying to pick up the rocks

"Here, let me try" Joe said.

Joe and Mike got on their knees trying to get the rocks to move. Beatrice paced around the boulder and the tree. Freezing when she reached Joe and Mike.

"Don't try to lift" She said "Try and slide them out towards you"

They both tried sliding them out like a drawer in a dresser. Nothing happened.

"The ground is in the way. Dig away some if the dirt first" Beatrice said getting to her knees to help dig.

"Are you sure about this?" Ron asked

"No, it's just a feeling I have" Beatrice said between breaths.

"Great, now we are going off of a female's feelings" Joe said rolling his eyes.

Beatrice reached over and punched Joe in the arm.

"Hey, I was just joking" Joe said with a smile

"You two done? This seems to be working" Mike said

Beatrice and Joe backed up and let Mike and Ron work the rocks. Slowly they started to loosen.

"What the hell, it's working" Ron said pulling and digging at the rocks

Mike retrieved his knife from his pocket, prying between the rocks and the boulder. Pulling and digging along with Ron and Joe. Beatrice stood by watching the men work. Twenty minutes later, the three rocks slid away from the boulder. Revealing a metal tray attached to the three rocks hidden inside the boulder. Ron reached down and picked up the metal box sitting inside the tray.

Mike turned on his flash light and shined it inside the boulder from the opening. "It doesn't look like anything else is in there. How on earth did this get this way?" Mike said

"I don't know" Joe said

"Let's see what is inside the box" Ron said sitting down on the ground with the box in his lap. He produced the necklace from his pocket and placed the heart inside the heart shape and the key in the key hole. He tried to turn the key without success.

"Try pressing the heart in and then turning the key" Beatrice said getting to her knees next to Ron.

He looked a Beatrice and then did what she suggested. Hearing a click when he pressed the heart into its place, he turned the key and the box popped open. Everyone took in a deep breath as Ron opened the box.

Beatrice reached down and picked up the envelope on top. Underneath the envelope was money. Ron picked up the money to reveal a large size key at the bottom of the box. Beatrice opened the envelope. Inside was a small key and the directions to a bank and a safety deposit box number on it. The letter states that the account and the box is in both Beatrice and Joe's names.

"How much money is there?" Joe asked

"Three hundred thousand dollars" Ron said placing the money back in the box

Beatrice placed the envelope and its contents back in the box and closed the lid.

"Let's try and put this back together and cover up any signs that anything was moved" Ron said

"That's not going to be easy" Joe said

"Yeah but let's give it a try anyways" Ron said

Joe and Mike put the three rocks back as best they could. Ron helped put the dirt and grass pieces back. Beatrice stood by watching holding the box.

"Let's get the hell out of here before someone spots us" Ron said taking the box from Beatrice and taking her hand leading her back to the car. Mike and Joe followed behind.

Reaching the car, everyone pilled in. Ron started the car and pulled out onto the road. Making a U-turn, he headed back towards the hotel. Beatrice sat in the passenger seat with the box on her lap.

"What are you thinking?" Ron asked Beatrice

"How I knew where the box was and how to get to it" Beatrice said rubbing her hands on the box.

"I was wondering that myself" Ron said

"You are doubting me aren't you?" Beatrice asked

"No, baby I'm not. Just the opposite. I'm in awe of you" Ron said taking her hand and kissing the back of it.

"I just keep getting more and more confused the further we go" Beatrice said

"Beatrice, I want you to hand the box to Mike and tighten your seat belt" Ron said in an even tone

"Why, what's going on?" Beatrice asked

"Just do as I ask please" Ron said putting both hands on the wheel and stepping on the gas making the car jerk as it picked up speed.

Beatrice did as she was told. Mike took the box and secured it under the seat of the car. Joe turned his head in time to see the speeding SUV hit the rear of the car.

Beatrice jerked forward as she screamed. The car fishtailed as Ron tried to correct the car. The SUV hit the car again and again.

"Shit, this rental car sucks. It doesn't have any power. Everyone needs to hold on" Ron shouted.

The SUV came up to the driver side of the car and banged the rear panel of the car sending it into a spin. Ron tried to recover the spin when the car went into a roll. It landed on its side, trunk down in a ditch. Beatrice blinked her eyes and saw a figure approach the car before she lost consciousness.

Chapter Twenty Three

When Beatrice woke up, she noticed the sun was setting and darkness was coming. She sat up noticing she wasn't in the car anymore. Trying to get her eyes to focus, she saw the car still sitting in the ditch. Beatrice stood and made her way to the car. Ron, Joe and Mike were gone. Leaning in the back seat of the car, she saw the back seat was cut up. She couldn't find the box. Rustling in the trees caught her attention.

As quiet as she could, Beatrice took off in the opposite direction of the noise. Moving through the trees and bushes, Beatrice kept going as best as she could. Tripping over rocks and tree branches hitting her in the face. She came to a small clearing so she started to run. The sun had set and darkness settled in making it harder to see. Beatrice slowed down feeling her way along. Soon she heard the sound of water. She froze thinking about her dream. Slowly making her way through the trees in front of her, she crept closer to the sound of the water. The moon appeared shedding some light. Beatrice stopped and looked down. "Oh shit" Beatrice whispered out loud. She turned to make her way away from the cliff when she heard the rustling.

Beatrice froze to her spot. If she could barely see her hand in front of her face, chances are this person won't be able to see her. Beatrice caught a sent as the breeze blew past her. She thought the smell was familiar. Trying to focus in the darkness, she thought she saw a figure move past her. Holding her breath, so her breathing wouldn't be heard she prayed they would go away. A hand reached out and grabbed her arm. Beatrice screamed and swung her arm to fight off her attacker.

"It's me, stop swinging" Ron said

Beatrice lunged into him and hung on tight "Oh thank God" Beatrice said into his neck

"Mike, she's over here. Mike, can you hear me?" Ron said in a soft voice

"Stop shouting, I can hear" Mike said standing behind Ron and Beatrice

"Shit man, sneaking up on me like that could be dangerous" Ron said

"Not with the way you are with her in your arms" Mike said chuckling in the dark

"Where's Joe" Ron asked Beatrice

"I don't know. Isn't he with you?" Beatrice responded

"No, we left him with you while we chased those fuckers into the woods" Mike said

"When I came to, I was alone. The only car that was there was the one we were in" Beatrice said "I heard someone coming so I took off"

"Shit, they must have come looking and took Joe. But why would they leave you?" Ron asked

"I don't know but I would like to get going. Staying out here all night is not high on my list of things to do" Mike said

"Right, lets get going back to the road. Call Carl and see where he is. If they are here, have them start making their way to us" Ron said to Mike

Mike wasn't able to get any signal on his phone until they hit the clearing. Beatrice held onto Ron's arm for support as they walked back to the road. Once they reached the crashed car, Mike had gotten a hold of Carl. He and Amanda were in a car heading towards the hotel. Mike gave him their general coordinates to come and get them. Beatrice, Ron and Mike hunkered down on the ground to wait for them.

"I guess they have the box along with Joe. He was in on it from the beginning wasn't he?" Beatrice asked

"No they don't have the box. I do" Said Mike smiling "And no, I don't believe he is in on anything. We had a long talk last night. I believe he is just as in the dark as you are. He just wants answers as well"

"What could have happened to him and why did they leave me alone?" Beatrice asked

"When we were at the bar with Aengus, he kept mentioning that Joe needed to learn some sort of a lesson. He might have him, but why not you I can't tell you" Ron said

"Here comes a vehicle" Mike said

Mike stood up to see if they were going to stop. The car went by slowly and made a U-turn and made its way back to them slowly.

"It's Carl" Mike said

Ron helped Beatrice up off of the ground and led her to the car. Ron, Beatrice and Mike got in the back seat.

"I leave you alone for a week and look what you get yourselves into" Carl said taking off down the road

"Shut up and drive" Ron said leaning his head against the head rest and closing his eyes

"Where to?" Carl asked

"Anywhere to get some food and drinks" Ron said

Amanda turned in her seat "You okay Bea?" She asked

"I am now" Beatrice said snuggling up against Ron while taking Mike's hand

Mike looked at Ron and shrugged his shoulders. He lifted Beatrice's hand, kissed her knuckles gently and let her hand go. Mike rode the rest of the way to the restaurant with a smile on his face.

Arriving at the restaurant, Ron nudged Beatrice "Baby we're here. Are you hungry?" Ron asked

"I'm starving and I need the bathroom" Beatrice said rubbing her eyes

"Me too" Said Amanda

"You girls do your thing us men will get us a table and some liquid" Carl said

"So how is married life treating you?" Beatrice asked Amanda on their way to the bathroom

"It's been great so far, except for the morning sickness. Every morning I spend in the bathroom." Amanda said laughing "How are things between you and Ron?"

Beatrice smiled while in her stall sitting down "He's told me he loves me several times" She said

"Wow, that's great. Do you love him?" Amanda asked

"I think so. I've never been in love before so I'm not sure. But I've told him I do so....." Beatrice responded

"Oh Bea, I'm so happy for you" Amanda said

Opening the door to exit the restroom, Amanda ran into Ron's chest and screamed. "What the hell, you scared me" Amanda said

"Sorry, you were taking so long, I had to check on you guys" Ron said laughing

"Is this what you have been going through without me?" Amanda asked Beatrice

"You have no idea" Beatrice said taking Amanda's hand leading her to their table.

"We've just been discussing what to do about Joe" Ron said assisting Beatrice into her chair.

"We have the box and the key so why would they take Joe and not me? I just don't get it" Beatrice said

"I have a theory" Mike said "Since they couldn't get the box or the keys to the box, they took Joe. They are going to suggest that we make a trade"

"I think that I would have been a better trade than Joe" Beatrice said

"Maybe something happened so that they only could get to Joe and not you" Carl said

"When I woke up, I wasn't in the car, I was on the ground a few feet from the car in the ditch" Beatrice said

"That points to Mike's theory. I bet Joe was trying to hide you when they came. Someone had to have come because the SUV that hit us wasn't there anymore" Ron said

"Let's eat and get back to the hotel. Maybe he made it back there" Mike said

"Sounds like a plan to me" Beatrice said digging into her chicken and broccoli fettuccine

"Wow Bea, I've never seen you eat like that" Amanda said on their way back to the car

"I know, I'm just hungry lately" Beatrice said shrugging her shoulders "and I'm tired too"

Amanda and Carl looked at each other for a second before digging in to their meals.

"What was that look for?" Ron asked

"Nothing" Carl said taking a bite of his steak "I believe we have the room next to one of yours"

"Oh, what number did you get?" Ron asked

"They gave us 217" Carl said

"Hey, that's right next to us" Beatrice said

After everyone had finished eating, Carl picked up the check and they all piled into the car. Mike, Ron and Beatrice in the Back seat.

Mike went up the stairs to the rooms first, Ron assisted Beatrice and Carl was with Amanda.

"There's an envelope taped to your door" Mike said

Ron reached the door and took the envelope from Mike. He opened it and read it. "It's from Aengus, he says he wants to trade Joe for the necklace tomorrow at noon. He gave an address and a phone number"

"Well are we going to do that?" Beatrice asked

"Let's talk inside" Ron said opening the door

Once everyone was inside, Ron said "No, we aren't trading anything. We're going to extract Joe and get to the bank to see what's inside this safety deposit box"

"Do you think that's safe?" Amanda asked

"No but there's no other option. That is if Joe is still alive" Ron said

"Well, you're not going without me" Carl said

Amanda gasped and brought her hands up to her mouth. "You're not serious are you?" Amanda said to Carl

Carl kissed Amanda "Yes, dear I am. I'm not letting them go alone. Especially since there will be more than two men there I'm sure. They will need all the help they can get"

"What time do we leave?" Mike asked

"Let me call this number and see what they say" Ron said picking up the room's phone and not his cell phone

Everyone waited and listened to Ron on the phone "Yes, this is Ron" He said when someone answered the phone. "You have made a big mistake old man"……. "Don't look forward to the time we meet again" Ron said hanging up the phone

"Well?" Beatrice asked

"That is one senile old bastard" Ron said shaking his head

"Extraction tomorrow?" Mike asked

"Yes, first thing in the morning" Ron said "I have clothes for you Carl. I'll get them now"

"Don't bother, I have my own" Carl said smiling

Ron and Mike smiled back "Here I thought you went soft living in those suits you've been wearing" Ron said

"Soft my ass" Carl said

"Everyone get some sleep, I want to be on the road by 0730 or so" Ron said

Beatrice opened the door so everyone could go to their own rooms. Closing the door, she walked over to Ron and wrapped her arms around his waist tilting her head back so she could look him in the face.

"What would I ever do without you?" Beatrice asked

"It's more of what would I ever do without you?" Ron asked reaching down to grab the hem of Beatrice's shirt. He pulled it over head, and with her arms over his shoulders, he started removing her pants.

"Am I to assume you only want me for my body?" Beatrice asked laughing

Her laughter got cut off by Ron's mouth, parting her lips with his tongue. He walked her backwards until they were at the end of the bed. Ron lay Beatrice down. Beatrice grabbed his shirt and removed it as he stood up to finish removing her pants and remove his own. Beatrice scooted up higher on the bed. Ron crawled up to Beatrice placing kisses along her leg and stomach so they were face to face. Starring into her emerald eyes while Beatrice massaged his back with her hands brought tears to his eyes. "Shh, I'm here. I'm not going anywhere" Beatrice whispered pulling him in for a kiss was all the reassurance he needed.

A series of knocks brought Beatrice out of her slumber. Opening her eyes, she saw Ron opening the door to their room. In came Amanda "Rise and shine sleepy head" She said to Beatrice

"What time is it?" Beatrice asked

"Time to get up" Amanda said

"Why where are we going?" Beatrice asked rubbing her eyes

"Carl and Mike are waiting for you in our room" Amanda said to Ron

"Okay, I'll be back" Ron said shutting the door behind him

"Get up and go pee on this" Amanda said handing Beatrice a pregnancy test

Beatrice took it "What are talking about? You think I'm pregnant?" She asked

"I sure do hot stuff. Now get up and pee on that stick. Do you need me to help you?" Amanda said

"No I don't need any help" Beatrice said getting up rolling her eyes at Amanda

Amanda paced in the room waiting for Beatrice to come out of the bathroom. She knocked on the door "Hey, did you fall in?" Amanda shouted at the closed door

Beatrice opened the door and stood in the doorway completely naked. She handed the test over to Amanda. Beatrice walked over to the bed and sat down starring at Amanda.

Amanda looked at the test "Yes, I knew it" Amanda shouted doing a dance with her arms in the air. She stopped dancing and looked at Beatrice "You haven't been taking your pill have you?" She asked

Beatrice thought for a second and shook her head 'no'. "I guess with all that has been going on I forgot" Beatrice whispered

"Unmarried and pregnant, who would of thought?" Amanda said laughing "I'd put some clothes on if I were you, I hear someone coming"

Beatrice grabbed the bathrobe she had been using and put it on as Ron came back into the room.

"I'll just leave you two alone. Is Carl still in our room?" Amanda asked Ron

"Yeah he's waiting for you" Ron said to Amanda

Amanda closed the door behind her, laughing all the way to her room.

"What the hell was that all about?" Ron asked Beatrice

All Beatrice could do was hand Ron the pregnancy test.

"What's this?" He asked taking the stick from her and looking at it

His eyes got big, his jaw dropped as he saw the two very pink lines. He brought his eyes up to look at Beatrice's eyes. "Is this…. you mean you…. we….?" Ron couldn't finish not one thought.

Beatrice shook her head 'yes' as tears started streaming down her cheeks. "I'm sorry" She whispered

"Oh baby no, why are you sorry?" Ron asked getting to his knees taking her hands in his

"We've only known each other for a short time. What if you don't want….." Beatrice got cut off with a kiss.

"You listen to me right now. I've told you that I love you. I'm not doing all of this for my health. I have a life now, a life with you. And if you happen to be pregnant when we get married, hey worse things have happened" Ron said

"Married?" Beatrice squeaked

"Yes, married. That is if you'll have me" Ron said holding his breath waiting for her response

Knocks on the door made Ron exhale and spit out some curse words on his way to the door.

Chapter Twenty Four

Ron opened the door to Mike, Carl and Amanda. Stepping aside to allow them entry.

"Is it alright that we come in?" Carl asked

"Sure, come on in" Ron said

"I thought we would give the girls some instruction on fire arms so they would be able to protect themselves incase while we were gone" Carl said.

"Um, I don't know that leaving them here alone is the best choice. I would feel better knowing they were closer" Ron said while starring at Beatrice

"Everything alright with you? You don't look so good." Mike said to Ron

"Actually could you all give us a moment?" Ron said taking Beatrice's hand leading her into the bathroom

"Talk to me" Ron said placing Beatrice on the toilet while he took a seat on the edge of the tub

"You're okay with this? With all of this? Me and a baby? I mean really are you? Cause we didn't plan this." Beatrice said

"If you're happy then I'm ecstatic" Ron said

"Really?" Beatrice said

"Really baby" Ron said scooping her up in his arms and holding her tight "Really baby"

"Oh Ron" Beatrice said crying into his neck

"Hush now baby. I've got you and I won't let go" Ron said letting her slide down his body so her feet were on the floor "Let's go join the others"

"Is everything alright?" Carl asked noticing the tears in Beatrice's eyes

Ron put his arm around Beatrice's shoulders pulling her close "Yes everything is fine" Ron said "What kind of weapons were you thinking about?" Ron asked

"I don't want to be left here" Beatrice chimed in "I can just see you all leaving and Thomas coming for us" Beatrice said after she blew her nose.

Mike and Ron looked at each other "He does know where we're staying. I wouldn't put it past them to have someone watching the hotel" Mike said

"I think you're right" Ron said

"Amanda and Beatrice get dressed for the day. Make it something comfortable. We will pretend that we are all going out for breakfast. Keeping us all together is the best bet I think" Carl said

Amanda went to her room to change and Beatrice ran for her bathroom to shower. Thirty minutes later the entire group was ready. Ron and Carl made sure that they had a conversation on their way to the car about breakfast destinations, loud enough for someone to hear.

Ron spotted the tail on the way to their destination. "You spot them yet?" Ron asked Carl

"Yeah I was just going to ask you the same thing" Carl said "looks like two in the front seat"

"While we're having breakfast, we'll disable their car" Mike chimed in from the back seat

"Works for me" Carl said pulling into the parking lot of a diner. The car following past the parking lot up and went to the next corner and turned left

"They're circling the block to throw us off" Mike said

"Hurry, you girls go inside, do whatever you need to to stay inside until we come for you" Ron said

"Wait, what?" Amanda said

Beatrice took Amanda's hand and pulled her towards the entrance to the diner "Come on we don't have much time" She said

"Good girl" Ron said to Beatrice giving her behind a smack as she went by causing her to giggle on her way

"Is this the shit you've been doing since we last parted?" Amanda asked

"You have no idea. Since then, Thomas kidnapped and beat me again. I've hardly slept where I wasn't knocked out. I've been followed, chased, in a car accident and left in a ditch. Ron has two other men at Kristy's house guarding her and the kids" Beatrice explained

"This is some crazy, serious shit" Amanda said

"Like I said, you have no idea" Beatrice said looking out the window

"Where are they and what are we supposed to do?" Amanda asked

"We wait for them to come for us" Beatrice said

"Something's wrong. They should have circled back already" Mike said

Ron and Carl looked at each other and said in Unisom "The girls" and took off running for the entrance to the diner. Opening up the door, Ron ran into a lady coming out. "Oh excuse me" Ron said

"Are you looking for the two ladies that came in a few minutes ago?" The lady said

"Yes, why what happened?" Carl asked

"I'm only telling you this because I hate that old man. He killed my husband. Anyway, Aengus's two men took them out the back door just now" The lady said "He has a lot of this town in his pocket because they're scared of him"

Before the lady could finish, Mike ran around the back of the diner and Carl went inside straight to the back. Both Carl and Mike reached the back in time to see the car pulling out of the lot, Mike could hear screaming coming from the car. He pulled his gun and fired at the car, blowing out one of the back tires causing the car to fish tail and hit a pole. Ron, Carl and Mike ran to the car. Ron taking the passenger and Mike taking the driver out of the car. Carl opened the door to the back seat to find Beatrice and Amanda tied up squished on the floor of the car.

"Are they alright?" Ron yelled

"Yes, they seem to be fine" Carl yelled back

After securing the two men, Mike ran around the front to retrieve their car. Carl and Ron untied Amanda and Beatrice then they went about changing the tire on the car Mike shot. Mike drove around and parked behind the other car. They put one man in one trunk and one in the other.

"Excuse me, hold on a minute" The lady yelled from the back of the diner

"Hey it's the lady we were talking to. Go see what she wants" Ron said to Carl

Carl walked over to the lady and took the box that she was carrying.

"Hi, I made you all some sandwiches and I put some sodas in there as well. May I speak to Beatrice before you all take off?" The Lady asked

"Um.... how do you know Beatrice?" Carl asked

"Trust me honey I know more than you think I do. And believe me when I say that I'm not on Aengus's side. My name is Lynda, Lynda O'Malley" She said

"Okay, let's step over to the car" Carl said

Lynda and Carl walked over to the car. As Lynda approached Beatrice she smiled.

"Oh my Lord, you look just like your mother" Lynda said "I hoped I would get to meet you someday"

"How do you know my mother?" Beatrice asked

Lynda smiled and said "She was my best friend"

"Wait just a minute. How do we know that you are not working with Aengus?" Ron asked

"I know you're suspicious of me and I don't blame you. Here let me show you something" Lynda said pulling a small book out of her apron pocket. Opening it she produced two pictures. "This is me and your mother taken a year before she left for the United States and this one is of you and your mother. She sent this to me a few months before she was killed"

Beatrice stood holding the pictures in her hand. Lynda reached out and touched Beatrice's arm.

"It's okay honey, breath for me" Lynda said

"If you'll excuse us we have some business to take care of" Ron said

"I know. Go get Joe out of that place. When you have him, come and see me. I think I can answer some of the question swimming around in your head. If you're anything like your mother, you can bat out one question after the other" Lynda said

"Oh she sure can" Ron and Amanda said at the same time

"This is my diner so you'll find me here from seven in the morning to about ten at night. Good luck to all of you. Oh and if you're going to Aengus's hang out, he has cameras set up all over" Lynda said

"We better get going so we're not late" Mike said

"I know you don't trust me and I get it. Please be careful, I've lost more family than I can mention at the hands of that old man. I hope you'll stop in to see me" Lynda said stepping backwards

Beatrice ran over to Lynda and hugged her before running back to the car and getting in. One last look behind her, Beatrice saw Lynda with tears in her eyes.

"What do you think of that?" Carl asked Ron once they were in the car

"I don't know what to think" Ron said

"Baby, what do you think?" Ron asked Beatrice

"I don't know what to think anymore" Beatrice said sinking down in her seat "Of all the places to stop it just happen to be hers. I don't know about this. What if she tipped of Aengus?"

"I was thinking the same thing" Ron said "We'll soon find out"

Ron got into their car with Beatrice, Carl and Amanda. Mike drove the other car after they fixed the tire.

"If my GPS is correct, our destination is 13.2 miles in this direction. The building should be on the right side of the road" Mike said into the radio

"Copy that" Carl said into his radio

"What will we be doing while you are getting Joe?" Amanda asked

"I'm not sure yet. Let's see what this place looks like first then we can decide" Carl answered

"Hey Amanda, look over there" Beatrice said pointing "See that castle sitting out there all by its self? Ron said we might get to tour one before we leave if you want to go?"

"That sounds like fun. I've never been inside a real castle before" Amanda said

"Yeah, me neither. I've only read about them" Beatrice said

"Hey what's happening up there?' I'm lonely back here by myself" Mike said

"We need to find you a girlfriend while we're out here" Carl said laughing

"Um... let me be the judge of that. Five miles to go" Mike said

"We drive by and check it out, then we meet a couple miles down the road" Carl said

"Copy that" Mike said

On a drive by the house, it showed to be three feet from the road. A metal fence with bushes surrounded the compound with one drive in and out.

Mike pulled up behind Ron and the others. Beatrice and Amanda stayed in the car.

"So did you tell Ron?" Amanda asked

"Yes" Beatrice said

"What did he say?" Amanda asked

"He's so excited. He wants to get married" Beatrice said

"And you don't?" Amanda asked

"I don't know. This is all happening so fast. We've only know each other for a short time" Beatrice said

"Yeah, but how are things in the bed? Must be something since you're knocked up" Amanda said

"Well, that part I have no problems or worries with" Beatrice said laughing

"What's so funny back here?" Ron asked leaning in the open window

Beatrice and Amanda looked at each other and started laughing. "Nothing dear" Beatrice said

"The plan is that you girls are going to drive the car down this road for an hour then turn around and come back this direction. Its 10:30 right now so that puts you back here about 12:30. If you need anything, call me on my phone. Only if it's an emergency. Do you understand? No stopping for anything." Ron said

"What if we have to go to the bathroom?" Beatrice asked

"It would be better if you go now to avoid that situation" Carl said coming up to the other window

"Like where? I don't see a bathroom" Amanda said

"Come on it's not like we've never done it on the side of the road before" Beatrice said

"Yeah when we were kids" Amanda said "Really?" She asked looking at Carl

"I'm afraid so dear" Carl said

"Well let's get this over with" Amanda said getting out of the car

"What about the guy in the trunk?" Beatrice asked

"We're taking him out" Mike said

"Oh good, we have an audience" Amanda said

"Pregnant women get cranky" Carl said

"I'm not cranky" Amanda snapped back at Carl

Mike put his hands up in the air and backed up. He went back to watching the compound through the binoculars. "We have movement" Mike yelled

Ron went to look through the binoculars "One car, two passengers, heading away from us. No doubt off to find the two we have with us. Now would be a great time to strike. They're four men down" Ron said

Carl put Amanda in the passenger side of the car and Ron instructed Beatrice to drive while placing her in the driver's seat.

"Like I explained earlier just drive this direction for one hour. Turn around and drive back here. Do not stop for anyone or anything. Do not stray off of the road" Ron stressed his point home with the look on his face.

"Please be careful. I don't want to do this without you" Beatrice said

Ron reached his head in the window and kissed Beatrice "Take care of my son until I return" He whispered

"You guys done making out? We really should move now" Mike said

"We really need to get him a girlfriend" Carl said as he stood waving at the girls driving away.

"Girlfriend my ass" Mike said making his way to the compound.

He went to the power box and cut the power and phone lines to the house. It knocked the cameras out as well. But not before alerting the rest of the house of their presence. Two men came around the side of the house with their guns drawn. The first man fired at Ron and Carl. Returning fire, Ron hit one man in the shoulder and Mike came up behind the other successfully knocking him out. They tied up and secured those two outside before entering in the front door.

Ron signaled for Carl and Mike to go left and search for Joe. He went right in search for Aengus. It was a single story dwelling making it easier to search. Ron swept through a kitchen and what looked like a living room. Coming up to a door, Ron slowly opened the door gun in hand. There he found Aengus sitting behind a large dark wooden desk. Leaning back in his chair cigar in hand watching the smoke swirl up to the ceiling.

"Have a seat" Aengus said in a raspy voice

"No, I'm here to get Joe and end this here and now" Ron said

"Sit down, please" Aengus said waving his hand towards the high back chair opposite of his chair.

Hesitantly, Ron sat on the edge of the chair. "Speak" He said to Aengus

"I have spent the last 30 years chasing that land. Land that should have been left to me. Instead Charles loses it in a poker game. Can you believe it, a poker game" Aengus paused to puff on his cigar "Join me would you?" Aengus pushed the box of cigars towards Ron

"No thank you, continue" Ron said

"Awe yes, before the transfer could take place, the deed goes missing. I spent the rest of Charles's miserable life trying to find out what happened to it. Charles had a stroke that made him a vegetable. So getting information from him was impossible. Since then I have acquired bits and pieces of information from different people. So tell me, did you ever find the box?" Aengus said

Ron sat quiet for a moment. Finally he stood and said "Beatrice and Joe are off limits to you and your rent-a-thugs. And from what I hear, you killed both of their parents. Leave them alone" Ron said

Before Aengus could answer Ron, Joe busted through the door. Clothes ripped, blood all over his face. He didn't stop his forward motion, lunging at Aengus "You bastard" was all Joe got out before he hit Aengus full force with his whole body. Both of them fell backwards hitting the floor.

Carl and Mike came running into the room just as they hit the floor.

"We couldn't stop him. He said that Thomas beat him, asking where the box is" Mike said out of breath from chasing Joe.

Ron, Carl and Mike stepped around the desk to try and get Joe off of Aengus. Mike and Carl took hold of Joe each took an arm and lifting. Ron bent down to help Aengus up and noticed he wasn't responding.

Chapter Twenty Five

"I DON'T LIKE JUST LEAVING them like that" Amanda said as she turned to watch the men fade off in the distance her and Beatrice were putting between them.

"I don't either but one thing I've learned being with Ron, is that he and Mike can take care of themselves and I'm sure Carl can to" Beatrice said checking the rearview mirror for anyone that might be following them

"I haven't seen this side of him. He told me a little bit about that part of his life, but to see it is weird" Amanda said sitting forward again in her seat

"So, are you hoping for a boy or a girl?" Beatrice asked Amanda deciding to change the subject as to get Amanda's mind off of the situation

"I want a girl and Carl wants a boy" Amanda said laughing

"Have you thought of any names?" Beatrice asked

"No not yet" Said Amanda

"Have you talked about where you are going to live?" Beatrice asked

"Kind of, Carl wants to start his own security business. We've talked about a few different destinations but we haven't settled on one yet. At first, we thought about both working on a cruise ship, but with me being pregnant........." Amanda stopped talking when her cell phone rang. "It's Carl" Amanda said looking at the screen.

"Answer it but put it on speaker" Beatrice said

Amanda did as Beatrice said "Hello?" Amanda said out loud

"Hey it's okay for you to turn around and head back this way. It's all over" Carl said

"What do you mean it's all over?" Beatrice said stepping on the brakes pulling over to the side of the road

Carl laughed "Just turn around a comeback, Ron and I will explain when you get here" he said

"On our way" Beatrice said turning the car around and driving back

"Beatrice and Amanda are on their way back right now. It should take them about forty five minutes" Carl said to Ron

"Good, that will give us some time to get things cleaned up around here" Ron said

"Joe has arranged for the ambulance and Dublin police. Their ETA twenty minutes" Mike said

"I'm not sure how they're going to react to two guys tied up on the front yard, Aengus dead and all of our equipment" Ron said

"I'm the one that killed him" Joe said

"Well, technically I believe it was a heart attack. But you did scared the hell out of him lunging at him out of nowhere" Carl said

"I just lost it after being beaten by Thomas and no one did anything about it" Joe said

"Understandable" Mike said

"Where did Thomas go?" Ron asked Joe

"I heard them say that these two were missing and couldn't get a hold of so he went out searching" Joe said

Ron and Carl went over to the two guys they tied up "How do you get a hold of Thomas?" Ron asked

The two guys looked at each other and smiled, then looked back at Ron saying nothing.

"I'm not going to ask again" Ron said

The guy on the right spit on Ron's shoe.

Bringing his boot up, Ron made contact with the guys face. Causing it to fly back and to the left. Leaving a bloody lip in its wake.

"We have company" Mike yelled "and it's not the girls"

Ron and Carl jogged over to Mike. "It's the car that took off to search for the other two and they are coming fast" Mike said

"Listen, I hear sirens" Ron said

"Look, is that lights following them?" Carl asked

"I'll be a son of a gun. They're in a chase with the police" Mike said laughing

Ron, Carl, Mike and Joe stepped off to the side to watch the chase. The car that Thomas was driving skidded into the driveway to Aengus's house. The police car came to a stop just behind the car. Thomas and the passenger got out of their car and ran inside the house. A second police car arrived followed by an ambulance.

"I'm going to find out what is going on. They should talk to me" Joe said walking over to the second police car.

Ron, Mike and Carl stood off to the side of the road watching and waiting for Beatrice and Amanda.

"It's been ten minutes, what could be taking Joe so long?" Mike asked

"Here he comes" Ron said pointing at Joe walking towards them

Joe had a great big smile on his face as he approached "You will never believe this" Joe said laughing

"What?" Carl asked

"Thomas wasn't being chased by the police, they were both racing over here because they heard the call over the radio about Aengus being dead. The police started questioning Thomas and Andy. Andy sunk to his knees crying saying he wants to tell all he knows. Thomas attacked Andy and the police almost had to shoot Thomas to calm him down" Joe explained

Carl's phone rang, reaching for it and looking at the screen, "It's Amanda" Carl said

"Hi honey" Carl said into the phone

"What the hell is going on? Why do we see all of the lights and an ambulance?" Amanda asked

"Don't freak out, we are all alright. Just pull up and we will explain" Carl said disconnecting.

"Let me guess, they see the lights?" Ron asked

"They sure do, here they are now" Carl said

Beatrice was out of the car and into Ron's arms in record time. She wrapped her arms around his neck while he put his around her waist and picked her up off of the ground in a tight hug.

"I thought you were hurt. What is going on?" Beatrice asked

"Aengus is dead and now that you are here, I want to go over and see what else we can find out. Are you up for that?" Ron asked Beatrice

"Hell yeah, let's go" Beatrice said trying to get down from Ron's hold

"I love it when you get all squirrelly on me" Ron said placing a kiss on Beatrice's lips before loosening his grip letting her slide down his body.

Hand in hand, followed by Joe, Beatrice and Ron walked over to the house. Carl, Amanda and Mike stayed behind with the car.

Approaching the house, one of the police officers spotted Beatrice, Ron and Joe. He started moving closer. Beatrice tightened her hold on Ron's hand.

"Beatrice, it's nice to finally meet you" the police officer said holding his hand out

Beatrice put her hand in his. "It's nice to meet you as well, I think" Beatrice said

"Don't be nervous, your father and I were friends. And you must be Joe" he said shaking Joe's hand "I haven't seen you since you were born"

"And your name is?" Joe asked

"Oh sorry, I'm Connor" He said

"Connor, can you tell us the cause of Aengus's death?" Ron asked

"I'm sorry, you are?" Connor asked Ron

"My name is Ron and I am here with Beatrice and Joe" Ron said

"Well, as far as the coroner can tell, it was a heart attack. We have taken Thomas, Andy and the other two that were tied up into custody. I'm assuming from the way you are dressed, that you have something to do with that?" Conner asked looking at Ron

"Yes, they were coming after Beatrice for Aengus. He has sent several men for Beatrice. One in particular, Thomas. He has kidnapped and beaten her twice and Joe once" Ron said

"From the things that Andy has said so far and the evidence being pulled from Aengus's files, things are going to be different around here" Conner said

"What do you mean different?" Beatrice asked

"Aengus was very careful in covering up after himself in the illegal dealings he has been doing for the last fifty years. As he got older, we think he started to lose his mind. He had been making slips here and there. We think that Thomas has been calling the shots for a while now in Aengus's name. We are going to be busy here for a while sorting this mess out. Is there anything I can do for you?" Conner said

"Um… not right now. But if I have some questions later I will get in touch with you" Beatrice said

"Here is my card. It has my number, call me if you need me" Conner said handing the card to Beatrice and he walked away.

Beatrice, Ron and Joe walked back to the car to join the others.

"What's going on over there?" Mike asked

"A whole lot of shit" Joe said

"Aengus is officially dead, Thomas and the others that were here are being hauled to jail and the police are going through Aengus's files and records. The one cop that we talked to said that they were going to be at it for a while. Shall we see what is in that safety deposit box?" Ron said

"I'm all for that, but can we please get some food first? I'm not feeling so good right now." Beatrice said

"I'll second that motion" Amanda chimed in leaning against Carl with her head on his shoulder

Mike and Joe busted out laughing "pregnant women" Joe said

Beatrice reached out and hit Joe in the stomach making him double over and laugh even harder.

"Alright, food it is" Carl said heading for one of the cars with Amanda at his side

The location of the restaurant was directly across the street from the bank holding the safety deposit box. Beatrice's seat at the table gave her access to view the bank out the large picture window at the front of the restaurant. She could hardly eat her chicken salad wondering what was in the box.

"Aren't you going to eat?" Ron asked Beatrice with his voice low and close to her ear.

This brought Beatrice back to the here and now.

"Oh, sorry. I was just thinking about the box" Beatrice said looking Ron in the eyes with a small smile.

"I know you are, but could you please eat something? You need to eat there are two of you now" Ron said giving her temple a small kiss.

Beatrice smiled and got down to the business at hand, eating.

* * *

"Do you mind if Ron comes in with us?" Beatrice asked Joe before they entered the bank

"No not at all. If it weren't for Ron here, I don't think that we would have made it to this point" Joe said

"We will do some shopping while you all are in taking care of business" Carl said taking Amanda's hand leading her in the opposite direction of the bank with Mike on their heels.

Approaching the desk they were instructed to, the man behind the desk stood and smiled.

"My name is Peter Smith, how may I help you?" He asked Beatrice, Ron and Joe

"Yes Mr. Smith, we need to get into safety deposit box 351 please" Beatrice said

"Okay, box 351. Hold on one moment please" Peter said walking away from his desk.

"If he has to walk away from his desk, this can't be good" Joe said

"Quiet, here he comes" Beatrice said grabbing Ron's hand

"Alright, here we are. Please have a seat" Peter said motioning to the chairs in front of his desk. "This box had some special instructions with it"

"And what might those instructions be?" Ron asked

"First, I need to make sure that I am speaking with the correct people. There seem to be only two that I am allowed to speak with so may I see some I.D's please?" Peter said

Joe and Beatrice handed Peter their passports and drivers licenses.

Peter looked them over and turned to Ron "And who might you be?" He asked

"This is Ron and he is with me" Beatrice said

"I understand, but the instructions for this box state that only two of you with proper I.D may enter the room with the box. I'm sorry for the inconvenience but I must follow the instructions as they are written" Peter said

Beatrice looked up at Ron.

"It's alright, I will wait here for you. Take as long as you need" Ron said to Beatrice standing up and stepping away from the desk.

"Thank you very much, now if you will please follow me" Peter said standing

Beatrice and Joe followed Peter into a room filled with boxes on three sides of the wall.

"Do you have the key?" Peter asked

"Yes we do" Joe said producing the key from his pocket.

"Please insert you key here and we need to turn them at the same time" Peter said

Joe did as instructed. Both keys turned together and the box sprung free of the wall it was enclosed in. Peter took the box and moved to another room just off of the room containing the boxes. He put the box down on a small table in the middle of the room.

"I will leave you two to your business. Please lock the door after I leave. Take as long as you need" Peter said as he backed out of the room closing the door in his wake.

"Are you ready for this?" Beatrice asked Joe

"Hell yes I'm ready. You do remember what it took for us to get to this point right?" Joe said inserting the key and opening the box.

Inside the box was three envelopes. One had Beatrice's name, one had Joe's name and one had both of their names on it. Looking at each other, they opened the envelopes with their names on it. Inside were instruction and numbers to a bank account in that bank. The letter stated that the account had been started twenty years prior. The starting balance in each account was $500,000.00.

"Holly shit" Joe whispered

"Yeah, um let's open this one" Beatrice said

"Go ahead" Joe said

With shaking hands, Beatrice picked up the envelope. Opening it, she discovered a letter to her and Joe from their father. Beatrice read it out loud.

> Dear Beatrice and Joe,
>
> If you are reading this than I must be gone. I'm so sorry we did not have the life I wanted to have with my two children. Please take these gifts from me and have a wonderful life. Know that I loved you both very much. Be careful of the people that you confide in and trust no one other than each other. It's up to you two to carry on the O'Riley name. Take care of each other.
>
> All my love, Your Father

   With tears in her eyes, Beatrice unfolded the other papers that were contained in the envelope with the letter.

   "Oh My God" Beatrice said

   "What, what's it say?" Joe asked

   "You're never going to believe this" Beatrice said with astonishment in her eyes as she handed Joe the paper work

About the Author

Growing up as an avid reader, I enjoyed several different styles of writing. My start with writing was with peoms. I have wrote several poems for my family.

I have been known for my imagination and decided to put my imagination down on paper.

I was born and raised in Stockton, California and up until now, I have worked with young children.

Printed in the United States
By Bookmasters